His Unicorn Alpha

Shifters Sanctuary Book 3

Anna Sparrows

Copyright © 2025 by Anna Sparrows

All rights reserved. No part of this publication may be reproduced, stored or transmitted in any form or by any means, electronic, mechanical, photocopying, recording, scanning, or otherwise without written permission from the publisher. It is illegal to copy this book, post it to a website, or distribute it by any other means without permission.

This novel is entirely a work of fiction. The names, characters and incidents portrayed in it are the work of the author's imagination. Any resemblance to actual persons, living or dead, events or localities is entirely coincidental.

Anna Sparrows asserts the moral right to be identified as the author of this work.

Anna Sparrows has no responsibility for the persistence or accuracy of URLs for external or third-party Internet Websites referred to in this publication and does not guarantee that any content on such Websites is, or will remain, accurate or appropriate.

Designations used by companies to distinguish their products are often claimed as trademarks. All brand names and product names used in this book and on its cover are trade names, service marks, trademarks and registered trademarks of their respective owners. The publishers and the book are not associated with any product or vendor mentioned in this book. None of the companies referenced within the book have endorsed the book.

Anna Sparrows acknowledges that all of her writing is 100% her own. No part of it is created by generative Artificial Intelligence (AI) software of any kind. Yes, that means that it's sometimes flawed, but she's okay with that.

Cover Design by Ky at Blue Brolli Graphics

For those who just don't fit in.
Welcome to the club. It's fun here!
(I like making my own rules)

Acknowledgements

Firstly, a huge thanks to Ky at Blue Brolli Graphics for designing the paperback cover for *His Unicorn Alpha,* and for being such a supportive friend *and* an awesome PA. Thanks to you, writing and releasing this book was a much smoother process than my usual squirrel-brained panic stations.

Similarly, thank you to my amazing alpha readers, Erin, Cindy, and Megan. Your feedback helped shape and polish this into a story I'm super proud of and excited to share.

Finally, thank you, the reader, for giving my books a chance. I know that time is a precious commodity, and I'm honoured that you've chosen to spend some of yours on my writing. I really hope you enjoy it!

Preface

While this is a predominately sweet & steamy mpreg Omegaverse romance with low relationship angst and zero miscommunication between the MCs once they meet, *His Unicorn Alpha* does cover some potentially upsetting topics and themes with hurt/comfort elements and some angst from external conflicts.

These include: infertility, pregnancy complications, premature birth, gender/breed disappointment, a postnatal depressive episode, body issues/self-confidence, size-related insecurity/anxiety (an MC with a micropenis), and implantation of embryos/conception without the donor's explicit consent.

Contents

Chapter One

"You're okay with doing the fertilization tests today?" Eric asked as I wandered into our shared clinic.

My life had both changed significantly and also not at all since I had moved to Shifters Sanctuary roughly two years earlier. I had always been a doctor and a researcher, honing my skills over my centuries of existence, but when I moved to the town my younger brother had established with the then-only known alpha in existence, I had been drawn into assisting him with his research into alpha/omega dynamics and omega fertility.

It had been the focus of Eric's research since the last known dragon alpha—our father—had vanished, presumably killed by dragon hunters, though his remains were never found. Eric was determined that we could save our species from extinction.

We were an all-male race, dependent on the existence of alphas to impregnate our omegas. Without alphas, there was no longer any way for our omegas to have babies.

When Eric had called me, excitedly announcing that he had discovered an alpha —albeit a wolf shifter and not a dragon— his hope was infectious. For the first time in centuries, I imagined that maybe our race had a chance after all.

Beckett Smith had grown up entirely human until he had met his omega mate and they had been thrown into a whirlwind mating heat and bonding experience. What followed was a series of events which upended a great deal of the shifter community, causing an even deeper divide between the 'new age' of shifters, who believed in social equality, and the 'old-school' faction, who appeared to be led by a cult-like religion called Moonmusic, whose reasons for keeping things the way they'd always been seemed to be driven purely by financial greed and a lust for power.

Because alphas, it turned out, were just as powerful as legends suggested.

They radiated power, in fact. Their very scents were electric, buzzing and energizing. And, as we had discovered, they had the ability to compel and control betas and omegas through commands alone if they so chose.

I imagined just how terribly things could go if the wrong sort of person had those abilities and I shuddered. No wonder the Moonmusic-founded sect had wanted an alpha of their own.

So, to cut a long story short, I was working for Eric in the hopes that we could save our species, as well as find answers to the questions raised by the existence of all the new alphas.

"Yes," I replied, making my way to our private lab, though I was convinced the task would be just as fruitless as with every other round of testing.

In the couple of years since Eric settled in Shifters Sanctuary with the first of the new alphas, people had been arriving in the hopes that they, too, were potentially affected by 'hidden alpha syndrome' or 'locked alpha syndrome', as Eric had called it. However, as time continued to pass, we were all losing hope that we would find more alphas.

From the start, I was skeptical that we would find any dragon alphas. Eric's theory that the locked alphas had some genetic throwbacks to shifter lines made the likelihood of finding someone with dragon genes even slimmer. After all, our father had been gone for hundreds of years: even if he had sown his wild oats in the human community, those lines were likely far too diluted by now. Additionally, I didn't believe that Eric, Sage, or I would be fated or compatible mates for someone within our genetic line. Yet, we still worked in hope. It was that or resign ourselves to extinction.

Eric and I had spent months working out the science on inducing egg production in omegas without being able to incite mating heats. In the end, it involved using similar chemical hormones to the birth control we had devised for Ollie, Damon, and Lena – mates to the town's alphas. Not that Ollie or Damon felt confident in relying on our science to prevent future pregnancies, much to Eric's frustration, and Lena was pregnant and unable to be our test subject for at least another six months.

With mild desperation to prevent our research from stalling, Eric convinced the Pack Alpha, Beck, to host social events between the growing numbers of potential alphas and the omegas in town, but none had sparked the kinds of connections that Beck, Rex, and Brandi had reported. Through a meticulous documentation process, we had decided to attempt blind insemination matches in the lab, using sperm donated from multiple potential alphas and even the town's betas, and ovum from omegas who had been willing to undergo the invasive procedure to donate them to science.

Eliminating the combinations of omegas and potential alphas who had interacted at the social events left us with possible combinations of ovum donors and sperm. The plan was ultimately to alert any potential matches should any of the insemination attempts become successful and allow the parties in question to make decisions on how to proceed from there.

We believed that, under controlled circumstances, potential mates could meet and ride out the initial mating heat while simultaneously avoiding pregnancy.

It was beginning to feel like we were throwing things at a wall in the hopes something might stick, though. There were too many variables, even if Eric was convinced that fate and magic would be on our side.

My youngest brother had always been the dreamer of our family.

Two hours after walking into the lab, I was staring open-mouthed at successfully fertilized eggs. Three of the four in the petri dish were viable. My heart hammered wildly. This meant that there was another potential alpha among us after all.

Eric was right.

I couldn't even be annoyed that he was.

I checked the numbers on the petri dish and pulled up the records to see whose samples had matched so spectacularly.

Chances were, I would be on a first name basis with the omega, given the ovum-retrieval process was run out of our clinic. I had less to do with the potential alphas than Eric, who conducted all their interviews and collected their samples, but I might have crossed paths with them in town.

My mouth went dry and I felt dizzy when I saw my own name staring back at me from our records.

It can't be, I thought. But, when I double checked the records, there was no doubt left.

They were my ovum. My eggs. The petri dish in front of me held *my* potential children.

Dragons.

I didn't rush to look up the potential alpha, too shocked at the realization that I had three viable, fertilized dragon eggs —from my own dusty womb— sitting right in front of me.

Eric, Sage, Dexter and I had all undergone the ovum-retrieval process out of a sense of desperation to save our species, but I had never imagined that one of us would find a match, especially not me. I was one-hundred years older than Sage and Dexter, and almost two-hundred years older than Eric. I was practically middle-aged by dragon standards! (I appeared middle-aged by human standards, too.)

The urge to ensure the safety and continued viability of my test-tube created young rushed over me in a wave of overwhelming determination.

Even if they weren't inside me, they were my babies. I had technically even made them, though through unconventional means.

But who was their other father? Who was my potential alpha?

Holy shit, I thought to myself, my heart hammering, *I have a potential alpha!*

After carefully returning my petri dish of hope back to the specialized, protected storage Eric had had manufactured for his lab, I turned back to our records and looked for the corresponding number for the sperm donor.

I blinked, then frowned deeply as the name registered in my brain.

Micah Hawthorne.

Beck's friend and former roommate.

A *beta.*

How is that possible?

Sitting back in stunned silence, I mused over the discovery. I'd never met Micah. Even at Beck and Ollie's wedding in front of the entire town, our paths hadn't crossed. But from what I knew of the man, the contents of that petri dish should not be possible. Firstly, he was a beta. Secondly, unlike Beck, Rex, and Brandi, he had grown up knowing he was a shifter and he had the ability to shift. Finally, and most confusingly, he was a horse shifter.

Beck and Ollie were both wolves. Rex and Damon were both mountain lions. Brandi and Lena were both rabbits.

I was a dragon. Micah was a horse. How could we possibly be compatible?

If we were, and if the fertilization of my ovum wasn't a fluke, this discovery would throw all of our theories to that point into the wind.

And, assuming Micah was also affected by locked alpha syndrome, did that mean inter-species breeding was possible between alphas and omegas after all, like it was between betas of different species? And, if so, would those fertilized eggs be dragons, or would they be horses?

I decided that, on that last question, I didn't care either way. They were still my babies, made from my ovum — something I'd honestly thought was a daydream at best. They were precious, regardless of their species.

However, another realization hit me like a punch to my solar plexus.

Eric and I did not have the facilities to freeze the embryos. After a few days, they would need to be frozen or disposed of.

I felt sick at the idea of disposing of them.

Especially when Micah didn't live in Shifters Sanctuary. As far as I knew, he lived in New York and traveled all over the world for work. Even if I contacted him, would he want to uproot his life to be saddled with a man he'd never met, or to have children simply because I was desperate to try to save my species and, if I was being honest, because I desperately wanted to be a father?

I'd wanted it for centuries, but had never imagined it possible.

The petri dish called to me, speaking to those desires like a siren.

I knew it was unethical. I knew it would be a breach of my Hippocratic oath as a doctor...

But I *really* wanted to be a father, and I didn't want to dispose of my embryos. As far as I could tell, this was my only shot.

It was fate, as Ollie would say.

And so, under my brother's nose, I prepared to break laws and oaths and ethics in order to fulfill that dream and potentially ensure my species would continue.

What was the modern saying? Seek forgiveness, not permission?

Well, I hoped I'd be forgiven for my next actions, because they were going to change history.

Chapter Two

"Can't you, I don't know, make the hair...poofier?" Bertram, the designer whose collection was about to walk out onto the catwalk in less than five minutes, stood back with his hands on his hips and a frown on his face as he looked into the mirror at the model I'd just finished working on.

He might have been great with fashion, but he needed to learn to leave hair and makeup to the professionals. That is, me.

Reminding myself that this was his vision, I plastered a not-entirely-real smile on my face and tilted my head, trying to see the model through his eyes. "Poofier?" I repeated.

"Yes," he nodded emphatically, "I see my collection as an ode to the '90s. Big hair, big makeup, big *everything*." He leered as his gaze switched to me and swept over my body from my feet to my face.

You'll be bitterly disappointed if you try to climb that tree, I thought, but kept the words internal.

Instead, I bit my lip and looked the model over again. I'd met the brief I'd been given. The makeup was bold, but not '90s tacky. She had what I thought was 'big' hair, however, as Bertram whipped out his phone and brought up a photo of '90s

Fran Drescher a la *The Nanny*, I realized too late that he wanted exaggeratedly big hair.

Grabbing the ridiculously oversized can of hairspray I carry in my kit, I nodded. Some extra teasing and an ozone-destroying amount of spray later, and I could definitely say that the model's hair was 'poofier'.

"Perfect!" Bertram cheered and even jumped up and down with his glee. "*This* is why you come so highly recommended," he said, ushering the woman from the chair and shoving her towards the group of people armed and ready to get her into the outfit she was debuting. "Micah, darling, you're magic."

"I'm not," I shook my head and headed towards the line of models waiting to step out onto the catwalk, double checking that none needed any touch ups. "I'm just good at what I do. Oh!" I plucked a soft brush and some translucent powder from the toolkit slung around my waist and leaned in to add a bit more coverage to one very pretty model's cheek.

They smiled at me and winked as I pulled back to inspect my handiwork. They were pretty, but not my type, so I smiled back with a little less enthusiasm, then moved on. When I reached the end of the queue, I turned to find Bertram standing far too close to me, his eyes level with my pecs. I neatly sidestepped him and headed over to my station to start packing up.

"You should come sit and watch the show with me," he said, the offer coming out smarmy and kind of gross.

I shook my head again and checked my watch. "I can't. I'm due across town in an hour. Besides, you should get out there now." I gestured with my chin. "Your first outfit has already hit the runway."

Eyes widening, the creepy little man rushed away without so much as a goodbye, and I breathed a sigh of relief. I enjoyed my job, but some people, like Bertram, often overstepped boundaries and made it very uncomfortable. However, because I needed the money, I had to be careful about how I rebuffed their advances. It was an exhausting balancing act and I felt sorry for any other professionals in the same position.

On days like that, I often wondered why I bothered. I knew that my pack, based outside of Susanville in California, would welcome me home with open arms...but that kind of life had never been for me. My pack, my *herd*, weren't the omega-oppressing kind, but I found life with them wasn't satisfying. I was bored there.

Then again, I was becoming bored with my life as a traveling makeup artist, too. It was almost as if I didn't know who I was anymore.

In my mid-thirties, I was unsettled. I missed my younger days, when I felt wild and free. I had an itch under my skin, not unlike the need to shift into my horse form and run, but...deeper somehow. More intense. Like even shifting couldn't fix it.

Maybe I just missed my friends. A couple of years earlier, my two closest friends and former roommates had moved to a no-name, speck-on-a-map town in freaking *Iowa* of all places. Beckett and Sandy, who were foster siblings growing up, were people I never had to pretend to be anything other than myself with.

I'd known Sandy was a wolf shifter, having been able to scent it on her the day I'd knocked on her door in answer to her ad for a third roommate, but Beckett had been completely human...until he wasn't anymore. His discovery that he was actually a shifter

—and an alpha at that— had been the beginning of the end of our stint as roommates. I couldn't blame them, though. Not with everything that happened after that.

Beck's omega mate had gotten pregnant, and then the cult religion that a lot of packs seemed to be indoctrinated into got wind of the existence of an alpha, and then *dragons* had gotten involved. It was a crazy time. Beck and Sandy had left and settled down in a shifter town where they could not only better defend themselves from the people who wanted to harm Beck and his mate, but also where Beck could raise his kids with a little more space than our poky little apartment in New York could provide.

I missed that apartment, though. And my friends. Keeping in touch via texts and messenger apps and the occasional phone call was not the same thing.

Also, I had started to feel a weird, unsettled feeling after visiting their pack-slash-town for Beck and Ollie's wedding. It had been great seeing my old friends and hanging out with them as they celebrated, and even Beck and Ollie's twin toddlers were fun to spend time with, and even though small-town life had never appealed to me before, I'd hated to leave.

Life had gone back to feeling unsatisfactory after I returned to New York for work.

At first I thought it was because I was just overdue a proper vacation, but now I wasn't so sure. My gut was trying to tell me something, but I wasn't great at listening to my instincts.

I kind of sucked as a shifter, to be honest.

I'd never felt like I was a *real* beta. That sounds dumb, I know. But I wasn't born with the crescent moon birthmark of an omega, and I didn't get slick like an omega, either. But I didn't feel right as a beta. I didn't have the confidence or grace of my beta brethren. I certainly didn't have the expected build, either.

Instead of being strong and masculine, I was just tall and lanky. Long-limbed (at least *something* was long) and awkward. Gangly. Like a perpetual teenager. I felt like a wobbly-legged colt and not a sure-footed stallion.

Plus, I was gay. Like *gay* gay. Gold star gay. For a beta, that's nearly unheard of. Omegas? It's expected. But betas? If anything, we're usually bi, though most beta men settle down with beta women to keep their packs growing. But not me. Oh no. I had to not only be physically unimpressive, but I had to also be solely interested in men. And, to the omega men in my pack, I was a dud because I, like them, preferred to bottom. I didn't fit in at all, and I was miserable because of that.

I mean, okay, let's lay it all out there right now. I have, in layman's terms, a micropenis.

Yep.

I'm a freaking horse shifter and I'm not hung like one. It felt like some kind of cosmic joke. And of *course* that was a source of disappointment to the omegas I attempted to hook up with...so, eventually, I gave up.

That's part of why I left my pack. My parents are amazing, supportive people. They're total hippies, actually. Always upbeat and never judgmental. But I could tell they were disappointed that I always felt out of place at home. And I hated upsetting them simply by existing, so...I left.

In the human world, my differences weren't as much of an issue. They were definitely something I had a chip on my shoulder about, but at least human men didn't automatically assume I wanted to top, and I had a pretty great sex life despite my (dear god, I'm sorry about this pun) *short*comings.

Still, it was all a part of the simmering concoction of emotions making me feel uneasy about myself.

Being flirted with by men who couldn't understand the word 'no' only seemed to make the feeling worse.

As I finished packing up my kit, I bid goodbye to the assistants who had been working with me behind the scenes and I headed out onto the busy Manhattan street. If I wasn't lugging around thousands of dollars' worth of makeup and hair products, I might have taken the subway to get to my next destination, but I opted to hail a cab instead. It was going to cost more, but was safer and easier.

Thankfully, the cab driver had just as little interest in talking to me as I did with him, and I used the drive across town —to the on-location filming spot for an episode of a new TV show— to relax and center myself.

I am calm.

I am content.

I am—

The shrill ringing of my phone cut into my silent affirmations and I sighed before looking at the caller ID. *Mom.* It was as if she had a sixth sense for any time I was getting too lost in my wallowing.

"Hey, Mom," I greeted with enthusiasm I didn't quite feel.

"Baby," she cooed, "are you well? I haven't heard from you in weeks."

For an airy-fairy hippie, she was still really good at laying on the mom-guilts, but I knew she only did it because she really did miss me. I missed her, too. Just not the rest of the pack.

This time when I smiled, it was more genuine. "I'm fine, just busy."

"You work yourself too hard, Mikey."

"I can't help it. I take the work when and where I can get it."

"You know if you need money, your dad and I—"

"Mom, I'm thirty-six. I am beyond the age of calling my mommy and daddy to pay for things."

She sniffed. "You'll never stop being our baby, Micah. You'd know how that feels if you ever hurry up and give me grandbabies."

I take it all back. She's a monster.

"Mom, I'm—"

"Don't give me the old 'I'm gay' excuse, Micah Hawthorne. Omegas in our pack have been known to adopt babies from all over the world. *And* Mitchell and his human partner, Daniel? Yes, I think that's his name. Anyway, they've just announced that they're having a baby through a surrogate. There's no excuse for you, Micah."

"Aside from the fact that those options are hella expensive, how about the fact that I'm single?" I offered her, along with a long-suffering sigh. "I like kids, Mom. I do. But I don't want to raise them by myself." I studiously ignored the cab driver's raised eyebrows in the rearview mirror. He could butt the hell out, too.

"Well, find yourself a man. The clock is ticking."

Oh, sure, because everyone *was lining up to settle down with the guy with the tiny dick and no money to his name.*

"What clock?"

"Your biological clock."

I laughed. "Don't you mean *your* biological clock? I'm content the way I am."

Liar.

Oh, great. My inner voice was ganging up on me, too.

"Forgive me for being blunt, baby, but that's not true and we both know it."

I swallowed and looked out the window at the grays and tans of the buildings swishing by as the cab weaved through traffic. "Mom..."

"The last time you sounded even close to happy was when you visited your alpha friend for his wedding a few months back. Oh, I got such good vibes from the universe while you were there..."

"I called you while I was drunk, Mom. It wasn't good vibes; it was too much tequila."

This time, the cabbie snorted, then averted his gaze when I caught his eye in the mirror and frowned.

I'm so glad I can provide someone with amusement today.

"I know what I felt, sweetheart," she dismissed me. "And I know you're not happy now, either."

I never really bought into my mother's hippy-dippy 'in tune with the universe' crap. I believed in magic to some extent —I was a man who turned into a horse at will, after all— but that was just a step too far. Still, I played along with her because it made her happy and it wasn't hurting anyone.

The conversation in the cab was no different. I sighed. "Fine. I'm feeling..." I searched for the right word and could only come up with: "unsettled, I guess." And she was right — the last time I felt content and settled had been at Beck's wedding months earlier.

"I knew it!"

"Mom…"

"Do me a favor, baby. Call your friends. Go visit them. I'm getting the feeling you're supposed to be there."

Shoulders slumping, I decided it wouldn't hurt to take a little holiday. Maybe I'd sublet my room and see if staying in a small-town for a couple of months might be enough to fix whatever misguided notion my instincts —and my mother and her *universe*— were stuck on.

"Fine, Mom, I'll go. But I reserve the right to say 'I told you so' when it's a bust."

"And I reserve the right to say it when it turns out that *I'm* right." She paused to blow air-kisses down the line. "*Mwah*, baby. I love you. Let me know when you get there safe and sound."

We said our goodbyes and I sat in awkward silence for the remaining few minutes of my car ride. When the cab pulled up to the curb and I paid, the driver turned in his seat and extended a card with his number.

He smirked and shrugged. "I'm not looking for anything serious, either," he said, adding, "and I get it: my Mom's Jewish. The guilt is strong in that one."

I took the card, sharing a chuckle of commiseration. The guy was cute, with dark curly hair and eyes that glimmered with mirth, but he was far too young for me.

Because that was my other issue: I had a type. It was just a pity that even the older men I'd dated had gotten bored of me for one reason or another.

I was destined for singledom and Grindr hook-ups.

I tucked the card into my jeans pocket as I climbed out of the cab with my makeup kit, reminding myself that, in the end, beggars couldn't be choosy.

My inner shifter huffed and my skin prickled with renewed unease. Apparently, he disagreed with my life choices more and more with each passing day.

"Fine," I muttered to myself, feeling like an idiot, "I'll text Beck."

Oddly, that seemed to settle my inner beast.

Weird.

Chapter Three

Brandt

I underestimated how draining pregnancy might be for a middle-aged shifter, and I quite literally had nobody to blame but myself. The alpha —who wasn't an alpha yet— hadn't even touched me. He'd donated his genetic material to science, and I'd abused his trust in us by implanting the resulting viable embryos in my womb. With my hormones running rampant, I struggled with nearly crippling guilt over that fact.

However, I was pregnant.

I was elated to be pregnant.

Me. A dragon omega. *Pregnant.*

Yes, there was a chance that the embryos I carried might take after their alpha parent and be born horse shifters instead of dragons, but even so, it meant that somewhere in their DNA, dragon genes would carry on. Maybe somewhere down the line, they might find mates also with recessive dragon genes and then spawn a new generation of dragon shifters after all.

But even if not, I was still fulfilling my dream of having children of my own.

I loved children. There was nothing more rewarding than watching them explore the world. They were innocent and enthusiastic about everything they discovered. Their wide-eyed joy never failed to make my own heart feel lighter.

Working in the clinic with Eric, and spending time with my new friends' children, was bittersweet for me. It was always a joy to interact with the town's small ones, but also left an ache in my heart for a future I desperately wanted and never thought I would have.

Until that fateful day in the lab.

I would be forever grateful to whichever fates saw me in charge of checking the results of our testing that day. I also counted myself lucky that Eric hadn't stumbled in on me as I had performed the somewhat awkward and uncomfortable transfer of the embryo into my womb. I was luckier, still, that our lab had even had the requisite supplies on hand, though I'd needed to sneak into the clinic room with the ultrasound machine and I'd been terrified my brother would catch me in a compromising position (we do not need to think too long on just *how* I needed to get the catheter into the right location).

It was an anxious six weeks of waiting before I gave in and, when Eric was called away to the Alpha's house for a town meeting, used the ultrasound machine to confirm that all three embryos had implanted correctly. Of course, the other symptoms I had been experiencing suggested that they had, but as a man of science, I needed to be certain.

I had cried upon seeing them on that screen, though they were little more than tiny specks of matter inside my womb.

Courtesy of the hormonal imbalance that three growing fetuses would cause, I expected that I would spend a lot of time crying from that point on.

They certainly caused a lot of nausea, too.

And exhaustion.

And really sore nipples.

And did I mention the exhaustion?

It was hard to disguise these changes from those around me, most notably my brothers, but also Damon, who was the clinic's main receptionist and who had become one of my closest friends since he had arrived to the town roughly eighteen months earlier. He'd been six months pregnant when he had arrived, seeking sanctuary and assistance, and the alpha he'd accidentally mated with (Rex) followed soon after.

Initially, Damon had been resentful of his pregnancy. As someone who longed for children of my own, I hadn't quite understood why. But he had been scared, felt rejected by his potential mate, and he had not been enjoying the symptoms of his condition. But once he and Rex sorted things out, he seemed happier. Their son, tiny little Cam, was adorable, and I ended up spending a lot of time with Damon and the baby.

Because of the close friendship we had developed over time, it was difficult to keep my secret from him. I knew that, eventually, there would be no hiding it. But while miscarriage was still a risk and a concern —particularly given my age— I wanted to keep my babies to myself.

It was selfish for more than that reason, though. I also knew that Eric would not be happy with me. Even Damon might be disappointed in my lack of ethics. As would Beckett, the pack Alpha.

After all, Eric and I had made promises to the alphas, both actual and potential, that we wouldn't use their sperm to impregnate anyone without their consent.

Micah had not given his consent.

Did I mention I was wracked with guilt? Because I was. Truly.

But I stood by my decision. I would make it again, given half a chance.

This was a mistake, I thought to myself as I sat in Beck and Ollie's living room.

I had volunteered to be one of the chaperones of the pack's most vulnerable members: namely children who could not yet shift and pregnant betas and omegas. The pregnant shifters could technically shift but, apparently for those further along in their pregnancies, it was such a drain on their systems that they spent their time in shifted form curled up and sleeping.

I bounced Cam on my knee, the near-toddler giggling delightedly at the funny faces I pulled for him, while I listened to Lena and Ollie bantering on the couch about having more children. Lena was heavily pregnant with twins, while Ollie was just joining us on guard duty. He was not, as far as any of us were aware, expecting any more pups of his own just yet.

However, the reason I was suddenly overcome by panic was Ollie's declaration that Beck's friend and former housemate would be coming to stay.

Micah.

The Micah.

The Micah whose children were currently gestating away inside me.

The Micah who I hadn't ever met. Not even during Ollie and Beck's lavish Christmas wedding a few months earlier.

Shit, shit, shit.

Catching Damon's curious gaze as he and Ollie switched to bantering about Damon's notorious dislike of my fellow dragon, Dexter, I attempted to re-engage in the conversation. I muttered something about Dexter going through his own issues—not that I knew what they were, exactly. He was Sage's best friend, and Sage was also being curiously tightlipped— but I'm not sure I did a fantastic job of sounding put-together.

Because, and I might not have been clear about this, Micah Hawthorne was going to be living in the pack Alpha's home for an unknown amount of time.

I thought I would have much, much longer before facing him became an issue.

"Are you okay?" Ollie asked after Rex and Damon disappeared outside. Something was going on there, but I was too distracted to pay much attention. It took a moment to comprehend that he was talking to me.

I cleared my throat and nodded. "Of course. Why do you ask?"

Ollie also assisted us in the fertility lab, though he worked more closely with Eric on the research than he did with me in the lab proper. He cocked his head and narrowed his eyes. "You seem...off."

"Off?" I repeated, playing dumb.

"Off," he nodded decisively. "I can't put my finger on it, but...you seem...distracted, maybe?"

Thinking quickly, I considered the conversation I was having with Damon before Lena walked in. "I'm just thinking about our research. Before you joined us, I was attempting to convince Damon to trial the omega birth control which we've developed."

"Yeah, good luck with that," he laughed and settled back against the couch cushions, shaking his head. "That man is one and done. Cam's a cutie," he waved at the baby I was still bouncing on my knee, "but not even that chubby cheeked smile is going to convince Day to open up shop again."

Glad to have overthrown his suspicion, I looked over at his twin two-year-olds who were currently wrestling with a stuffed wolf toy between them. "And you?"

"And me what?"

"Have you...shut up shop? Or would you be amenable to trialing our birth control? You've seen the science yourself. It worked for the ovum collection."

Lena grinned wickedly at him and rubbed her gravid belly. "What's the worst that could happen, Oliver?"

"You" —I pointed my finger at her— "are not helping."

She cackled while Ollie snorted and shook his head. Then he looked back over at his kids wistfully and sighed. "Like I said, I'm not completely opposed to having more," my spirits lifted until he continued, "but I promised Beck no more unplanned pregnancies in our lifetime. Birth control failing counts as unplanned in my books."

"Amen," Lena agreed emphatically.

I snorted. "I told you, keeping up with your implant was your responsibility."

She poked her tongue out at me, then winced and poked at her stomach. "Behave in there."

"That doesn't work," Ollie told her wisely. "It doesn't work on the outside, either." He proved his point by looking at his still brawling children and saying, "Hey, you two. Behave!" They ignored him. "See?"

"Yes, you put a lot of effort into managing their behavior just now," Lena sassed back.

"Having two at once is exhausting," he complained. "Thank god I've got Beck and Sandy living here with me. I don't even think I could handle one on my own."

I looked down at Cam and smiled. "You're not that difficult, are you?"

He responded with an assortment of babbled sounds that warmed my heart. Hormones going wild, I had to blink back tears at how cute he was. I couldn't wait to hold my own and get the same sweet, gurgled replies.

"You get to hand that one back to his parents," Ollie told me, seemingly oblivious to the unwelcomed emotional moment I was experiencing. "Be thankful you haven't had an oops moment with an alpha, is all I'm saying."

"Hey, the results of your oops moment are adorable," Lena argued.

Rory chose that moment to let out an ear-piercing yowl and fling herself bodily at her brother, who burst into tears.

Ollie winced and pushed to his feet. "Yes," he replied, deadpan, "so adorable." Then he turned to his kids and swept one up under each arm. "Come on, monsters. It's about time we get you ready for bed, anyway."

Their cries only got louder at his declaration. He turned to Lena. "You sure you're ready for this?"

With her nose scrunched up against the sound, Lena looked at her belly. "Nope."

I bit my lip and worried it.

I was ready for it, though.

Wasn't I?

"What's this about you trying to land me with more kids?" Beckett asked me a few days after the monthly pack run.

Not expecting anyone else in the lab, I just about jumped out of my skin. Spinning my chair around, I found the alpha grinning at me from the doorway, where he leaned against the door jam with his arms folded across his broad chest.

He was young, still in his early thirties, with olive-colored skin and dark hair. He kept a stubbled jawline, and he was tall, though not as tall as me. I'd heard more than one omega and beta swoon over him. But it was the electric alpha scent that really worked in his favor. Despite his generally easy-going nature, he was powerful.

But, to me, the pack Alpha was a friend. I guessed there was something about rescuing a man from his abductors and flying him back to his laboring mate that formed an instant bond between people.

"Well?" he prompted with eyebrows raised. "You gonna explain yourself, Brandt?"

Snorting, I sat back in my chair and only *just* managed not to splay my hand across my abdomen. I'd taken to touching my belly more often, as if the touch would reassure the tiny fetuses that I was thinking about them.

"I was actually trying to prevent that, *alpha*," I responded drily.

"Uh huh," he sounded amused. "By offering my mate untested medication?"

"How else are we supposed to test it if the only omegas with alpha mates refuse to use it?" Despite understanding Ollie and Damon's misgivings, my frustration on the issue was building. I put that down to hormones, too. Trying not to pout, I added, "Besides, Oliver said that he wouldn't be opposed to having more children."

"Yeah, planned ones, preferably."

"Does it make that much of a difference? Really?" I gestured around us. "When you weren't financially secure and were newly mated, I understand. But you've got a spacious home, an entire pack at your disposal, endless resources funded by dragon hoards—"

"It's not just about the financial strain. There's an emotional one, too." His answer was gentle, and he wandered into my little lab and sat down on the spare chair beside me. I casually closed the window I'd had open on my computer screen, not wanting him to see the records I was keeping of my own pregnancy. "Kids take a lot of energy and attention, too. There's the sleepless nights, the diapers, the potty training...which I am *not* loving, by the way." He scrubbed his hand over his face. "Plus being constantly worried that I'm giving them enough attention, enough love, that I'm not screwing them up for life...It's a lot, Brandt."

I hadn't expected the brutal honesty, nor to hear about his self-doubt. I had to bite my lip to prevent it from wobbling. Clearing my throat, I averted my gaze. "I apologize," I told him. "I suppose I've idealized the concept of having children. Many children. With our species on the brink of extinction..." My throat tightened and I clenched my hand into a fist to once again prevent it from wandering to my belly.

Unlike Eric, who was muscular and defined, and Sage, who was long and lean, I had a more average build. I am tall, and broad shouldered, but my stomach had never been flat or muscular. I was glad for the additional padding, the slight softness and roundness which had always existed, because it would allow me to hide my secret just a while longer.

Beck's expression softened and he leaned forward, placing his hand over my own. "I get that. And, like I've told Ollie, I would love any kids we have together, even if they're a surprise like Rory and Duke were. It does seem unfair that we have the luxury of choice where you don't." He gave my hand a squeeze and sat back again. "But I didn't actually come here to make you feel bad about asking us —*again*— to be your guinea pigs."

Still struggling against the tumultuous emotions inside me, I managed to croak, "You didn't?"

"A couple of years ago, this badass dragon saved my life. I told him that I owed him. That I'd have his back. So..." he took a deep, steadying breath, "this is me saying that I trust your science, Brandt. Ollie and I talked about it, and we agreed that we can't keep relying on condoms during his heats, anyway. The last one..." Beck's cheeks flushed and he averted his gaze. "Let's just say it was a close call and leave it at that, yeah?"

His sudden change in tune almost gave me whiplash. I sat up straighter. "You're serious?"

"About being your guinea pigs?"

I nodded.

He sighed and scrubbed his hand over his face again. "Yeah. I am. Like I said, I trust you."

Oof. I wasn't feeling particularly worthy of that trust in that moment.

But, I *did* stand by the calculations and the research Eric and I had done.

I licked my lips and clapped my hands together. "Okay. In that case, bring Ollie down later and Eric and I will run through everything with you both. I promise, we believe it to be just as effective as The Pill for human and beta women. As long as he takes the medication like clockwork, it's likely even more effective."

Beck squinted a little and nodded slowly. "Alright," he agreed slowly. Then he sighed and offered me a small smile, "If it fails, you and Eric are going to be our on-call babysitters for eternity."

I grinned. "Deal."

Chapter Four

"There he is!" Beck's voice was loud and joyful, rising over the small crowd of people at Sioux City airport.

I dropped my bags, just gathered from the baggage carousel, and crouched with my arms extended as his two-year-olds barreled towards me on chubby toddler legs.

Even though I'd only met them in person a couple of times, I Facetimed with Sandy, Beck and the kids often enough that they recognized me on sight. My heart thumped as their solid little frames crashed into my sides, chipmunk voices excitedly greeting me as "Unca' Micah!" in unison.

Immediately, some of that awful buzzing under my skin seemed to fade. This felt *right*. Being here with my old friend felt right.

I straightened up, lifting Rory and Duke as I stood, and Beck grabbed my bags from the ground.

"How was your flight?" Beck asked, and I shrugged as best I could with two small shifters in my arms.

"It was fine. A little bumpy at the end there, but still uneventful." I smirked at him, remembering how *he* got to Iowa. "Better than by dragon, I bet."

"I don't recommend flying by dragon if you can help it. Though, I will say, the legroom is usually better."

I snorted. I was taller than him and, yeah, squeezing into cramped economy seats was a bitch. "I'll stick with commercial for now." After a beat, I added, "Thanks for coming to pick me up. I could have hired a car."

"It's fine. The monsters like going for long drives. Besides, I think Ollie was looking forward to us being out of his hair for a while. He and Eric had some sort of research-y breakthrough and I'm pretty sure he would bury himself in whatever books they unearthed if he had half a chance."

The way he talked about his mate was fond and affectionate. He even rubbed at his chest, and a part of me panged with jealousy. As a beta, even if I did find someone to settle down with, I wouldn't ever get to experience a full mating bond. That magic was reserved for alphas and omegas.

"Well, that answers my question about how he's doing," I laughed lightly as we continued our way towards the exit. "And how's San?"

"Still flying in and out for work. We're lucky that she's able to work remotely most of the time, but they still like having her in the office for fuck knows what reason."

Duke and Rory giggled, and Beck groaned. "Please don't tell Papa."

Looking very much like Beck, Rory practically smirked as she leaned across my chest to tell her father, "Bad word."

"Yes, I said a bad word."

"Buck." That was Duke's contribution.

"Thank god he can't make the 'ffff' sound yet," Beck muttered. Then, as we came up to the exit doors, he stopped and turned to me. "Potty before we get in the car."

I blinked at him. "Uh…"

"Not you, *them*." He pointed at his kids, both happily looking around the airport with all the wonder of being at a carnival. "Come on," he reached for Duke, "potty time."

"Aren't they still a bit young for potty training?" I handed the now squirming kid over, and we both ignored his protests and determined 'no's.

Beck shrugged. "Ollie read something that said the average age is just over two. I don't know. It's a pain in the a—uh—butt," he hastily censored himself as we walked together towards the bathrooms, "but Rory's getting it. Duke's…a little slower on the uptake. But I've got them both in pull-ups anyway. Still, *if we don't stay consistent…*"

I bit my lip against my amusement as Beck clearly parroted his mate's words. "Sounds like *you're* well-trained," I teased.

"Do you want to shift and run from here back to the pack? Because that's still an option."

It was not an appealing one, so I bounced Rory on my hip. "So, potty time?"

He snorted and reached for Rory with his free hand. "I've got this. You should enjoy the wonders of not having kids."

"Oh, yeah. All the wonders of standing outside an airport bathroom." I rolled my eyes and kept Rory tucked into my side. "I don't mind helping. Besides, two of them against one of you seems like unfair odds anyway."

"Being outnumbered does sometimes suck," he agreed as we strolled towards the bathrooms. "It *is* getting easier as they get older, though. Sometimes. Maybe. Well, until they run in opposite directions. And, no," he gave me a pitiful look, "Ollie isn't a fan of the whole 'backpack with a leash' idea. I don't judge parents who use them, but Ollie has a thing about being a wolf on a leash...it doesn't matter that these guys can't shift yet. It's a whole thing with him. I don't argue."

It was tempting to joke about him being well trained again, but I really did prefer to be driven to the pack, so I kept those thoughts inside that time.

Getting the kids to use the bathroom was a relatively painless affair, and they were excited to be 'rewarded' by using the automatic hand soap dispenser and hand dryers after they were done.

"At least they're easily entertained," I mused, and Beck chuckled, ruffling Duke's light-brown hair.

"Yeah. They're easy to please."

"Most kids are."

Beck eyed me curiously as we left the bathroom with my bags and the kids still in tow. "How do you know so much about kids anyway? I didn't think you were a kid person. I wasn't. Not before these guys came along, anyway."

"I've actually always wanted kids," I admitted easily. It was always easy talking to Beck or Sandy. They were my pack away from home, even if we no longer lived together. "I came from a large, supportive pack. Nothing like Ollie's. We were one big happy hippy commune, mostly. So I was always surrounded by the pack kids, I guess."

"So, why'd you leave?"

We exited the main building, and Beck led the way towards the parking lot while I considered my answer. While it was easy talking to him about some things, others remained too personal. "I love my family, but I didn't really fit in. The small-town commune life wasn't for me. I wanted to travel. I wanted to live somewhere big and eclectic." I'd wanted to find people who could work around my less-than-impressive physical traits. Somewhere where I wouldn't be seen as a disappointment as a beta. "I stumbled into makeup artistry and the rest his history, I guess."

"And now? When you called, it sounded like you wanted to escape for a while. Not that Sandy and I aren't thrilled to have you back with us, but...why not go back to your pack?"

My instincts revolted against the very idea, but I didn't know how to explain it. I didn't fully understand it myself. Why would I feel more drawn to staying with my friends instead of my family? It was a small-town existence either way. The only difference was my shifter side was telling me I'd be more at ease in Beck's pack than in the one I'd grown up in.

"Honestly?" I found myself answering. "This is where my gut is telling me I need to be. I've wanted to be back here since your wedding."

Beck raised his eyebrows. "Really?"

"Really. I can't explain it, but...I guess you've got a good thing going here. Shifters of all shapes and sizes. Potential alphas. *Dragons.*" I paused. "Maybe that's it. You and Sandy were my family away from family—shut up, that's as sappy as I'm getting," I rolled my eyes at the expression on his face; something between amusement and fondness. "But on top of that, your small-town pack is actually pretty exciting behind the scenes. However, I'd like to avoid any culty ambushes while I'm here. Think you can keep those at bay?"

The Moonmusic people had made two separate attacks on Beck's pack since he and Ollie had moved there, but ever since Beck and the rest of his town council had reached out to neighboring towns, they'd made allies of the mixed lot of humans and shifters who lived nearby. In doing so, they'd taken a gamble by making their status as a shifter pack known, but the Moonmusic cult had seemingly backed off.

It didn't hurt that Joe Morstein —their weasel shifter leader— was losing followers at what felt like a breakneck pace. More people were starting to realize that they didn't *have* to pay his cult tithes, that his 'religion' did nothing for them, and that perhaps the 'neo-shifters', as Beck's lot were being referred to, might have the right idea when it came to treating omegas as equals rather than minions.

After all, it was only 'neo-shifters' who had the fortune of discovering alphas again. Perhaps that said something about magic and fate favoring those who treated each other properly?

Of course, if that were true, why hadn't any alphas appeared in packs like the one I had grown up in? They weren't cult-ridden lunatics. They were hippies, yes, but they were all about equality and love.

Well.

Except for betas like me. But I hadn't exactly helped myself to fit in with them, either. I'd resented my pack and I couldn't wait to graduate high school and leave for greener pastures.

"We've got proper security measures in place now," Beck was saying in response to my teasing, and it took me a moment to remember why we'd been discussing it at all. "You'll be safe in Shifters' Sanctuary, Micah."

I nudged his shoulder with my own and grinned. "I know. I hear the pack has a pretty awesome alpha."

And dragons.

I had no idea why I was so fixated on that part of the town, either. I mean, sure, what kid didn't grow up loving the idea of the mythical creatures? They could fly and breathe fire, after all. And learning they weren't as mythical as I'd thought was a trip, though I still hadn't actually seen one with my own eyes.

I supposed that was why I was still so drawn to the idea of them. When I visited the town for Beck's wedding, I was hoping to meet the four dragons that lived there, but two of them (Sage and Dexter) were travelling, researching magic of all things, and I kept *just* missing the older one, Brandt, any time someone came close to introducing me. I did get to meet Eric, the dragon who had also been Ollie's boss in Manhattan, but he was unable to join the pack during the celebratory run as he had been designated as the on-call emergency doctor for the night.

But I was planning on staying for a couple of months at least this time. Surely I'd get to see a dragon during this visit.

My inner horse whinnied at the idea, practically prancing around in my soul.

I didn't understand his excitement, but I couldn't help but share in it.

"Oh, sorry, I need to make a quick stop before we get home," Beck told me as we pulled off Main Street in the quaint little shifter town. We headed down the country road which I remembered led to the farm he and Ollie lived on, but he took an earlier driveway than the one I knew belonged to his house. "I need to grab Ollie's meds from the clinic. Brandt said they'd be good to go today."

"Meds?" I cocked my head to the side. "Is he sick? I wouldn't have come if—"

"No," Beck looked into the rearview mirror, and I looked over my shoulder, smiling at the two sleeping toddlers in their car seats. "We're, uh, trialing Eric and Brandt's omega birth control."

I blinked. "Trialing?"

The truck rumbled over bumpy gravel, and some part of my soul sang as I looked out over stretches of green grass and copses of fruit trees. It would be magical to shift into my horse form and run through acres of fields. I didn't get many opportunities like that in New York or LA.

"Yeah. We're the first test subjects. There hasn't really been a way to test whether they work for omegas because, y'know, there are only three known alphas in the world. But Brandt and Eric worked for over a year on the science. They even used the same principals as part of whatever it was they did to extract eggs from the omegas for their research." He put the truck into park in front of the little cottage which had a new sign on the door declaring the space as the town's 'Fertility and Birth Center'.

"Well, you *are* the Pack Alpha, too," I reasoned. "It makes sense that you're taking on the responsibility of testing their effectiveness. But, I have to admit, after a run of three of you alphas all appearing so quickly, I'm surprised there haven't been more."

"That we know of," Beck unbuckled his seatbelt. "We're actively trying to reach out to shifter communities overseas —Sage and Dexter are supposed to be helping with that while they're traveling— but if new alphas are popping up in situations like me and Ollie faced, outside of known packs, well...who would know? Damon set up a few Facebook groups and stuff, but so far it's mostly been trolls and pranksters joining." He looked over his shoulder, then back at me. "Can you watch the kids? I won't be long."

Then he was out of the truck and trotting across the tiny gravel parking lot to the clinic's front door.

When the door swung open, I inhaled sharply. The man standing just inside was *magnetic.* He was about my height, but broad and thickly built. I wouldn't describe him as muscular, though his biceps did look impressive. He had a bit of a tummy, but I had a thing for cuddly men. Then there was his gray-speckled goatee and the long, thick, silver-streaked dark hair on his head.

Then we locked eyes, and I swallowed thickly, my heart suddenly going wild.

His eyes widened, though, and I swear he looked almost...*panicked?*

With my hand on the handle to open the passenger door and climb out of the truck, I watched as the man said something hastily to Beck, shoved a little package into his hands, and then shut the door in his face without another glance my way.

I sat there, stunned as my shifter side brayed and hoofed at the ground, wanting me to charge into the clinic and after that man.

What the fuck was that about?

Chapter Five

Brandt

*S*hit. *Shit. Shit shit shit.*

I paced the length of the clinic's waiting room and waited for my heart to calm itself. When Beckett had said he'd be picking up Ollie's medication after running other errands, I hadn't realized that those errands included collecting his friend from the airport.

But there he had been. Micah Hawthorne. While I had never met him, I had seen photos.

After his sperm had fertilized my ovum, I *might* have stalked him online somewhat, too.

What? I was curious. I wanted to get some idea of what my children might look like should they take after their beta (or was he actually an alpha?) father.

He was handsome. Young, but then everyone was young to me. He was tall and lean, with striking light brown eyes and long sandy-blonde hair that reminded me of Farrah Faucett's style in the 1970s, wavy on the ends and styled to flick away from and frame his face.

Then there were his lips. His beautiful, pouty, perfectly kissable lips.

Gods above, I was in trouble.

It was all well and good when he was an abstract concept. A man who had left a specimen for our research and who had unknowingly left me the most precious, priceless gift in history. He was *supposed* to remain that way.

From everything Beckett and Sandy had said, Micah had zero interest in staying in the middle of nowhere. His work was dependent on being in a big city. He was a makeup artist. There wasn't much call for such a thing in our pack.

And yet, here he was. Sitting in the passenger seat of Beck's truck mere feet away from where I stood.

From where I carried his children.

Children he had *not* consented to creating.

I was torn between closing the space between us and thanking him effusively, and also bursting into tears and begging for his forgiveness.

Instead, I did neither. I rambled the reminder for Ollie to take the pills within the same hour window every morning, thrust the packet into Beck's hands, then slammed the door and started to pace.

I was almost twelve weeks along. I was almost through the first trimester. Through what was largely considered the 'danger zone'. But I was old, even for shifter standards, and I was carrying triplets. The entire pregnancy would be risky.

Already, I was beginning to develop a bump. It was disguised by my pre-existing belly, but I knew my body. I knew my shape. I knew it was changing.

Sooner than I would like, it would be unmistakable.

For almost three months, I had considered what I would tell people. How I would justify my (admittedly shitty) behavior to my brother and to our Pack Alpha. I hadn't banked on having to face the man whose genetic material I had absconded with at the same time. I had really thought that I would have a little longer until then. In fact, I had hoped that Beck would inform him, given their friendship, and that Micah would opt to remain in New York and that I wouldn't have to face him at all.

I was a terribly cowardly dragon. I blamed the hormones coursing through my body.

Sadly, I couldn't blame them for the choices I had made to begin with.

Not that I ultimately regretted the decision itself.

I'd always wanted children of my own. Whether to save my species or not, I wanted babies. I wanted to watch them grow and learn and explore. I wanted to experience the wonder of seeing the world through new, pure perspectives. I wanted someone to love unconditionally and to be loved in return. I wanted purpose and happiness.

By breaking oaths and the trust of the people around me, I had hopefully secured those dreams for myself. I couldn't possibly regret that.

But I could regret that it was going to hurt people.

There was a saying: you have to break a few eggs to make an omelet. That's how this felt. I wasn't sure I quite liked the metaphor, seeing as my eggs being whole and accounted for as they grew into healthy fetuses and then children was kind of the point, but it was the best analogy my scrambled mind could come up with.

No, that was not an intentional egg pun.

Gods, I was going mad.

The guilt was getting to me.

Think of the babies, I told myself firmly. *Think of why you are doing this.*

My hand drifted to my tiny bump. I couldn't wait until I could feel them moving, until I could be reassured by their presence inside me.

They *were* the reason I had done what I did. No matter what happened, I needed to remember that.

The dreams started that night. They were vivid, but I couldn't recall them when I woke. They left me achingly hard and dripping with slick — not a sensation I was used to anymore, despite being an omega.

On the third morning of it happening, I *needed* to sate the desire. I was desperate to be filled and fucked. In the stillness of the house I had purchased years earlier, though it was too large for just me alone, I closed my eyes and reached beneath the waistband of my pajama pants. I slept without underwear, preferring the extra breathing room, and as I bypassed my aching cock, I slid my fingers beyond my taint and to my wet hole.

I whined as I circled the rim, spreading my slick and teasing myself with the light touch. I imagined long, tanned fingers in place of my somewhat chunky pale ones. Then I pressed inside and caught his forbidden name before I could sigh it out loud in my relief.

It was wrong to think of him —I did not have the right, especially with the secret I was concealing— but I could not stop myself.

The position I held was awkward, my frame too bulky to properly pleasure myself, and I withdrew my fingers after only a couple of unsatisfying thrusts. In the pre-dawn darkness of my bedroom, I rifled through my nightstand for the toy which would hopefully dull the desperate need building inside me, grateful for its long, curved handle.

With my prize secured, I kicked my pajamas off beneath the thin blanket and then spread my legs like the wanton beast I was. Lying back, I notched the blunt head of the toy at my hole, not requiring any more lube than the slick I was leaking, and slid it inside me.

"*Fuck,*" I exhaled, relishing the sensation, imagining warm flesh instead of flesh-simulation silicon, "fuck yes, just like that."

I did not want to acknowledge who I imagined I was speaking to, but it was more satisfying to imagine a long, lean body hovering over my bulk, lovingly rocking in and out of my slippery passage.

I readjusted the toy and nudged my prostate. Curved up against my belly, my cock dribbled precum while I felt myself release a rush of slick at the sudden burst of pleasure from the toy.

"M—" my breathing hitched and I bit down on my tongue, refusing to say his name, "*Mmmm.*"

I writhed in my bed, fucking myself on the toy, imagining long, sand-toned hair brushing my skin as fantasy kisses were pressed to my lips, my cheeks, my jaw...

"Fuck," I growled again as the fantasy cock pressed against my prostate, "there, darling. *There.*" It nudged the spot over and over again, and I grunted and growled with every sparking touch to that sensitive bundle of nerves. "Mi—" No. I couldn't. This fantasy man couldn't have a name. "M-my darling, *fuck*, yes, perfect..."

Imagining his hand in place of my own, I teased at my still-sensitive nipples and then down my furry chest and soft, growing belly. Then I grasped my own cock and—

"Oh, *fuck*, I'm coming!" I warned my imaginary lover, my back arching from the mattress as I coated my own hand and stomach with cum. As my hole spasmed around the toy inside me, copious amounts of slick spilled down my ass cheeks and onto the sheets beneath me.

I discarded the toy carelessly at my side, on the empty space where I wished my imaginary lover would collapse and join me in the gentle come down from our mutual orgasms. I was sticky, wet, and even though I was physically satisfied, my racing heart felt empty and sad.

I lamented that I had given in that time. The dreams were my punishment, after all.

I knew that Micah's presence was to blame. Even though we hadn't spoken, hadn't even gotten close to each other, just locking gazes was enough to trigger...*this.* Whatever this was.

I had my suspicions, naturally. His sperm had fertilized my eggs in a petri dish. He was my fated —or at the very least compatible— mate.

My soul ached with the potential for so much more and the knowledge that, once he discovered what I had done, that was all it would ever be. *Potential.*

This...*thing* went on for days, turning into vivid daydreams as the yearning to leave the clinic and walk up to Beck and Ollie's house, where Micah was staying, became an incessant itch beneath my skin.

It made me irritable and sad in equal measures.

Thank the gods my job was mostly solitary. It was easier to hide away in the lab, poking at test results dazedly, than to have to interact with people.

Especially when those people knew me too well.

"Alright," Damon said, folding his arms and staring at me with arched eyebrows, "what gives?"

"What gives," I drawled, "is that you burst into my lab and are now asking me frustrating questions when I should be working."

He leaned against the bench running along the side wall, his lip quirking. "You're being snippy, Bran. And you are *never* snippy. You might look like a big, scary dragon man, but you're the teddiest bear of your siblings. So, I'll ask again. What gives?"

"Teddiest bear?" I cocked my head. "Does that mean you think of Eric as a teddy bear also?"

"Eric's a golden retriever," he shrugged. "But you're the one who is secretly the softest and cuddliest, and not just on the outside."

Though his descriptions left a lot to be desired, he wasn't wrong.

I sighed. "It's a work thing." It was not a lie.

"I don't buy it. Try again."

Relaxing my shoulders, I tried a different tactic. "Day, I am fine. I am just tired and frustrated."

A flash of memory struck me of when he had been six months pregnant and stressed over his alpha, Rex, reacting somewhat poorly to the news of his pregnancy. He had unleashed a tirade of all the things ailing him, from heartburn to hemorrhoids, and I had felt sympathy for him, but little empathy. I had wanted what he had and couldn't understand why he was so resentful.

But now, I understood.

He had been scared. Scared and sad.

I hated to admit it, but I was beginning to feel the same way.

Omegas weren't designed to go through pregnancy alone. After observing Ollie, Damon, and now Lena, Eric was theorizing that the presence of the alpha provided some kind of magical stabilizer to their omega's physical and emotional health. While I wasn't entirely convinced that it was magical, I did agree that having a supportive partner was beneficial for anyone while pregnant.

Now that I was experiencing it personally, some part of me selfishly wished I could share the experience with a partner myself.

But I had chosen to be alone from the outset. My alpha (beta?) hadn't even been present for the conception. He wasn't even remotely responsible for my choices or for the embryos his DNA had had part in creating. I had no right to desire his support.

Knowing as much didn't prevent me from wishing for it, though.

Once again, I lamented the draw to him. I wished that we hadn't locked gazes across the small parking lot. I wished that I hadn't even opened the door that day.

"Earth to Brandt," Damon waved his hand in front of my face. When I blinked and focused on him, he was frowning in concern. "I'm worried about you, Bran," he said softly, his words matching the expression on his face. He tucked a stray lock of his long, dark hair behind his ear. "You're tired. Frustrated. Zoning out. It's not like you. And if you don't want to talk about it, that's fine. We all know I'm not the world's biggest sharer," he chuckled with a modicum of self-deprecation, "but I think you need to at least take a break. You've worked nonstop in this lab for years now, right? When was the last time you took a vacation?"

"A...vacation?" The idea had never occurred to me. I enjoyed working with Eric. Even though most of our test results were disheartening and got us nowhere, I loved researching and hypothesizing. The lab was usually my happy place. My escape.

It was funny that the idea of leaving Shifters' Sanctuary had never occurred to me.

I gave it a moment of consideration, but to hide away would only make things worse in the long run. I needed to come clean. To confess what I had done and to wear whatever consequences came my way.

I was just too cowardly to say anything.

After I completed my next ultrasound and confirmed that the pregnancy was still viable, I told myself that I would put an end to my anxiety. I would tell Eric and Beckett.

And Micah.

"...a beach?" Damon was saying, clearly still offering ideas for the vacation he had suggested. "Or what about a ski chalet somewhere? What kind of places do you find relaxing?"

"My lab," I grumbled, and he snorted and pushed off the bench, shaking his head.

"Just think about it," he told me as he walked out the door. "A break might do you some good."

No, I thought to myself, absently running my hand over my tiny bump, *facing the inevitable will.*

I just needed to confirm that there was something worthy of confessing first.

"Hello, my beautiful babies," I murmured to the monitor, amazed at how much my children had grown.

At just over twelve weeks gestation, they were no longer amorphous blobs, but proper human-shaped fetuses. They had defined fingers and toes, rounded heads and curved spines, and perfectly beating hearts. I could see them all flickering away, and a quick check had them averaging around one-hundred and fifty beats per minute, which was well within the expected range.

Swallowing, I flicked the switch on the ultrasound machine that would produce the sound, and I sat back on the bed to bring the wand to the first of my children. The rapid *whoosh-whoosh-whoosh* brought tears to my eyes.

Performing my own ultrasounds was an awkward affair, but I managed. I knew that the rounder I became, the more difficult doing so would be. But I would be telling Eric soon —once I worked out exactly how I was going to tell him— and I was certain that he would assist me, even if he was disappointed in my actions.

But, until I gathered the courage, I was going to enjoy my private joy on my own.

I moved the wand to the next baby, my eyesight blurring as more *whooshing* played over the speaker. I listened in rapture, losing myself in the steady, strong rhythm.

It was an addictive sound.

Finally, I shifted my hand, seeking out my third baby. But, at that moment, the exam room door swung open with Eric's voice speaking mid-way through a sentence.

"...there soon, I just forgot to grab—*what the fuck?*"

I whipped my head around to face him, watching as his phone slipped from his hand to the floor, and I winced as it clattered on impact.

He scooped it up, his blue eyes never leaving mine as he spoke into it. "Beck, change of plans. Something's come up. No, no, it's fine. I'm sure I'll be there soon." Then he terminated the call and stared at me with shock and hurt plain on his face. "Please tell me I'm hallucinating."

I swallowed, and I didn't very much feel like I was the eldest in that moment. I shook my head.

Eric stepped further into the room, shifting his gaze from mine to the monitor, then to my exposed belly —covered in gel and with the transducer wand held awkwardly to my skin— then back to my face. "You're pregnant."

It wasn't a question. I nodded anyway.

He took another step forward, running his hand through his blonde curls in agitation. "What...how...*Brandt*." He looked at the screen, at the still images I had managed to capture for my records, and then frowned. "You're at least twelve weeks."

I nodded again, trying to find my voice. Almost five centuries old (I'd lost count of the specific years at that point) and I felt like a chastened toddler.

I deserve his ire, I reminded myself, though I was still trying to avoid it.

"Twelve weeks and three days," I managed to croak. But it had only been ten weeks and three days since they had been implanted. It was frustrating that we were measuring omega pregnancies by human and beta female standards, but considering our young appeared to gestate at the same rate, it made sense to include the standard two weeks for ovulation.

Eric sat heavily on the rolling stool and took the wand from my hand, pushing me back to complete the check-up himself. He took measurements —likely more accurate than my own, seeing as he didn't have to contort his body to do so— and studied my children's organs and development with a practiced eye.

Once he was done, he set the wand aside, handed me a wad of paper towels to wipe myself off, and sat back, watching me in silence as I hurriedly slipped my shirt back on.

Eventually, he folded his arms and stared me down. "Start. Talking."

So, with no other choice, I did.

Chapter Six

Green grass flattened beneath my hooves as I cantered across the lush field behind Beck and Ollie's home. The air here was fresh and free of smog or exhaust fumes or the body odor of thousands of tourists and city residents alike. It felt good to be stretching my long, golden-colored limbs, to be feeling the sunshine on my coat. To shake out my mane and my tail and run free and uninhibited.

I was hoping that doing so would settle the restlessness beneath my skin. I no longer felt uneasy, and my shifter side was appeased to be back in Ollie's pack, but ever since we had stopped at the fertility clinic, my horse had been stamping its hooves, demanding...*something*.

I was also hornier than I could ever recall being, and no amount of jerking off in Beck's guest bathroom shower was helping with that.

Beck had picked up on my anxiousness and suggested that I go for a run. He'd offered to join me, and it would have been cool to run alongside his wolf, but I had ultimately felt like I needed to be alone. Plus, I was weird about getting naked in front of other shifters in order to shift. I always had been. Ever since I'd realized I hadn't developed like all the other betas.

In shifted form, as far as I knew, I was anatomically correct. But in human form? I felt...defective.

I knew I wasn't. I knew there was nothing wrong with me. That the size of my dick had nothing to do with how good I was in bed. But aesthetics were still aesthetics, and I didn't want to be laughed at or, worse, pitied.

I knew Beck wouldn't laugh at me, by the way. But I couldn't be as certain that he wouldn't pity me.

Not wanting to risk it, I turned his offer down and opted to run by myself.

With the breeze blowing through my nearly peroxide blonde mane, I listened to the leaves in the trees rustling and the birds chirping. I breathed and ran, my hooves thundering across hard packed ground.

It was helping. I was beginning to feel more in control of myself and my emotions than I had in months. My beta still demanded that I should seek Brandt out, but I got the distinct impression that he didn't want that to happen. Over the week that I had been at Beck's, the oldest dragon had been noticeably absent from any gatherings or meetings.

I'd spent time getting to know his youngest brother, Eric. I had also been properly introduced to the other alphas, Rex and Brandi, and their respective omega mates, Damon and Lena. I'd met several members of the rest of the pack, too. But any time Beck attempted to introduce me to Brandt, the eldest dragon was nowhere to be found. Coupled with the look on his face when he saw me sitting in the car, I was taking it personally.

He was avoiding me.

I couldn't work out why. We had never met. Never spoken. I couldn't imagine Beck or Sandy would have said anything negative about me, but I didn't know what else would have caused his avoidance.

I was still mulling over this when movement from the path connecting the clinic and the main house caught my eye. Eric emerged from the small orchard of apple trees, gesticulating wildly. I couldn't understand his shouts, but I could tell he was unhappy. Enraged, even. A few steps behind him was a tall, bulky, dark-haired figure. *Brandt.*

Brandt's posture made the back of my neck prickle, even in my shifted form. His shoulders were rounded and hunched forward and his head was hanging in defeat. It appeared, to me, that his younger brother was raving at him, and he was taking the tongue-lashing.

My heart thumped and, before I had even processed it, I began racing towards the main house, to the spot in the empty stables where I had left my clothes. I shifted inside the stables and dressed as quickly as I could, not bothering to fix my hair or make sure I was neat and tidy. I didn't know why, but I needed to find out what was wrong.

I need to make sure he's okay.

I had no idea where that thought came from, but I felt it deep in my soul.

By the time I burst in through Beck and Ollie's back door, I knew that Eric and Brandt were already in the house. I could scent them, though it was faint.

"Whoa," Ollie put his hand to his chest in surprise as I rushed through the kitchen and dining area and into the hallway, almost knocking him over. "Where's the fire?"

I couldn't explain why it was so important that I find Brandt, but my shifter side was screaming at me to get to him. Still, I couldn't be rude to my host in his own home.

"Sorry," I apologized quickly, scanning the main hallway which led to Sandy's room, a bathroom, and the room which had been turned into— "The meeting room!" I blurted in an excited rush. It had apparently been soundproofed when Beck and Eric had converted it so they could hold the shifter council meetings there.

"There's a fire in the meeting room?" Ollie asked, and I frowned.

"What?"

He shook his head. "Never mind. What's got you so shaken up?"

I scrubbed my palm over my face. "Eric and Brandt went in there, right? With Beck?"

"And Rex, yeah," Ollie nodded slowly. His eyes narrowed. "Why?"

His confirmation made me feel even more unsettled. Brandt had looked so broken and defeated, and Eric had been shouting and angry...whatever they needed the involvement of *two* alphas for couldn't be good, could it?

"I just...I just have this...this *feeling*." I couldn't describe it. I looked at him pleadingly. "I've got to head in there."

Ollie grimaced. "I'm going to be honest with you, I've *never* seen Eric look more like he wanted to watch the world burn...and I've seen him half-shifted after fighting off some of Morstein's cronies. I think we need to stay out of whatever it is he's on the warpath about. At least until Beck and Rex have had a chance to talk it out with him."

I sighed and glanced longingly down the hallway.

"Come on," Ollie tugged me in the opposite direction, towards his living room. "Damon's watching all three kids right now, and I think he could use a hand wrangling them. I'll get us some iced tea and we'll wait for the others to get us when they need us, okay?"

It wasn't okay, but short of breaking the likely locked door to the meeting room down, it was probably my best option, especially when I couldn't explain —not even to myself— why it was so important that I get in there. My shoulders slumped and I nodded. "Yeah, okay."

Chapter Seven

Brandt

"What's going on?" Beck asked as Eric shoved me forcibly into the meeting room with the two alphas.

The very second I had finished telling him what I had done, he had held up his index finger, instructing me to wait, and he had called the Pack Alpha and requested an audience with him and the other alphas.

I could hear Beck's confused response that Brandi and Lena were not available, which was unsurprising considering how close Lena's due date was, but that he would call Rex to meet us at the house.

Then Eric had thanked him, ended the call, and had finally addressed me. He had been berating me for my selfishness ever since.

If it had been anyone else on the receiving end of his vitriol, I might have been impressed. Of the three of us —myself, Sage and Eric— Eric was the least likely to lose his temper so completely.

It turned out that breaking scientific and medical oaths was his trigger.

In the Alpha's meeting room, Eric pointed to a chair at the long table and barked, "Sit."

Aware of Beckett and Rex exchanging raised eyebrowed looks, I did as I was told.

Eric waved his hand in a sweeping gesture towards Beck and Rex, who were both leaning casually against the buffet unit running along the opposite wall from the door. They straightened as my brother demanded, "Tell them. Tell them what you've done."

I had known Eric would be disappointed in me, but I had hoped that, as a dragon shifter also desperately trying to save our species, he might have some empathy.

I'd been wrong.

It hurt that he didn't see it at all from my perspective. That he wasn't even remotely supportive or even excited.

I also knew that the upset I was feeling over that realization was mostly hormonal. As were the tears that blurred my vision. Still, I couldn't stop them.

"Jesus, Weldman," Beck snapped, and I flinched from the harsh rebuke until I realized that he was glaring at Eric as he rounded the table to stand between the two of us, "he's clearly upset. Why are you—"

"He's pregnant, Beckett," Eric announced, despite his insistence that I tell them what I had done myself.

"Wait," Rex stepped forward, cocking his head, excitement building in his voice, "does that mean there's another alpha 'round here? Another dragon?" Then he frowned. "And why is that a bad thing? Unless..." His blue eyes widened with horror. "You don't think one of us..."

"No," I interrupted, shaking my head and bringing their attention my way. I felt miserable. The one person I had hoped would at least somewhat understand what I had done had reacted with far more anger than I had anticipated. And if Eric was so upset with me, I doubted I would get a gentler reaction from either of the alphas.

Perhaps I should have listened to Damon after all. Perhaps I should have taken a vacation and given birth to my children in private. Perhaps I should have kept them a secret from the entire world, including my family and the pack I had come to think of as home.

No. That would have been wrong and I knew it. I had known from the outset that my actions would have consequences. I had just hoped that Eric would understand. That he would be on my side, despite his misgivings.

It would break my heart if Sage also hated me for what I'd done.

"No?" Rex repeated. "No what, exactly?"

I looked up at him, knowing my expression was pitiful. For all of the hundreds of years that separated us, I considered Rex one of my closer friends in this pack. He was Damon's mate, and we spent a lot of time together socially. It was going to hurt to have him loathe me for my choices, too. Not that I didn't deserve it.

Licking my lips, I told him, "No, Eric knows it wasn't either of you, nor was it Brandi. But," I steeled myself and cupped the small swell of my belly gently, taking strength from the conviction that I had made the right choice even if it hadn't been the ethical one, "there isn't any other alpha."

Both Beck and Rex frowned. Beck gently pushed Eric further away so he could sit on the edge of the table in front of me.

"Explain," he urged, but his tone wasn't accusatory like Eric's had been. I didn't know if that was better or worse.

I picked at my thumbnail, unable to look him in the eye. "You know about the compatibility tests we have been running, attempting to fertilize donated ovum with sperm samples from potential alphas."

"Yeah?"

I swallowed. "A couple of months ago, I discovered that we had a successful match. Viable, fertilized eggs." Licking my lips, I finally dared to meet his dark gaze. "*My* eggs."

His eyes widened almost comically, while Rex sucked in a breath and murmured, "Oh boy."

"I...you must understand, we don't have the facilities to store fertilized ovum. They would either be destroyed or—"

"Or you could turkey baste 'em," Rex finished for me. "Which is what you did."

"I used a catheter and the ultrasound machine to ensure my success, but...yes. I...I knew it was wrong, but—"

"It was a breach of trust, Brandt!" Eric burst out, unable to hold his tongue any longer. He began pacing the room, his arms flailing wildly, repeating the things he had already yelled at me at least five or six times already. "We made promises to each and every person who donated their samples. We specifically swore that if matches were found, we *wouldn't* impregnate anyone. Do you really think anyone is going to trust us going forward once news of this gets out? Do you really think our science won't be questioned? Our research?"

"They were *my babies!*" I finally snapped back at him, slamming my fist on the polished timber of the tabletop beside Beck's leg. "I have lived *hundreds* of years dreaming of being a father, wanting nothing more than to carry my own children and knowing it was nothing more than a pipedream and there they were." My voice cracked as I recalled the hope that had swelled inside me. The realization that my hopes were not futile or impossible after all. "My three precious little embryos. My babies."

"But they weren't just yours," Eric snapped, storming back to my side as he raised his voice in anger. "They're fifty percent someone else's and you took that choice from him. You made that decision *for* him. Selfishly."

I curled around my belly as he loomed over me. Beck slid off the table and insinuated himself between us once more.

"Enough!" he cried, and I flinched again. "Eric's right," he spoke again after a moment, but his voice was gentle and full of the empathy I wished I could have heard from my brother himself. "What you did definitely broke the promises you made. However, I know you're a species on the edge of extinction and I understand why you would choose to take the chance in front of you. But why not reach out to the potential alpha?"

Once I answered that question, I doubted he would sound so understanding for much longer. Micah was his friend. His former found family. Not only had I broken the Pack Alpha's trust, I had also done the unimaginable to his friend.

"He wasn't here. He's not a member of the pack and I didn't want to risk the viability of the embryos on time spent attempting to contact him. It was only a small window of time and..." I hung my head, "I was selfish, Alpha."

"*Ugh,*" Beck groaned. "Stop that. I'm your friend, Brandt, not your...overlord."

Rex snorted and repeated "Overlord" with a significant degree of amusement, his Texan accent curling around the word pleasantly.

"Shut up," Beck directed at him with a smile in his voice. "You all know this Pack Alpha thing makes me uncomfortable."

"But that's *why* I brought him here," Eric cut back in effusively. "What he's done is...well, it reflects badly on our research. On what we're trying to achieve for shifters and potential alphas everywhere. You're our Alpha. You get to decide how to handle this."

"I understand that," Beckett was back to sounding reasonable but serious, "but this isn't some super simple 'right vs wrong' issue. There are complex emotions involved, too, and I'm not a dictator."

"Okay," I watched as my brother nodded, then he met my gaze and gestured towards Beckett again. "Tell him *who* you've involved without consent, Bee."

"Micah Hawthorne," I admitted, watching as the Alpha blinked and processed my confession.

He coughed. "What?!"

"Micah?" Rex repeated, then looked at Eric. "*Micah*, Micah? As in Beck's beta friend? That Micah? The one stayin' here right now?"

"That Micah," Eric nodded.

"Well," Rex licked his lips, "that complicates things some more, doesn't it?"

Beck was silent for a long moment. Eventually, he looked me in the eye and, directing his words at the others, said, "Can Brandt and I have the room, please?" As Eric and Rex moved to leave, he added, "And don't say anything to anyone else.

Especially not Micah. That's up to Brandt and we're not taking that from him." He narrowed his gaze at Eric. "Understood?"

Eric held up his hands in the universal sign of surrender. "Okay, okay. Yes. Understood."

I loved my brother, but he often got tunnel vision when it came to things he was passionate about. To some extent, it could be argued that I was the same. I had underestimated his passion for his research, just as he had underestimated the lengths I would go to for my children.

After he and Rex left, with Rex patting my shoulder and squeezing it reassuringly on his way out, Beck continued to stare at me in silence.

It was unnerving.

Despite my advanced age, I felt like an errant schoolboy.

I fidgeted, and, unable to take the tense silence any longer, said, "I had no idea if it was a fluke or something more. But...they were *my* embryos and I...I couldn't..." The thought of destroying them —of letting them waste away in that petri dish, of *losing* them— had me curling my arm protectively around my abdomen once more. Tears clogged my throat, making my voice thick and gruff. "I *know* it was wrong. I know that he will hate me. And when he was only an abstract idea that was fine. You and Sandy had both described him as someone who would never willingly stay in a small town or in our pack and I thought..." I trailed off, shaking my head.

I didn't need to tell him that I had planned on raising my children without ever having to worry about explaining myself to the unwitting sperm donor. Shakily, the rest of my confession bubbled up, and out spilled the fears which had been brewing ever since I had looked into Micah's eyes a few days earlier.

"But now I believe that it was not an improbable fluke. I think...I think he is my compatible mate. Perhaps even my potential alpha. And he has every reason to loathe me now."

The hold I had on my tenuous emotions slipped and tears trickled down my cheeks. I hung my head, trying to at least keep the sobs contained. It was largely hormonal, but also my emotional reaction to the reality of what my actions had cost me.

My mate. My *alpha*.

From where he was still seated on the table, Beck sighed heavily, then I heard him move. The chair beside mine rolled towards me and then dipped as he sat in it. With his hand on my back, he patted consolingly.

"For the record," he said after I had calmed somewhat, "I don't think Micah has the capacity to hate anyone. He's always been pretty chill. But this is...something else."

Swallowing roughly, I nodded. "I know."

"And I'm caught in a pretty tight spot here because he's one of my best friends and you...well, I owe you my life, Bran."

I shook my head and finally forced myself to look him in the eye again. "We were never going to allow the zealots to harm you. You owe me nothing for doing the right thing when you were taken."

"You still saved me," he argued. "And you made sure I was back here for Ollie as he gave birth. I—" Stopping suddenly, he gave me a sharp look. "Did you say children? Plural?"

Throat working convulsively again, I nodded.

"Twins?"

I shook my head.

He paled.

"More than twins?"

"Three," I acknowledged, shifting my palm over my bump. "Triplets. I couldn't..."

How was I supposed to explain that I couldn't choose to save only one or two of the fertilized ovum? That the very idea hurt my heart and made my stomach roil?

"Hey, shh," I hadn't realized I was breathing heavily, on the verge of an anxiety attack, until Beck's hand began rubbing soothing circles over my back. "It's okay. I'm not pissed, Brandt, and Micah...well, I think this might give him a heart attack, but—"

"I don't expect anything from him." I don't know why I said it, but I needed Beck to understand that I wasn't trying to...what was it the humans said?...baby trap his friend. "He...he can pretend they don't exist. I have centuries of savings, and—"

"If he's your mate, that's not going to make a difference. The way I felt after I met Ollie..." He paused and rolled his shoulders, then shook his entire body as if throwing off an uncomfortable feeling. "Are you feeling drawn to him? Like...a desperate need to find him and, uh, *be* with him?"

"Yes...and no. It's...strange. For you and Ollie, I know your meeting set off his heat and your rutting instincts. But I am already pregnant, so going into heat is unlikely." I inhaled after I said it, realizing it was the first time I'd said the words out loud, despite thinking them many times over. I cupped my belly and softly repeated, "I am pregnant."

"Yeah, that's still a mindfuck," Beck chuckled lightly. "You're a brave man going for triplets. I still get palpitations at the thought of adding even one new one on top of our two little gremlins, and they're becoming kind of self-sufficient. Sometimes."

"I've always dreamed of having children," I responded in the same, quiet, near-reverent tone as when I'd repeated myself moments earlier. "As many as I could. Not just because of our species being close to extinction, either. But because...I felt born to it, you know? I have yearned to carry my own young since I was barely considered an adult myself."

"Well, that explains the impulse decision even more, doesn't it?" I didn't bother answering and, after a beat, he mused, "Micah is a beta. And a horse. Both of those things are so different to everything else we've experienced with the locked alpha stuff..."

"I know," I dropped my chin. "These children may not even be dragons. But I will love them fiercely no matter what."

He was silent again. Then his tone was low and serious as he said, "You have to tell him, you know that. And if he's feeling the same pull towards you that I did when I met Ollie..."

I nodded. "I've already broken his trust. And I have put you in an awkward position should he demand some kind of restitution through pack law."

"I'm telling you, Micah's not like that. I mean, I can't say for sure that this isn't going to freak him out...but he's got a leg up on me, seeing as he's already a shifter and the concept of alphas and omegas isn't new to him. Learning that he might be an alpha himself, on the other hand..."

"We don't know that for sure," I cautioned, though I couldn't imagine that a stock standard horse beta could impregnate a dragon omega. That made zero sense. But then, neither did an alpha horse shifter, either. Unless he had recessive dragon genes?

But how could such a thing be possible? Until now, we had theorized that mixed matings between alphas and omegas was unlikely. Past alphas mating with humans, resulting in human children with recessive genes, on the other hand...

I was getting lost in hypothesizing.

"Well, we're not going to get answers by hiding in here." Beck pushed to his feet. "I'm going to talk to Eric. I'm sure, once he calms down, he'll be excited to have new data and theories to work with. In the meantime, I'm going to find Micah and send him in here so you two can meet properly. You don't have to tell him today, but you know he deserves to know soon, and he does deserve to hear the whole story from you."

I was back to feeling like a chastened schoolboy caught vandalizing school property or something to that effect. I chewed on my bottom lip and nodded. "This is why you're a good Pack Alpha, Beckett," I told him as he reached the door. "Thank you."

"Yeah, well," he shrugged and gave me a lopsided grin, "I told you a couple of years ago: I've got your back, Bran. No matter what." Then he paused and scrunched his nose. "But that doesn't extend to babysitting. You're on your own for that."

For the first time in weeks, I laughed loudly and freely.

It hadn't happened quite the way I had planned, but my secret was mostly revealed. I could focus on the future instead of hiding, and I swore that I would do whatever I could to rebuild my brother's —and my pack's— trust in me.

Chapter Eight

I didn't know what to make of the strange looks Rex and Eric kept shooting me and, even with my shifter hearing, I couldn't make out any details of their hushed, murmured conversation over the din of three toddlers playing loudly on the living room floor.

Beck still hadn't come out of the meeting room, and neither had Brandt, and my instincts kept telling me I needed to get my ass into that room.

I didn't understand what was going on with me at all.

But then Beck appeared in the archway that led into the hallway, and he asked me to come with him to finally meet Brandt. Almost immediately, it felt like the tension inside me was uncoiling in one way and then building in a completely different —and kind of inappropriate— way.

What the hell was happening to me?

I didn't have a lot of time to wonder about that, though, because Beck led me into the meeting room and made introductions between me and the oldest dragon, but I was too busy cataloguing every single visual detail I could.

His dark eyes, brown like my own but so much darker, were rimmed red, and his cheeks were flushed pink. His goatee wasn't as immaculately trimmed as it had been the day I'd seen him through the windshield of Beck's truck, and his hair seemed longer and more disheveled, too. It had only been a week, but it was almost like I was looking at a completely different man.

Even though I knew he was hundreds of years old, he didn't appear to be older than his mid-to-late forties. He looked tired, and sad, and his dragon scent was smoky, like Eric's, but also kind of sweet, too. Like sugar cubes. Or apples or...something equally as tasty.

When we shook hands, an electric shock traveled straight up my arm and seemed to wake up every nerve inside my body. My inner horse whinnied and stamped its hooves.

Mate, a voice inside my head whispered, and I gave myself a shake because...weird.

"I've gotta go talk to Eric, but you guys have the room for as long as you need it," Beck said, like it was totally normal that two complete strangers would need a soundproofed meeting room for a casual introductory chat.

I turned to ask him what, exactly, he thought we would need it for, but he was already gone.

Also weird.

Inside, my shifter side was elated to finally meet Brandt. He was the dragon who had rescued my friend from a grizzly end, and also the elusive figure who had always evaded introduction. And now he was right there in front of me, almost literally a captive audience for my curiosity, and I...wanted to jump him?

Seriously, what the fuck was going on with me?

"Take a seat, Micah," Brandt purred in an accent that made my heart thump, "we should...talk."

It struck me, as I complied with his request to sit, choosing the chair at the head of the table and leaving the one to my right free, that I might get answers from this delicious older man. Perhaps starting with the reason he had been so dead set on avoiding me?

"I'll confess," he said as he sat down as well, "that I'm not entirely sure where to start. I don't even know if you're feeling the same pull that I am, but—"

"You're feeling it, too?" I rubbed at my chest, in the spot at my sternum just beneath my heart, where the strange tension seemed to be building.

Attraction and arousal thrummed in my veins, and I blushed because I'd never felt this intensely horny before. I had been sexually frustrated since I arrived in town, but now I was getting hard just by being in Brandt's immediate presence.

It didn't make sense.

Nevertheless, he nodded. "Micah..." he began, and it felt *good* to hear him speaking my name in that sexy as fuck accent. "I have reason to believe that we are...compatible —or fated— mates. Like Beckett and Oliver, or Rex and Damon, or Brandi and Lena."

The words made sense, but they didn't compute. I blinked at him and leaned forward, steepling my hands on the table's smooth surface. "Say what now?"

He arched an eyebrow. Gods, he was hot. "You heard me."

"I did," I tilted my head in acknowledgement, "but...I'm a beta. I'm a horse and you are a *dragon*. Your lifespan alone..." I sighed. "I don't understand how that would work."

Inside me, my instincts insisted he was right, but logic said it was ridiculous.

"I know," he swallowed, then looked away, "but aside from feeling this pull towards each other, and that electric shock when we finally touched, I...have scientific proof as well." He shifted uneasily in his seat. "When you were last here, you submitted a sample to aid us with our research. You remember that, yes?"

Nodding, I could feel heat rising up the back of my neck. Jerking off into a cup for *science* was a memory which would stay with me forever. "Yeah?"

"Yes, well," he shuffled around again, and I didn't think it was because he was feeling the same desperate need to touch again like I was. He didn't want to look at me. "During one of our tests, your sperm reacted positively with an ovum sample." He cleared his throat, and finally met my gaze. "*My* ovum sample."

"Reacted positively? What does that—"

"In layman's terms, your sperm fertilized my eggs."

I could feel my eyes widening. "*Whoa.* But...I'm a beta. And a horse." I couldn't help repeating my misgivings. "How did that even work? Are you sure it wasn't just a weird, like, glitch in the matrix, or something? Do you need to repeat the test?"

Was that why he was being so strange and awkward? Was it that he needed me to fill another cup with another sample? Because with the way I was feeling right then, still wanting to strip him out of his jeans and button-down shirt and take him right there on the table...well, I could probably fill a couple of cups for him.

"Micah..." The apologetic tone should have been a giveaway that I wasn't going to love whatever else he had to tell me, but I was still too busy marveling at the idea that my sperm —from my smaller-than-average dick— had fertilized *dragon eggs.*

I mean, yeah, I was more than aware that the size of my dick had nothing to do with the quality or even quantity of my sperm —that it was my balls doing the hard work on that front— but this still felt supremely ironic to me.

"I..." he looked away again. "I made a decision when I discovered those fertilized embryos. One which you have every right to resent me for."

I frowned. Were we finally about to get to the reason he had been avoiding me? Maybe the fact that I was a horse shifter was distasteful to him. The gods only knew omegas had been disappointed in me as a potential partner for less understandable reasons.

"You didn't want us to meet," I said, fighting against my continued biological drive to touch him, to kiss him, to make him *mine.* The sadness at feeling rejected helped keep my head on straight. "You knew that I was, uh, *am* a horse, and—"

"What? No," Brandt's interruption was quick and vehement. He sighed and pinched the bridge of his nose, taking a deep breath before saying, "I chose to implant the embryos. *Our* embryos. Inside me."

Wait.

He...what?!

I watched in stunned silence as he placed a shaky hand over his soft midsection, stroking his thumb lovingly over his own belly. "I...I've wanted children for hundreds of years. I never dreamed..." Trailing off, he shook his head again, then looked me in the eye. "I am aware it was not ethical to use your genetic material in such a manner without your consent. That I have created life —*children*— without your knowledge. But I had very little time to make a decision before they became non-viable, and I couldn't let my potential babies just...slip from my grasp."

Inside me, my beta was cheering. He was delighted, the chant *'mate, mate mate!'* practically thundering in my soul and in my ears.

My heart was racing, and my mouth was dry.

"Micah." There was that stupidly sexy accent again. "I apologize for breaking your trust. For taking such a large choice out of your hands. I understand if you resent me. If you hate me. And I understand if that means you don't want to pursue whatever this...this...mystical connection between us might mean. However, I would still make the same choice a thousand times over."

I knew that I should be upset. That I should be freaking out. That I should be asking what the actual hell he meant by *children* in the plural sense.

But the first words out of my mouth were "My mom is going to be *so* happy about this."

Brandt's mouth dropped open, as if he couldn't believe that *that* was my reaction.

To be fair, neither could I.

Then again, hadn't I been lamenting the fact that I wanted kids but had to acknowledge that they just weren't in the foreseeable future for me? This resolved that issue, if nothing else.

I mean, it wasn't in the conventional way, or any remotely believable way. Also, it meant that I didn't have a whole lot of time to prepare for having kids, either, seeing as they were already inside this ridiculously sexy dragon omega. But

I couldn't help thinking that maybe my mother and her hippy-dippy connection to 'the universe' were right after all.

I started to laugh at that thought while Brandt looked on with an expression that suggested he thought he might have pushed my sanity beyond its reasonable limits.

"This isn't a joke, Micah. I—"

"No," I managed to wheeze out between near-hysterical laughter. "No, I know. I just…" I couldn't actually explain why the situation had tickled my funny bone. "It's…it's just ironic to me, is all. In so many ways. I…God, Brandt, you're getting the short straw here."

At my own unintentional, self-deprecating size pun, I lost it again, slumping on the table as I laughed the myriad of conflicting emotions out of my system.

When I felt calm enough to face him again, he was staring at me as though I was the one likely to turn into a dragon and eat him. "Sorry," I wiped at my eyes, feeling like the inappropriate hysteria had done me a world of good. "I needed that."

"I am extremely confused," he said, but his own shoulders were no longer tense, and he even seemed mildly amused. "You…you're not…repulsed by me? By what I've done?"

"Not even a little bit," I answered honestly. "My beta is thrilled. I'm…well, not gonna lie; I'm going to need some time to actually wrap my head around the fact that I'm apparently going to be a dad because that was *not* on my bingo card for this year, or at all, but…no. No repulsion. No anger. And I still feel this…this *pull* to you. Not that that's influencing how I feel about the baby thing."

"It's…not?" He didn't sound like he believed me.

"No," I assured him. "I, uh, I've wanted kids of my own for a while. But I never thought I'd find a man willing to settle down with me."

He scoffed, looking me up and down with skepticism. "You are a very attractive man," he said, "and you are being quite kind and understanding when you do not have to be, so forgive me if I find such a thing difficult to believe."

Shrugging, I told him, "I'm not as impressive as I am pretty."

He frowned. "It sounds to me as though you have been seeing the wrong kind of men if their expectations are purely based on your appearance."

I shrugged. "There's that, too."

Snorting, Brandt shook his head. "You're not at all like I anticipated you'd be."

"What? You thought I'd freak out?" I supposed most men in my situation would, and it would be understandable. But then, I had often been accused of being too chill.

It wasn't that things didn't get to me, because they did, but I picked my battles. Besides, if this gorgeous man really was my mate, it would be counterintuitive to get upset over starting a family together when it was clearly something we both wanted.

Yes, in my mind, I'd always thought I would get to know someone before we actively planned a family. However, I had seen Beck and Ollie's connection, and Rex and Damon's, and even Brandi and Lena's, too. Some part of me —the part that sounded like my mother— said that I should trust fate. I should trust the universe.

"I am pregnant with your children," he replied slowly, in a tone that suggested he most certainly did expect me to flip my shit, "and you didn't even have the benefit of…well, the *traditional* and, I'd assume, enjoyable method of conception."

And then I was right back to wanting to lay him out on the table and claim him all over again. I cleared my throat at the images in my head, amazed that my beta desperately wanted to top him when I'd spent the better part of my sex life bottoming for men who looked like him, and enjoying it, too.

"Yes, well, you'd probably enjoy a test tube more than me anyway," I muttered, then cringed as the self-flagellating thought slipped past my usual filters and out of my mouth.

He frowned. "Seriously," he asked with irritation, "what kind of men have you been involved with that you think so poorly of yourself?" There was an edgy, angry growl to his voice that did things to me.

My omega was the hottest man *ever*.

Despite not actually having a claim on Brandt, and him not even suggesting that he would be interested in pursuing whatever mystical connection existed between us, my beta was determined to think of him as mine. I should probably fight those instincts, but even my human side wanted to be selfish and possessive.

I didn't think I could be blamed for that. I mean, Brandt was stunning. And he was a dragon. An honest-to-God dragon! He was *perfect*. The embodiment of every fantasy I'd ever had, all rolled into one.

"I…" I started, then faltered as he pushed from his seat and loomed over me. I swallowed and my mouth ran dry, even as my cock woke all the way up, straining in my underwear.

Over the years, I'd told myself that size didn't account for skill or enthusiasm. I'd even started believing it once I left my pack and started sleeping with human men. But with the desperate, all-encompassing need to impress this vision of a man —of a *dragon*— standing over me, I had never wished for a larger dick more in my entire life.

Sadly, even our shifter magic didn't work that way. The organ straining in my pants, while harder than he had ever been, didn't suddenly grow any extra inches just because I wanted my mate to be happy and, more importantly, satisfied with the hand (or, rather, cock) fate had dealt him.

"Stand up," he demanded in that same, sexy growl, and I complied.

Standing nose to nose with Brandt, his eyes searched mine before he closed the scant distance between us and slanted his lips over mine.

If I had thought that shaking hands with him had been electric, the feeling had nothing on the fireworks his kiss ignited.

Kissing him was indescribable.

It was as if a thousand lightbulbs were bursting to life above my head. The sheer *rightness* of this connection, needy and fiery and raw, was a revelation.

My beta was right; Brandt was mine. He was meant to be mine.

Only mine.

I let my omega control the kiss. I parted my lips and let his tongue tangle with my own. I let his big, beefy hands cup my jaw while my useless, awkward fingers dug into his hips.

He tasted delicious, almost exactly as he smelled. Smoky and sweet; like burnt caramel or a marshmallow which had been left just a *little* too long over the flames of a fire. He was decadent and passionate, and I knew without a doubt that I would never find another man whose kiss could live up to this one.

His hands slid down from my jaw, beginning a slow, sensual exploration of my body. Meaty palms caressed my shoulders, my toned —but comparatively puny— biceps, my lean torso, and my not-exactly-fleshy ass. Then those same hands slid around to my thighs and I gasped, pulling away before they could reach for what I was certain would be a disappointing bulge.

"Shit," he cursed, then stepped back. I immediately hated the space he created between us, missing the radiating warmth from his soft belly against my flat one. "I apologize. I...the pull was so strong, and the hormones..."

"Don't...don't apologize. I want this —*you*— too. But..." I closed my eyes and sighed. "You should be warned, I guess. I'm not...uh...it's just most shifters assume that because I'm a horse, I'm hung, but..."

Fuck, explaining my issue was difficult. *This* was why I didn't date other shifters. Humans didn't make the same assumptions, nor did they seem as concerned about what I was packing, especially not as a bottom.

"You realize that I am half a millennium old, don't you?" he spoke gently into the awkward silence I'd left hanging, still trying to spit out what I saw as my biggest (no pun intended) personal failing. "And I am a doctor. I have seen it all, and then some. And I am more aware than most that one's species does not correlate to one's physical attributes in human form. Besides, we all have something we are self-conscious about. I am...cuddlier...than either of my brothers. And, now that I am carrying triplets—"

I'll admit that I *might* have collapsed back down onto my chair, dramatically gasping, *"Triplets?!"* while my hand covered my racing heart.

Some naïve part of me had assumed 'children' plural equated to twins, like Beck and Ollie had. Like Lena and Brandi were having. Not *three*.

That part where I said I was chill? That I wasn't going to freak out? I might have spoken too soon.

Brandt bit his lip, appearing far more adorable than a man who looked as intimidating as he did had any right to be. "Surprise?"

Chapter Nine

Brandt

I *probably should have started with how many children we're having,* I thought to myself as Micah stared back at me with wide, almost terrified eyes.

His throat worked convulsively, and I felt guilty all over again for the situation I had put him in. However, I had just given in to the biological draw between us, to the incessant desire to press my body against his and taste his mouth, and I knew that to do even that much without him knowing the entire story had been wrong.

I tried to ignore the slick that threatened to leak from me at the lingering tingles on my lips. My omega railed inside me, wanting my mate's long, elegant fingers digging into the soft flesh of my hips once more.

But to give in to those instincts without being completely honest had been a mistake. *Everything* I had done to this man had been a mistake.

When Micah had been an abstract stranger —a man disinterested in pack life— I had imagined that he was likely immature and vain. These past minutes talking to him had disabused me of that notion. Unfortunately, in doing so, it had only proven Beck and, to some extent, Eric to be correct.

My choice was unfair to Micah in every possible way imaginable.

"Three feels like *a lot* more than two," he eventually managed, his voice sounding strained and marginally panicked.

This was the reaction I had anticipated. Still not as volatile, or as upset, but certainly more understandable than his original calm collectedness.

"I know," I looked to my feet in a moment of weakness, needing to brace myself for the rejection which would hurt a hell of a lot more now that I knew what he tasted like. "I...I couldn't bring myself to...to...*reject* even one of the embryos. They were too precious."

"Yeah...yeah, I get that. I just...*wow*. Three is..." Micah chuckled again and I dared to peek up at him. He shook his head, a bewildered smile on his face. "It's kind of unheard of for horse shifters, y'know?" Running his hand through his hair, the sandy-blonde locks fell back around his face messily.

Why was that so sexy? Courtesy of my raging hormones and whatever pull was happening due to the connection we had sparked upon physical contact, I almost asked him to do it again. In slow motion. Like a shampoo commercial.

Maybe it's Maybelline, maybe it's a mystical shifter connection.

"Do you think that means they'll be dragons?" he asked, and I blinked, embarrassed at my thoughts having drifted so wildly.

"Pardon?"

"The...the babies. Because there are three of them. Do you think that means they'll be dragons? Because horses usually only have one? On *very* rare occasions sometimes two?" He winced, then looked at me beseechingly. I almost got lost in his beautiful eyes. "Not that I care if they're not horses. Because dragons are *way* cooler. Not that I've ever actually seen a dragon. I mean, a shifted dragon. I can see you just fine. I have twenty-twenty vision. Because that's a thing doctors think about, right? What kind of medical issues might be passed down? Aside from the, um," he gestured vaguely at his crotch, "I don't have any issues, I don't think. And...I'm rambling. Awesome."

Fuck, but he was delightful, wasn't he? Though I was beginning to get more than a little concerned about his body image issues.

"We will not know what their species is —are— until they are born, I imagine," I answered once I wrangled my rampaging hormones back into submission again. "But, for the record, I do not care one way or the other. They're my babies. I will love them even if they scent completely human at birth."

"Is that a possibility?"

I shrugged. "I am not sure of anything right now. I have to assume that mixed matings between omegas and...their mates," I was careful not to refer to him as an alpha, as our situation was completely without precedent, "are the same as mixed matings between beta males and females." They weren't known to happen often, but when they did, the offspring had a fifty-fifty chance of taking after their mother's species or their father's.

Well, it was more complicated than that, depending on whether either parent had come from a mixed-mated line themselves...but I wasn't going to get technical.

"Right, okay," he nodded and swallowed again. "How far along are you?"

"Twelve weeks and three days." I couldn't contain my answering smile. "They're all developing perfectly."

"Yeah?" I watched as his lips curled into a gentle smile, too, and it made my heart flutter. "That's great. If, uh, if you have photos...like, ultrasound print outs...maybe I could see them?"

Once more, he took me by surprise. I hadn't expected him to show any interest in the children I had taken it upon myself to conceive. But there he was, asking to see their ultrasound images, as if he was a proud expectant parent and not the man who had only just learned that an omega he hadn't even slept with was carrying three of his children.

"I do," I answered slowly, "but you don't have to..."

He narrowed his gaze as I trailed off. "I don't have to what?"

"Pretend," I finished, grimacing at the frown the world seemed to elicit. "I do not expect anything from you, Micah. I understand if you want nothing to do with me or my children. You had the right to know what I did, however you have no obligation—"

"Did you miss the part where I said I never thought I'd have kids? That I do, actually, want them?" My potential mate rose to his feet, standing in front of me so he could look me in the eye. The mirth was gone from those beautiful brown eyes. They were glinting determinedly now. "That I want you? Because I meant that. It's taking all of my self-control not to grab you and finish what we started a few minutes ago. That doesn't change because there are three babies instead of two."

My heart began to race as hope welled up inside me.

I had never dared to even dream that Micah might want these children. That he would feel even slightly the same way as I had. That he would be willing to overlook my morally gray behavior.

That he would want me.

It seemed ludicrous that a young beta would be at all interested in a middle-aged omega like myself, but I had no cause to believe he was lying. Of the two of us, I was the one who had lied and kept secrets, not him.

"What might it take to break your self-control?" I asked lowly. "Because, if you are amenable, I would like to explore this...*connection* between us. This pull. For...science."

His gaze shifted to my lips and his own quirked as he looked into my eyes once more. "For science?" he asked with amusement.

I believed we both knew I couldn't give a rat's ass about science right then. Still, I nodded. "Science, yes. The others all unlocked their alpha abilities..."

Some of the lust cleared from his expression as he shook his head sadly. "They all thought they were human, though. I was born a shifter. I'm able to shift."

"Hence exploring for science," I insisted, though I did not reach for him. I wanted him to close the space between us willingly. I wanted some part of this to be his choice.

"I see," his little smirk was back, and seeing it made my belly tighten with anticipation. "And what's your hypothesis, Doctor Weldman?"

Shivers raced down my spine at the sultry question, and slick pooled in my underwear. Unable to tear my gaze from his, I answered, "I suspect you will be able to knot me." Even just thinking it made my heart race and my cock stir. Licking my lips, I continued, "I believe your scent will change to that of an alpha. Beyond that...I am unsure. I doubt you are secretly a dragon, or that either of our species will change to match the other. But...this...this *need* to be with you...it's too strong for this to not be the same thing that the others experienced. By their descriptions, this urge matches."

"What about the urge to bite? To bond?" He asked, his darkening gaze dropping to the juncture where my neck and shoulder met. "We...we shouldn't do that, right?"

I shrugged. "That is up to you. I have lived a long time, and the prospect of having a bondmate is...comforting, though I am still unsure how that might even work with our lifespans being so drastically different."

It took all of my willpower to not mention that precedent had shown that delaying a bonding bite would only delay the inevitable. I wanted a decision of that magnitude to be his choice, too.

Micah nodded, then stepped into the remaining space between our bodies. His long-fingers threaded into the hair at the back of my head as he initiated our second kiss, this one just as intense as the first. While we no longer seemed to create sizzling, crackling energy when we touched, I could feel it bubbling in my veins. It was under my skin and inside my ribcage, making my heart dance and my soul sing.

Mate, my omega wanted to throw his head back and roar. *Mine.*

Whether my hypothesis was correct or not —whether we'd be able to enact a bond like the other couples or not— this man was most certainly my mate. I knew that better than I knew my own name.

I grew slicker with my omega body's natural lubrication. It trickled out of me and dampened the seat of my underwear. My cock swelled and pushed at its confines as well, while desperation to lie back and allow my mate to take me and knot me had a ball of tension forming in the pit of my belly.

Micah's lips tore away from mine, but only enough to trail open-mouthed kisses over my cheek and jaw and down the column of my neck. I trembled, overwhelmed with joy and relief that my mate wasn't rejecting me for what I had done.

"You're so hot," he whispered, smoothing his hands over my shoulders and down my arms. "So insanely sexy."

I chuckled. "I could say the same about you. You are exquisite, Micah. Prettier than the models you doll up." He was even more attractive to me now that I was aware of how kind he was.

Kindness was an incredibly attractive quality.

"Fuck, I love your accent," he muttered, moving his head to my other side and repeating his exploration of my skin with his mouth, "and your beard, and your body…"

"I haven't been this slick for anyone in…fuck…in my entire life," I admitted, squirming under the attentions of his hands and his mouth. I whined as he dropped to his knees in front of me and popped the button over the fly of my jeans. I swore I was going to create a puddle when he looked up at me from beneath long, surprisingly dark eyelashes, his hands braced on my thighs.

"Is this okay?" he asked. "You sure we're not going too fast? We've only just met."

"You are my mate. I can feel it in my soul. If anything, this is not progressing quickly enough. Though that could be the hormones talking…"

His pretty, plump pink lips lifted into another one of those lazy smirks. "Horniness is a better pregnancy symptom than nausea."

"Except for the fact that I feel as though I might combust if you do not do *something* immediately."

Sitting on his haunches, he shuffled around the floor on his knees and gestured towards the table. "Lean against that, sugar. Let's make sure you're nice and stable before I take care of you."

Sugar.

The endearment made me feel weak in the knees and I was glad for his instruction to brace myself on the strong slab of timber.

He unzipped my fly and pulled my jeans and underwear down. I had taken to wearing a size larger than I required, disliking tight waistbands around my growing stomach, and they slid to my ankles with very little effort.

"Gods," he breathed, staring at my cock as it strained to greet him. He wrapped his hand around its base and stroked slowly, looking up at me as he said, "I can't wait to ride this."

Chapter Ten

The moment the words left my mouth I wanted to snatch them back. Brandt's eyebrows were furrowed, his lips parting in confusion.

"Forget I said that," I pleaded, still stroking the glorious, long, thick length in front of me. The purpled tip glistened with precum and I wanted to lick it, to get my first taste of him.

"That is not going to be possible," his tone was gravelly and filled with the same lust that was coursing through my veins. "I assumed...I mean, I am an omega...betas have never..."

Shame suffused me, making my cheeks heat. I looked away. "I told you. I'm a disappointing beta. In more ways than one, I guess."

"Disappointing?" Brandt sounded incredulous. "Darling, the very idea that you want *me* inside *you* is incredible in all the best ways. Not to continually remind you of how much older I am, but...there is not much I have not done in my hundreds of years of existence. And humans tend to expect that I prefer to top. As such, combined with my omega desires, I am happily vers."

I should have known that the universe would gift me a mate whose sexual preferences were compatible with my own.

Nevertheless, I could have sobbed with relief. With my hand still wrapped around his dick, I squeezed and stroked him with renewed vigor.

"You're *so* fucking perfect for me," I told him before finally giving in to the urge to suckle at the tempting head of his cock.

"Oh, *fuck*," he gritted out in his deep, sexy rumble of a voice, and his hands came to land on top of my head, thick fingers grappling at my hair. "*Yes*, Micah, more. Please. Give me more of your beautiful mouth."

I couldn't deny him when he asked so nicely, especially not with that irresistible accent.

Relaxing my throat, I controlled my breathing and focused on taking him all the way in, wanting to impress him, wanting to *satisfy* him. He gasped as I took all of him in until his fuzzy balls were resting against my chin. Then, because I was a fucking show off, I swallowed around him.

"Holy mother of...*fuck*, Micah. Fuck. Fuck...your perfect mouth."

I groaned and attempted to nod as I slowly drew back and then sucked him all the way back in again.

I wanted exactly that. For him to fuck my mouth. To take his pleasure from me.

My eyes watered when I repeated the movement a bit faster, and drool slipped from the corners of my lips and down my chin. I probably looked like a mess, but when I peered back up at Brandt again, his eyes almost rolled back in his head.

"*Look* at you, darling," he practically purred. His fingers tightened their hold on my hair and he thrust his hips, making me choke momentarily. But instead of apologizing, he only groaned, proving that we really were on the same wavelength. "Oh fuck, I'm getting close."

I shifted my hold on his hips to cup his fleshy, hairy ass cheeks, and I must have made a choked off sound of surprise when my fingers dipped into his crack and found wetness.

For a moment, so lost in how much I was enjoying myself, I had forgotten that he was an omega.

My omega.

My *pregnant* omega.

Before I could register what I was doing, I pulled all the way off his cock with a slurp and, sliding my fingers further between his cheeks until I was teasing his hole, declared, "I want to be inside you."

He widened his stance as best he could, constricted by the jeans around his ankles. "Fuck, yes," he practically pleaded. "I want that so badly. Fill me up, darling."

I didn't know just how full he would feel, but I was beginning to believe that fate —*the universe*— had paired us together for a reason. That was probably my mother's influence finally getting to me, but everything else seemed to be pointing towards our connection being evenly matched, so why would this be any different?

I stood up and glanced around the room, not wanting our first time to be on the boardroom-style table. He deserved better than that. Ideally, I should try and sneak him up to the guest room I had been staying in, but I knew there was a literal horde of shifters in Ollie and Beck's living room and that would make things awkward.

At least at that moment, they probably just assumed we were talking things out. None of them had any reason to believe I wouldn't freak out about Brandt's news —assuming they all knew about it— and this space was soundproofed. It was like Pandora's box.

Hey, that sounds kind of naughty...

I blinked and forced myself to focus on the task at hand. Sometimes, I swore I had the mind of a teenager. How on earth could I be a good match for a man literally hundreds of years my senior?

After weighing up my options, I decided that the rolling office chairs would work better than the table. They were the fancy kind with the arm rests that could be lifted up, which meant that if I sat down, Brandt could comfortably straddle me with his legs draped over the sides of the seat. And, hopefully, with him on top, the angle might get me a bit deeper inside him.

I kissed him again, then helped him out of his shirt while he toed off his boots and jeans. I slid out of my sneakers, too. Then he tugged my shirt up and over my head, and I swallowed when his fingers popped the button of my jeans.

"Stop overthinking. You will be perfect because you're you," he murmured, his dark eyes locked on mine. "I promise."

Before I could tell him that he couldn't actually be sure of that promise, he was shoving my pants down and his big, warm hand was wrapped around my cock. As desperately as I wanted to look, I knew I'd feel self-conscious seeing the unimpressive length dwarfed by his large palm.

The universe wouldn't match you with him if it wasn't right.

"Oh *God*." I exhaled shakily, wondering how a simple, dry hand job could feel so good. "Sugar, I'm going to get addicted to your touch."

"I am going to become addicted to that endearment," he rumbled into my ear before he returned to nuzzling my neck. His beard added a scratchy, ticklish sensation which was driving me wild. "Please don't stop."

I checked behind me before I sat down, tugging him with me. The chair rolled with our momentum, coming to a stop against the wall at my back. I let out a grunt, clutching at Brandt's hips to steady him, even though he had reflexes enough to splay his hands against the wall to prevent toppling down over me and the chair.

I moved the armrests up, opening up the sides of the chair before I tapped my palm on my bare thigh.

He stared down at me, a wry smile twisting one side of his goatee before he snorted. "I could make a joke about riding a horse right now."

I laughed, loving his corny sense of humor. "Giddy up, sugar," I encouraged, then sucked in a breath as he did exactly what I'd asked him to.

With his solid legs splayed out over my hips, he lowered himself down onto my cock, and I slid inside his slick, welcoming heat as his ass cheeks came to rest on the tops of my thighs.

"Oh...*fuck*..." My head fell back, resting on the chair's padded leather headrest. "Fuck, Brandt...you feel amazing."

And he did. He was warm, slick, and *tight*. When he hummed in agreement and bounced experimentally, clenching around me, I practically saw stars.

"*Micah*..." his voice was rough and needy, his breath hitching as he started to ride me in earnest, "You...you feel..."

"I know." I closed my eyes, recalling far too many attempts to please the omegas of my pack before I gave up. I wriggled my hand between us to squeeze and stroke his erection, determined to give him some kind of pleasure. "But I'll make it good for you, sugar, I—"

This time, he did growl. The sound startled me enough that my eyes flew open, and I had to blink a few times to process what I was seeing. His face was contorted into a scowl, but it was the dark red scales erupting around his hairline which really had my attention.

"I swear," he ground out in a dark, gravelly tone, though he wasn't stopping his movement, "I will track down each and every man who has made you feel inadequate, and I will eat them, because" —he paused to whimper and rock his hips, just as his cock dribbled precum in my hold and extra slick escaped from his hole to drip down my balls— "you. feel. phenomenal." Each final word was punctuated with a sharp bounce in my lap.

Oh, Gods, I'm going to come.

There was only so much I could take, and between the sensation of his wet heat around my cock, and his sexy angry words, and the fact that he was so emotionally charged that he was partially shifted —not something I had known he could even do!— I was losing whatever minor control of my body I had left.

"Fuck, sugar," I panted, my fingers digging into the soft flesh of his hips as I tried really hard not to finish so soon, "I'm close. You're too perfect."

"Do you feel how slick I am for you?" Brandt continued, staring down at me with such intensity that, under other circumstances, I might be afraid that he could shoot flames from his eyes. "Do you, Micah? Because I am a middle-aged omega and that does *not* usually happen naturally. That is *all* you. It's how much I enjoy having you inside me. It's how aroused just being near you makes me."

Letting out an embarrassing whimper, I nodded. To be honest, I had never felt quite as hard before, either, but I thought maybe that was just my imagination playing tricks on me.

"Your cock was made for me, darling," his growly, gravelly voice had smoothed out again, but the scales on his face were still there. They were such a dark shade of red that they were almost black. I reached up to stroke one at his temple, finding it smooth and warm to the touch, and he shuddered, his hole clenching even more tightly around my dick.

"*Again*," he breathed, tilting his neck. "Touch them again."

When I did, he whined and lost his rhythm.

Interesting.

While I continued to pump his dick, I used my free hand to cup his jaw, stroking the scales I could reach with my thumb over and over again.

"*Ungh*," he writhed, no longer bouncing on me but grinding and rocking, "M-Micah..."

His cock was leaking precum almost constantly, and I was pretty sure his hole was attempting to cut off the circulation to my dick.

"*Darling*—" he practically purred, then pressed his mouth over mine.

The second his tongue slipped between my parted lips, I exploded.

My orgasm was sudden and unexpected, and I wrenched my mouth from his to cry out a sharp "Fuck!" as my release poured out of me in jets. I couldn't recall the last time I had come so hard, or so prolifically, and then I felt the tingling.

It started at the base of my cock, and then I *swore* I felt my dick swelling up, getting harder instead of softening.

"Fuck, Micah," Brandt swiveled his hips, grinding down on me and making me yelp with how sensitive my dick was. "Oh, *Gods*. You *are* knotting me. *Nnnngh*." He closed his eyes and tilted his head to the side, exposing that tempting juncture at the base of his neck. Then he opened his eyes, which were gleaming with joy and wonder. "We were right. *I* was right. You are an alpha. *My* alpha. Oh *fuck…*"

I assumed my knot was pressing on his prostate with the way he cursed and writhed, his cock jerking in my hold.

I would never feel like this with anyone else, I realized. Inside me, my shifter side —my *alpha* side— practically roared with satisfaction that we were giving such pleasure to our mate.

Mate, my inner voice repeated happily. *Mine*.

"Can I…*nnngh*…" I groaned as his clenching stimulated my knot and encouraged another orgasm from me. My brain was borderline scrambled by the pleasure which was beginning to hint towards pain from overstimulation. "C-can I bite you?" I asked, forcing my gaze to meet Brandt's. "Can I claim —*oh Gods*— c-claim you?"

His pupils were dilated to an inhuman degree, but his eyes welled with tears and he nodded readily, then tilted his head again. "Yes, my alpha. Please. *Please*."

I didn't need any further encouragement. Sliding my free hand up his sweaty back, I cupped his head to hold him in place and then bit down on his neck.

He *roared* and sticky warmth spread between our bodies and dripped out from beneath my knot as I felt his orgasm *inside* my soul, almost as if it was my own. Then he wrenched my head further to the side and bit down on my neck and I *did* come again, starbursts of bliss exploding in my chest and radiating throughout my extremities.

It became a feedback loop of pleasure on pleasure, until my balls ached from coming so hard and so much. We kissed slowly and sensually as we attempted to come down from the continual loop of orgasms, flinching and giggling against each other's mouths with every hypersensitized movement.

"Holy shit," I breathed, feeling elated. The entire situation was surreal. "We're mated. We...*I* have a mate." He nuzzled his face into the crook of my neck, his beard brushing my mating mark, and I grunted through another tiny, mildly painful orgasm as he contracted around my knot. "I'm...I'm an *alpha*."

That part was probably the most mind-blowing of all. Me, the most unimpressive beta ever, an alpha.

"Mmm," Brandt hummed, then yawned sleepily. "My alpha."

"My omega," I stroked his back, unable to hide the burst of pride and affection that welled inside me. I felt him smile against my skin, and a similar feeling radiated back at me.

Feeling his emotions was going to take some getting used to.

Of course, Beck and Ollie seemed to have gotten the hang of it. I might need to ask my old friend for pointers.

The thought of Beck had my eyes widening as alarm spiked through me.

"What?" Brandt sat up straighter, and we both shuddered through the resulting stimulation as it reverberated through our new bond. "What's wrong?"

"Beck," I said, then waved vaguely around us. "This is his house. His meeting room." A blush traveled up my neck and over my cheeks. I could feel it heating my skin. "We've been in here a while."

"I hate to break it to you, darling," he was back to sounding amused instead of concerned, "but you're already beginning to scent like an alpha. If you were hoping to keep this a secret..."

"No. Gods, no. I want to shout from the rooftops that you're my mate. But..." I sighed. "I've mostly been with humans, you know? So I guess I bring a more human sort of mentality to sex. And, on top of that, my alpha side doesn't want any of them thinking about you having sex, even if it is with me. It's a weird, possessive sort of feeling and it's making me feel all...*blech.*"

"It will take a while for your new instincts to settle," he advised me calmly. "It did for all three of the others, too. And, if anyone is going to understand what you are feeling, I would wager that it is those three." He leaned forward to rub our noses together, then he looked away as a mild wave of melancholy and guilt washed over me from his side of our newly unlocked mystical connection. "They are more than likely going to be concerned that we rushed into this. That my condition might have been the catalyst for you to make a choice you otherwise might not have made."

"What kind of idiot would avoid bonding with his fated mate?" I asked him lightly. "There's literally nobody else in the world better for me than you. I mean, you even enjoyed riding my tiny—"

"It is *not* tiny." His sexy growly voice was back, but this time I felt his frustration at the same time as watching it play out on his handsome face.

Nevertheless, I rolled my eyes. "A micropenis," I informed him, trying to sound as clinical as the doctor who had sat me down and given me the name for my condition, "is a penis which has a stretched penile length of three point six seven inches or less. My doctor measured me: it qualifies."

He scoffed. "It certainly doesn't feel tiny."

"That's my knot. I've obviously never had that happen before."

"Regardless," he insisted, "I *did* enjoy your cock very much, even before you knotted me."

"You'd be the first," I muttered a little darkly, then I remembered that that was the whole point I was trying to make in the first place, "and, yeah, because of that, it sort of cinched the deal that you're it for me. I mean, you didn't even freak out when I told you I like..." I cleared my throat. "That I'm vers. Other omegas..."

"I would very much like for you to not mention other omegas while you're still locked inside me." He pouted and it was adorable.

I guessed the possessive vibes went both ways.

"Sorry, sugar," I soothed and ran my hands over his skin. I was careful not to move us too much. I didn't want to trigger more orgasms. I wanted my knot to deflate so we could get dressed and face the firing squad. "Nobody I've been with before has been anywhere near as perfect for me as you, even if we do have a lot of getting to know each other to do."

"Yes, well," his expression softened out again, "the feeling is mutual."

The admission had me smiling long after my knot subsided and we got dressed, even after we opened the door and made our way into the main part of the house to be greeted by the bewildered stares of his pack.

Or, I wondered as questions were asked around us, *are they my pack now, too?*

Everyone's eyes were wide as they looked at us. They scented the air, and jaws grew slack. Then all hell broke loose as they started asking questions over the top of each other.

"Are you...is that an *Alpha* scent?" Rex asked.

Meanwhile Beck shook his head and scented the air again, as if trying to put the pieces together.

"That's definitely an alpha scent," Ollie confirmed. He grinned over at Brandt. "Go team dragon." A moment later his eyes landed on my neck and grew impossibly wider. "Holy shit, is that a mating bite?!"

"What?!" Beck cried, and a burst of renewed questions and chatter came flying our way, most of it difficult to discern considering they were all speaking at once.

"Are you telling me you willingly just bonded? With a complete stranger?" Damon's question rose above the rabble of surprised voices. I wasn't sure if he was asking me or Brandt. "*Knowingly?*"

"Hang on, did...did you just *mate* in my meeting room?" Beckett demanded on top of that, sounding marginally scandalized.

I felt my cheeks burn and I rubbed the back of my neck and offered him a sheepish smile. "Yeah...I'm sorry about that. I...we..."

"It is not unlike the time I caught you and Oliver in the lab," Brandt informed him.

"Hey!" Ollie protested. "I was going into heat. That was a spur of the moment thing."

"So was this," I spoke without thinking, then cringed. "I mean, not the claiming. I knew what I was doing. But...it felt kind of urgent, so...yeah."

"I guess I can relate to that," Beck admitted. "But...I have to sit at that table, Mike." He scrunched his nose. "Please tell me you, like, sanitized it afterwards, or something."

I opened my mouth to tell him we actually christened one of his chairs, but I was interrupted.

"Didn't you knot Ollie on your dining table once?" Damon asked my old friend, and it was fun to watch him balk.

He looked to his mate with round eyes. "You told him—"

"We were having an omega chat. It came up." Ollie shrugged.

"I've eaten at that table," I told him with exaggerated horror, more to tease him than because I was actually appalled. The shifter vs human-raised mentality about sex and propriety would always fascinate me. After spending so much time with humans, I felt like I related more to Beck and Rex than I did the other shifters.

Under his breath, Rex muttered, "Apparently, so has Beck."

Damon guffawed and offered his alpha a hand to high-five.

"As amusing as this chat is, I am feeling somewhat drained," Brandt interrupted, and I immediately felt concerned. He looked around at his pack —*our pack?* — and, without looking at his brother, asked, "Can we discuss these latest developments later? I would like to return home and rest for a while. It has been an intense day."

"That's putting it mildly," Damon murmured, but even his mirth had morphed into concern. "You've got yourself an alpha now."

"We'll talk," I assured Beck when I could see that he wasn't quite as willing to let it go. "But, for now, I'd like to take care of my mate."

The vaguely possessive words sent a thrill of excitement through me.

My mate.

I had a mate.

That had not been on my bingo card for the day. If I was being honest, I never imagined I would have a mate of my own. I never imagined that I was secretly an alpha.

"Come, darling," Brandt took my hand and guided me towards the door, and I thrilled int he reciprocal possessive vibes coming through the bond, wrapping me in his own desire. "Let us go home."

Home.

My inner alpha liked the sound of that, too, even if it wasn't quite what I thought Brandt intended.

But, considering we had bonded and we had triplets on the way, maybe it would be soon.

Chapter Eleven

The knock at my front door did not come as a surprise, though I was a little shocked that it took my brother more than an hour to show up.

My little house was only situated a couple of miles away from Eric's cottage (the same cottage which housed the fertility clinic), and I knew that he wouldn't be able to fight his curiosity after learning that Micah and I had bonded. We were the fourth known couple to do so, after all, and in a unique situation again.

Unlike Beck and Ollie, or Lena and Brandi, we had bonded outside of a mating heat. While Rex and Damon had also bonded out of choice, they had done so after the birth of their son.

And unlike those alphas, Micah —my alpha— had already known he was a shifter before he had knotted me.

Gods, but I wanted to experience that again. My omega practically purred at the notion of being locked together and filled by our mate.

But, even though I would happily spend hours in bed with Micah, we had to talk properly. To get to know each other as people, not just as compatible mates who had impulsively decided to agree with the hand fate had dealt us.

So, once we had acknowledged to our friends that, yes, we had bonded, and yes, Micah was an alpha, I had taken my mate by the hand and led him out of the Alpha's home and to the clinic to retrieve my car. From there, I had driven us to my house, and we had sat and talked about everything and nothing.

It was a strange feeling, to be tied to the man for as long as he would live, but to not really know him. My omega felt as if we had known him forever, but I still wanted to know the basics. His favorite color (red), his favorite food (apple pie), his favorite human pastime (riding a pushbike or mountain bike surrounded by nature), and other odds and ends. I knew his birth date and age from our clinic's records, but there were so many things still to learn.

He came from a pack in California, and it didn't sound as though they were the same kind of people as Damon's or Oliver's packs. They sounded more like naturists or, as he called them, 'hippies'. They treated all their pack members equally, and it sounded to me that they had a lot in common with the dragon clans of old. They even seemed to believe in the old magics and fate, or at least it sounded as though Micah's mother did.

"It sounds as though she and I will have some very interesting conversations," I told him as I pushed myself from the couch to answer the door.

He sighed behind me. "She can be a bit...intense...with the hippy stuff. And I know you're an actual scientist..."

I opened the door, not bothering to greet Eric as I turned to tell my mate, "I am a five-hundred-year-old man who can turn into a dragon, darling. I believe in some degree of magic in addition to science. And it will be nice to see what —if anything— she knows of the old ways. We have lost a lot of knowledge over time."

Eric cleared his throat, and I finally turned to face him, satisfied to see contrition and apology on his heart shaped face. I knew he had a right to be upset with me, however his reaction had still hurt.

"Can I come in?" he asked.

Nodding, I stepped back and gestured for him to enter.

After I had closed the door and led him into my little open-plan living space, I resumed my seat beside Micah on the two-seat couch and Eric sat tentatively on the matching gray armchair on the other side of the coffee table. I did not have a television, preferring to read or play computer games on my laptop. Micah and I had that in common as well, though we agreed it might be best to buy a television knowing we would soon have three babies and it might be nice to watch a movie while we held them or nursed them.

"Bran," Eric started, then stopped and sighed. "We both know what you did was wrong. And, yes" —he held up his hand to stall the protest on the tip of my tongue— "I know you apologized, and I know why you did it. But...this is my life's work. This is *my* baby. And it sucked that you disrespected that. It also hurt that you didn't come and tell me when you found the fertilized eggs." My heart squeezed and renewed guilt roiled at the betrayal and pain I could read on his face. "Did you really think I'd just make you get rid of them? That I wouldn't have at least found a way to store them safely?"

I...hadn't thought about that, actually.

I had just automatically assumed that Eric would want to study them before allowing them to become no longer viable.

I had also assumed that Eric would then contact Micah to perform a barrage of tests. I was honestly surprised that he hadn't demanded the right to perform such tests before Beckett left Micah and I alone, knowing that there was every possibility that we might act on the draw between us. I felt a little guilty for that, too, even though I honestly had never dreamed that Micah's response to my confession would end on such a positive note.

Shoulders slumping, I shook my head as I let it hang. "I wasn't thinking," I admitted. "I suppose, on some level, I did assume that you would use the embryos for research and then discard them when they were no longer viable."

"I might have liked to keep one for research purposes," he answered calmly and honestly, but the thought of giving up even one of my babies made my stomach churn with unease. "But," he continued, as if he could read my mind. He'd known me for nearly three hundred years, so I assumed he knew me better than most. "They were —*are*— the only hope for our species right now. I *do* get that, too. I was just pissed that you didn't tell me. That you've kept me out of the loop for almost three months." He leaned forward and looked me in the eye, his tone turning soft and compassionate. "I would have liked to have been a part of everything, Bee. Including helping you implant them, if that was what you really wanted."

My throat constricted as tears threatened to blur my vision. "You would have gone against your own ethics?"

With the corner of his lips quirking upward, he nodded. "I could have done some mental gymnastics. Justified it as necessary research." He cringed and glanced to my side towards

Micah. "Sorry. For what it's worth, I would have had Beck call you, too. If only to get your verbal consent."

"I would have given it," Micah told him without hesitation. "And, no, that's not the bond talking, sugar." He leaned into me and nuzzled my face with his own. "Even if I didn't want to acknowledge the pull back here, just the idea that consenting might help save your species —to save dragons— there wouldn't have been any reason to say no."

His words were supposed to be reassuring, but they just added to my guilt. I had been so afraid of all the possibilities which might prevent me from having my babies that I had willfully chosen to do the wrong thing.

"Whoa, *sugar*," Micah crooned, likely feeling the overwhelming emotion spilling over from the bond between us, "it's okay. It is. I promise."

Bile rose up the back of my throat and I groaned, then leapt from the couch and raced down the small hallway to the ensuite bathroom attached to the primary bedroom. I landed on my knees in front of the toilet with bruising force, but couldn't care too much about it as the contents of my stomach forced their way back out of me.

I heaved and tried not to fight it, knowing that doing so only made it worse.

Tears trickled down my cheeks, namely from the assault against my sinuses as I retched, but also from the guilt which still plagued me.

Micah was a good man —a sweet, kind man— and I had done nothing to deserve his kindness or understanding.

I jumped when his long fingers stroked through my sweaty hair before he rubbed calming circles over my back. He didn't speak for a while, just lent me his soothing presence as I rode the wave of nausea to the bitter end.

When I finished, he passed me a glass of water and a damp washcloth. I rinsed and spat, then wiped my face with the cloth as he flushed the toilet for me.

"Is it always that bad?" he asked softly as I brushed my teeth.

I spat again, then looked into the sink, unable to face my own reflection. "Yes," I answered simply, then added, "however, it has been decreasing in frequency."

"You're just past the first trimester, so that checks out," Eric's voice interrupted from the doorway. "Plus, with multiples, the hormonal fluctuations can be stronger. I wouldn't be surprised if it doesn't go away entirely."

I nodded, already aware of the fact. But this was probably all new to Micah.

"I don't expect you to deal with all of this," I told my mate, even while my omega whined at me. For an enormous, scary, flying reptile, my omega felt very much like a desperately needy puppy. "This was my choice and you—"

"We're not going around in circles on this," he cut me off, the firmness of his tone doing wonders for my hormones, despite sounding very odd given his usually relaxed demeanor. "I didn't bond with you just to take a backseat for the baby stuff. I know I wasn't there when my little swimmers did their thing. And I wasn't there when you did your thing with them, but you gave me the facts before I signed up for the mating bond and I'm accepting everything that comes with it. Are we clear on that?"

My omega was ready to go belly up for him then and there. With my brother present, that just felt awkward and weird. So,

I merely nodded and ignored the renewed slickness developing inside me.

"Crystal clear," I replied.

"Does that mean you're moving to Shifters Sanctuary?" Eric asked him without any tact. "Joining our pack?"

I didn't have time to tell my brother that he was out of line because Micah was already nodding. "Yes. I don't think I could move back to New York now. Not with this bond." He rubbed at his chest, where I knew he could feel the link between us. I felt the same inside me, too.

"But...you dislike small-town life," I argued softly. "And then there's your work. There aren't many calls for makeup and hair artistry here."

Micah shrugged, and his pretty long hair swayed with his movement. "So maybe I need to travel interstate occasionally. This will still be my home base." His expression became uncertain. "Unless you don't want me here."

I couldn't call what we shared 'love'. Not after barely knowing him for a day. But I still felt affection for him: a draw from our fated connection which I couldn't quite explain, but which felt right regardless of its inexplicability. "I most certainly want you here," I confessed, feeling vulnerable despite knowing that he had just told me exactly what my omega wanted to hear. What *I* wanted to hear. "I want to get to know you as my mate. As the father of my children. But I only want this if you truly do, too. If you can be happy with a life here."

"My bet—*alpha*," he corrected himself with a bewildered sounding chuckle. "Man, that feels weird to say. Anyway, my alpha has felt settled here since I arrived. I wasn't happy in

New York. Especially not after coming here for the wedding at Christmas."

I frowned. "We never met. It is strange that you felt the pull of the bond even without any sort of encounter to spark it."

"Can we move back to the living room so I can ask questions about all of that?" Eric prodded, reminding me of his presence. I had gotten so wrapped up in my discussion with Micah that I had forgotten we had an audience.

A suddenly gleeful, invested, and hyper-curious audience.

"Should you maybe eat or drink something with electrolytes in it or something?" Micah fussed at me as we followed my brother back down the short hallway. "All that throwing up might make you dehydrated, right?"

"Oh, I like this one," Eric declared, pushing me to sit before he headed into the kitchen on the other side of the cozy combined living and dining space. "Good thinking, Micah. Looks like the alpha urge to protect and nurture is already kicking in. Or is that just your usual personality?"

Eric opened my refrigerator and barked a laugh, likely at the multiple bottles of ginger beer I had accumulated. Sure enough, he pulled a half-empty bottle of the amber colored liquid from a shelf and twisted the lid, releasing a hiss of effervescence. He found me a glass and filled it, then returned the bottle to the refrigerator before bringing the glass to me. I sipped at it and immediately felt the remaining turmoil in my belly begin to fade.

Micah seemed to be considering Eric's question, and he shrugged. "I wouldn't say I'm any more nurturing or protective of people than most. But when I care about people, yeah...I can be, I guess."

Eric hummed and tugged his phone from his pocket. I knew he was opening his notes app, ready to ask us plenty of invasive questions.

He looked up at us expectantly, fingers poised over his keypad. "So, first thing's first; the pull between you. You say you felt it before you met?"

Micah nodded while I shook my head. "I didn't feel it until we saw each other across the parking lot the other day. Before that…no. I didn't feel any need to seek him out."

"But you, uh, you said yourself that you couldn't wait to get those embryos implanted, right?" Micah suggested cautiously. "What if that satisfied the instinct for you? Because I started feeling it after I was here for Beck and Ollie's wedding. Not in the same way Beck and Ollie talk about being desperate to find each other again, but after I left, it was like…like this itch under my skin. Like I had to turn around and come back, but I didn't know why."

"I can see the logic in that argument, actually," Eric straightened in his seat, his eyes taking on their usual gleam when it came to his research. He turned to me, "And it would also explain why you didn't stop to think a bit more rationally before you acted. Some part of you was being driven to be bred by your alpha in whatever way was available to you."

I was not going to argue with him. It might have been selfish of me, but if it meant that he would feel less hurt by justifying my actions in such a way, who was I to tell him it was unlikely? Besides, I could also see the logic and, looking back, I could acknowledge that my irrational behavior was out of character. I *had* felt as though I needed to act urgently. While I wasn't certain it could be all attributed to the pull towards my mate, it was possibly a contributing factor.

I nodded. "It is possible, yes. I was not thinking clearly once I realized they were my ovum. My eggs."

I felt Micah's amusement travel over our bond before he snickered out loud. "Dragon eggs," he said, by way of explanation.

I felt fondness for him even as I groaned. "Please tell me you are not under the impression that my kind lay eggs."

"Well, I'm not *now*. But I was obsessed with the mythology of dragons as a kid." His cheeks flushed pink. "I was actually kind of disappointed that I didn't get to see you or Eric shift when I visited."

Concentrating on sending him back my continued feelings of fondness and some reassurance, I told him, "I will gladly shift for you, Micah. And I would very much like to meet your horse, too. In my human form as well as in dragon form."

The pride and excitement which radiated back at me was adorable.

Eric cleared his throat and eyed us both. "This is fascinating," he told us. "You're practically strangers, but you're already so comfortable with one another. How does the bond feel?"

"Good," Micah answered. "It feels...right. Like it was a piece of myself I didn't know was missing." He scrunched his nose. "Which *should* be weird. Like you said, we were strangers a few hours ago. And now..."

"Now we are deeply connected," I finished for him. Then I looked back at my brother. "It feels right, however we are still both autonomous. We will have to work towards maintaining an amicable relationship."

"Just amicable?" Micah asked teasingly, and I snorted.

"That was my chosen euphemism, yes."

"So you don't feel like being fated —or extremely compatible— mates has forced an instant attraction or affection between you?" Eric's question was direct, and while it caused my omega to bristle, I understood that he was asking for scientific reasons, not to offend.

Micah, on the other hand, growled under his breath. "Brandt is the embodiment of my type," he responded defensively. "I would have found him hot with or without this connection between us. As for affection? I already cared about him before I met him because he's Beck's friend. After our...*talk*" —he shot me a wink which went straight to my cock— "I'll admit I started feeling *something* deeper...but, I don't think much of that can be attributed to the bond. I don't get emotionally attached often, but when I do, it happens fast. And, like he said, it will take time to get to know each other. Real affection —*love*—will take time."

Squeezing his hand, I nodded. "I could not have phrased it better myself."

"Fascinating." Eric tapped away at his phone screen. "It does seem as though these matches occur between people with compatible personalities and ideologies. The bizarre thing is that you are the first alpha/omega pairing of mixed species. It sometimes happens with betas, as well you both know, but until now we were operating under the assumption that alphas only mated and bonded with omegas of their own species."

"Are you working towards a question, little brother, or do you simply enjoy the sound of your own voice?" I asked playfully, not realizing until I did so that, only hours earlier, I had been afraid that I had lost the privilege to joke with him at all.

As he rolled his eyes, I felt a renewed wave of guilt and regret. Micah's hand releasing mine to rub circles on my back was the only sign telling me that he'd felt my surge of emotions.

"I'm just saying that this completely shakes up all of my —*our*— theories," Eric responded. "And, with Micah already knowing he was a shifter, it opens up a whole new world of potential matches. I would love to know why Micah is the first beta to manifest as an alpha. Why, if it has been possible all along, has it not happened until now? Or is Micah an anomaly?"

"I am not sure how we would even begin to research any of that," I said, adding, "however, I agree that it would be good to have the answers."

Eric tilted his head and smiled at my mate. "Is there anything distinguishing you from the other betas of your pack? Any physical or even mystical differences?"

I could feel Micah's unease, but he shook his head as he answered Eric smoothly. "None that I'm aware of."

I had to agree that, scientifically speaking, the size of his dick was not likely the kind of difference Eric was asking about.

My brother hummed, as if anticipating such a response. "Did you have any birth marks before you bonded with Brandt?"

Micah shook his head again. "No."

Eric smirked. "You'll probably find you have one now. A misshapen circle. Like a waxing or waning moon."

Micah groaned, leaning his head back to complain to the ceiling, "Why is it always moons?"

I snorted. "The mystical symbolism dates back to very early times. Shifters believed in the magic of the moon — it controlled the tides, the coming and going of the sun, the seasons etcetera, etcetera. Now, of course, we understand the science behind all of those things, but combined with our birthmarks and abilities, moons were and remain synonymous with magic, even for humans."

He nodded, then sighed. "Well, we dressed kinda' fast earlier, so I can't confirm the birthmark theory."

Eric shrugged, then sat back and waved vaguely over my mate's body. "Strip now, then."

I growled, then blinked at the possessive heat which had risen up the back of my neck and through my throat. My brother stared back at me in equal surprise.

"Scales, sugar," Micah's fingertips stroked over my forehead and down the side of my jaw. "Fuck, these are sexy."

I squirmed, feeling slick threatening to dampen my underwear at the touch to my scales, and to the low, sexy words my mate spoke.

"Fascinating," Eric repeated again. "The last time I saw that kind of possessiveness was when Ollie was newly bonded and pregnant. Oh, no, wait — it was after Lena and Brandi bonded. But I don't recall Damon ever being like that." He bent over his phone again, thumbs flying over the keyboard. "Hmm, the early days in the bond, coupled with pregnancy hormones, must make omegas extra territorial."

"Or, perhaps you have just made some particularly insensitive requests with us all and you did not get the opportunity to do so with Damon."

Eric looked up, rolled his eyes at me, then bent to look at his screen again. "They're not insensitive. I'm a doctor. A scientist. I'm asking these things for research purposes only. I have zero interest in your alpha, Bran." He glanced at Micah and grimaced. "Sorry."

"Yeah, you're not my type, either," he scoffed right back. "But I'm still not taking my clothes off for you. Brandt can go looking for a birthmark later."

"Mmm," I practically purred, my omega enjoying the suggestion very much, "I look forward to it."

Eric scrunched his nose for a moment, then narrowed his gaze, swinging it from me, to Micah, then back again. "You're not in heat," he began slowly. "You can't be, because not only are you pregnant, you're in your second trimester." He held up his index finger before I could crack the same joke about his lack of a question. "So," he continued, "I can only assume the lust pouring off you both in waves has something to do with continuing to build the bond. To...feed it and reassure it, if you will."

"Or, being in my second trimester, this is purely hormonal."

"On your part, sure," Eric shrugged, "but that doesn't explain him." He gestured at Micah, who blushed adorably.

"Can't that be chalked up to the standard honeymoon phase of any new relationship? Sex is always exciting and new with a new partner. Even most humans can't keep their hands off each other when they first begin dating."

Eric huffed. "Well, you do have a point there." He brought his phone back up again. "I'm making a note to ask the others. Damon and Rex in particular. They didn't bond until after Cam was born, so if they report the same feelings—"

"It is still possible that it is a honeymoon phase thing." I repeated.

My brother tilted his head in acquiescence, but still argued, "And it's possible that it's exacerbated by the bonding."

"That would mean you're both right," Micah said smoothly. He had such an easy-going attitude. It was calming, instantly soothing my growing irritation with my stubborn brother.

"You're a smart little pacifist, aren't you?" Eric asked with amusement.

Micah shrugged, not bothered by my brother's jibe. And, in that moment, it struck me that this was Eric's way of testing my bondmate. His, for all intents and purposes, brother-in-law.

I was going to strangle him.

"Well," I slapped my palms on my thighs and pushed to my feet, eyes locked on Eric's blue pair, "I believe that is enough interrogation for today."

"But..." he protested, and I shook my head.

"Eric, I am newly mated and hormonal, and I wish for some time alone with my alpha."

After a long moment where I was concerned that I would need to eject him from my home via force, he got to his feet and nodded. "Fine. But tomorrow, you and I are talking properly." His expression softened. "And I'll give you a proper checkup, too. Bring your notes and records. I know you have them."

Rolling my eyes, I nodded. After he left, I turned to Micah. "You would think he was the eldest, the way he speaks to me."

"It's cute," he mused as he pulled me in for a hug, which instantly seemed to relax something inside me. "I'm an only child. I always wanted siblings, but my parents had enough trouble getting pregnant with me, so...it's just me."

"Well, I believe your brothers-in-law will make you wish I was an only child, too," I joked, and he laughed.

"Nah, they're alright. But," his hands slid down my back to cup my ass and squeeze, "I'm glad we're alone now."

Chapter Twelve

It had been a long time since I was in the kind of relationship that involved sleeping over in someone's bed. But, after performing a thorough search for my alpha mark (which we discovered on my inner thigh) and subsequently indulging in the urges from our bond again, I was too tired and too happy to even suggest returning to Beck and Ollie's house, even though that was where all my stuff was being kept.

But waking up wrapped around my omega —and wasn't that a mindfuck? I was an *alpha*!— was an experience I wanted to repeat over and over again. It felt odd, at first, not being alone…but my inner alpha radiated contentment and pride.

And that was odd, too; feeling so blissfully content with a veritable stranger. We had so much to learn about each other, but I meant what I had said the previous day: I trusted that the universe wouldn't lead me astray when it came to my mate.

My mom was *never* going to shut up about being right.

I snorted to myself.

Brandt grumbled and cracked a dark brown eye open. "What has you so amused at this hour?"

"Not a morning person?" I asked him as I leaned over to check the time on my phone screen. His bedroom windows were covered by blackout curtains, so I couldn't see if the sun had risen or not. My phone told me it wasn't quite seven yet.

"I can be," he practically purred and rubbed his morning wood into my hip, "with the right motivation."

Arousal flared low in my belly and my dick stirred to life without any other prompting. I wasn't sure if it was the bond between us or just the newness of our relationship causing the reaction, and I didn't care.

Beneath his sexy goatee, my mate's lips quirked and he wrapped his large hand around my shaft. I groaned as he observed, "This is fine motivation indeed."

"Fuck," I muttered when he started to slowly stroke me. "That's it, sugar."

"Hmm," he practically purred into my ear, "I believe I can do better than that."

Before I could ask what he meant, he shuffled down the mattress, taking the sheets with him. After sex and a shower the previous night, we had gone to bed naked, and I had surprised myself by not feeling self-conscious about being so vulnerable and exposed. I assumed it had something to do with the bond, and the obvious proof of Brandt's appreciation of my body, but it was still a novel sensation to not want to hide away behind at least a pair of briefs.

However, I was glad for our choice when, moments later, Brandt's warm, wet mouth sank down on my dick.

"Oh my god," I breathed, closing my eyes when he began to suck and bob his head. "That feels...*nnngh*."

He hummed around my cock, presumably in pride or agreement, and the vibrations made the tingly feeling which I was beginning to associate with my knot start to tickle the base of my shaft.

I wasn't accustomed to getting such enthusiastic blow jobs. I hadn't lived a life without head, but it was usually an afterthought, or a half-hearted, quick and easy way to get me off if I didn't come during sex. But with Brandt, I could feel how much he wanted to do this for me. *With* me. His arousal and enjoyment were obvious, not only through the bond, but through his actions themselves.

I glanced down my body to watch him, to take in the dark eyelashes resting on his cheeks as he lost himself to his ministrations.

He was gorgeous.

He was gorgeous, and he was *mine*.

"Shit," I cursed, my back arching from the bed at the delicious suction, "I'm fucking close already..."

He hummed again as a sense of satisfaction traveled through the bond and I groaned, one of my hands moving to the back of his head, my fingers tangling in his dark tresses.

"B-Brandt," my breath caught on his name. "Sugar, I'm...oh, fuck, just like that..."

He slurped as he bobbed, and he twirled his tongue around my dick like it was a lollipop or a popsicle or—

"Fuck!" I cried out as he took the whole thing into his mouth again without warning, and I felt my balls meet his chin. I knew that in and of itself wasn't exactly hard to do, but those thoughts filtered away as he swallowed around the head of my cock. The suction and the relatively new sensations, combined with the enjoyment I could feel through the bond, made my eyes roll back in my head. "Oh, god," I groaned, no longer able to prevent the inevitable, "I'm coming. Fuck, I'm...*unnnggh.*"

I slammed my head back onto the pillow as I came down his throat, and then the tingling started up for real. "Pull off," I demanded. "M-my knot..."

I didn't know how large my knot could possibly be, but I didn't want to risk getting stuck in his mouth, with his jaw unable to open wide enough to release me. I doubted that was really a possibility, but I'd rather be safe than sorry.

Brandt seemed to gag before he pulled away, but as I looked down to check on him, shock rocketed through me.

I hadn't seen my knot the previous day, as the two times I had knotted Brandt, I had been buried as deeply inside of his body as possible. But now I was getting a good look at it and—

"Holy shit," I blurted, staring wide-eyed at my dick as though I'd never seen it before. Because, technically, I hadn't. Not like this. "What...?"

The bulbous swell of the knot, I had expected. The extra length, on the other hand...

"How is it bigger?" I demanded, reaching to grasp it, then slamming my eyes shut as I remembered belatedly just how sensitive the knot was. Cum spurted somewhat weakly over my hand and I watched, fascinated, as the practically entirely-new-to-me appendage twitched and dribbled out the last of my most recent orgasm. I looked at Brandt, knowing he could probably feel the spike of mixed emotions inside me. "Did...did either of the others...?"

My omega shook his head. "Neither Beck or Rex mentioned anything changing other than the knot itself." After a beat, he cautiously added, "However, Brandi's body changed significantly…"

Looking back down at my still rock hard, still significantly larger than usual dick, I sighed. "I guess it probably needs to be a certain size to knot properly, or whatever."

It was strange, but for as many years as I'd lamented how small I was, it seemed like even more of an insult from fate that my dick had to magically grow to accommodate my mate's needs. I'd genuinely believed that my body was enough for Brandt…but, apparently, it was only enough because it had grown without either of us knowing it.

"Whatever it is you are thinking, you need to stop," his voice dragged me from my musings with a growl. When I blinked and focused on him, he was scowling.

Why did that expression make him look even hotter?

"I was just—"

"Assuming I only enjoy having you inside me after your knot forms?"

It was a scarily close guess to what I had been thinking. Swallowing roughly, I tried again, "I—"

"You would be wrong if that was the case," he continued, crawling back up the mattress until we were face-to-face again. "I know that you do not know me well enough to believe me, but I am not so shallow that the size of your cock makes a difference to me one way or the other. Do I enjoy your knot? Yes. Did I enjoy riding you before we knew if you would even be able to knot me? Also yes. You are perfect as you are in every possible way, Micah. But you are most likely correct that it changes purely to facilitate the size of the knot." Then he smirked. "Besides, none of that makes any difference to how you will feel impaled on my cock, does it?"

Just like that, I was completely distracted. Because, really, he was right, wasn't he? We'd known that if I was an alpha, my body would change during sex. I couldn't control that, and the sex had been phenomenal even before I popped my first knot.

And speaking of phenomenal sex...

"I'm ready for you any time, sugar," I told him, reaching down to stroke the appendage in question. He hadn't come yet, and I felt like I had been an inconsiderate lover. "Do you have lube?"

He nodded, jutting his chin towards the nightstand. I released him to go digging around in the drawer, smirking at the toys in his limited collection. We could have fun with those. But, for the moment, we had each other's bodies to explore thoroughly first.

I tossed him the bottle and he opened the cap with a satisfying *snap*.

"How do you want me?" I asked him, spreading my legs in invitation.

"Like this," he said, waving his hand over me. "I want to be able to see you."

"Sounds perfect."

He bent to kiss me and I melted for him, more than happy to let my big, brawny omega take the lead. I reached between us to stroke his dick again, thrilling at the jolts of pleasure that echoed through our bond.

It was all I could do not to whimper and complain when he pulled away, but then his lubed fingers were nudging my hole and I had to grip the pillows behind my head to prevent myself from reaching for my cock. I'd only experienced stimulation to my knot twice before, but I knew that if I bumped it now, I would probably regret it.

I relaxed into the stretch and burn of Brandt opening me up, letting go of the pillow with one hand so I could slide my fingers into his silky dark hair instead. I watched the movement of his large bicep as he fucked me with his fingers, and I marveled at how stunning he was.

His large, hairy body, with its softening pecs and soft belly, was my favorite kind of catnip. The silvery specks in his goatee and through his hair made my mouth water. And those eyes! Such a deep, dark brown that they were almost black. I swore they could see into my soul.

"Get inside me," I demanded when the desperation to connect with him became too much to bear. "*Now*, sugar."

"Gods, you know what that endearment does to me," he muttered, but he did as told regardless, withdrawing his fingers and positioning his thick, slicked-up cock at my entrance. He groaned as he nudged his way in, and the pleasure inside me seemed to double as I felt his echoing mine through the connection between us.

That was still going to take some getting used to.

"Fuck," I cursed when he pulled out and slammed back in without warning, making my cock bounce against my lower abdomen — a wholly novel sensation. But I wasn't able to focus on the strangeness of that feeling for long, because the movement also stimulated my knot, forcing another short orgasm out of me.

It bordered on painful, and Brandt moaned as it ricocheted through the bond. "That is...intense," he mused through panted breaths.

I nodded and carefully gripped my shaft above the knot, hoping to prevent it from bouncing against me with his next thrust. "But fucking awesome," I replied. "Keep...keep going. Yeah, that's it. Just like that, sweetheart. Oh, fuck, you feel so good."

"*You* feel good," he told me, his voice strained as he carefully closed the space between us —probably afraid of jostling my knot— and pressed a sweet kiss to my lips. He continued to rock his hips, resting his forehead against mine as he confessed, "I'm close. Too close."

I shook my head. "No such thing. Come for me, sugar. Come for your alpha."

I felt the moment he lost control, the spike of bliss rocketing around the magic that tied us together. As he cried out his release with a loud, growly "Fuck!", I felt it as a multi-sensational experience.

Even without touching my knot, I came again, pushed over the edge by the phantom orgasm which didn't actually belong to me. When I opened my eyes, it was to find Brandt's dark pair staring intently at me, warmth and awe painted on his face. He brought a trembling hand to the side of my face and stroked my cheek tenderly with his thumb.

No words needed to be said as we took a moment to bask in the afterglow of this first for us — the first time my omega was inside me, making my inner alpha sing. The first time of many, if I had my way.

Brandt pulled out and flopped down at my side, working to catch his breath. Resting his head on my sweaty shoulder, he pressed lazy kisses onto my skin. I kissed the top of his tousled hair, nuzzling my cheek over the top of his head.

"That was most certainly the right kind of motivation for waking early," his voice rumbled through his chest, and I chuckled.

"I'm happy to motivate you any time, sugar."

"Are we going to talk about it?" Beck's voice startled me. I turned from where I was re-packing my suitcase on the bed inside the guest room I had been staying in and found my former roommate leaning casually against the doorframe.

"About the alpha thing?" I asked him easily, still finding it all a bit surreal.

After our morning spent *motivating* each other, Brandt finally admitted that he did have work to do at the clinic, and I knew I needed to head back to Beck and Ollie's to gather my things and, also, thank my friends for their hospitality. I also knew that Beck and Sandy would want to talk about the huge and sudden changes I was making in my life, but neither had been around when I let myself inside the house.

Beck crossed the room and sat on the edge of the bed's mattress, making my suitcase bounce. "Yeah, about the alpha thing," he agreed, matching my light tone. Then he cocked his head and looked up at me. "But also about the bonding thing. And the baby thing. Because, I gotta tell you, man, I wasn't expecting..." he trailed off.

I understood where he was coming from. A few years earlier, when he had told me and Sandy about his impending parenthood, I had reacted with shock on his behalf. But back then the whole concept of alphas existing, of magical bonds being more than simple legends or slowly-forgotten history, had been mind-blowing on its own. Now, it was rare, but not a complete anomaly. Even so, I had embraced the idea of my omega carrying my babies with a lot less freaking out than me-of-three-years-earlier would have, and we both knew it.

"Yeah, well, he's my omega," I shrugged and rolled a pair of jeans up into a neat cylinder shape, placing it into the open case beside him. "I realized that if I wanted him, I needed to be okay with everything that comes with that."

"Yeah, but...*triplets*, Mike. Twins have been..." he shuddered, then looked instantly shamefaced. "I mean, I love my kids, don't get me wrong. But...two has been rough, and you're having *three*. And you didn't even—"

"If you're about to say 'enjoy the sex that made them' or something along those lines, I think it's safe to assume that Brandt and I have made up for that."

My friend snorted. "No. But thanks for the mental imagery, asshole."

"You're welcome."

Shaking his head, Beck ignored my snarky teasing. "I was going to say that you didn't even get a choice...I mean, I guess you *did*, but...Ugh, I'm not saying this right." He huffed out a breath of frustration, then stared up at me with a whole bunch of emotions on his face. "I'm just saying, it would have been totally understandable if you were pissed with Brandt, or if you weren't ready to have kids. *Three* kids, Mike."

"Yeah," I sighed and pushed the suitcase further up the bed so I could sit beside my friend, "it would have been understandable. But I didn't feel like that. And that doesn't make your freakout when Ollie got pregnant any less valid, by the way."

Beck scrunched his nose. "Except—"

"Nope. No exceptions. And if you're still feeling guilty about that, that's something you need to talk to him about."

"I'm not. Not really. I mean, this whole thing with you and Brandt has kind of shaken up some of those old feelings, but I guess I just assumed...I mean, *three babies*, Micah. You'll be outnumbered."

"We, uh, we're talking about employing help, actually. Like...a nanny." I cringed as I said it, associating the word with the rich and affluent. "Not to, like, do all the work or raise them for us or anything. But I will have to travel for work, and Brandt wants to keep working at the clinic, and...what?"

Beck was staring at me with wide-eyed surprise. "That's...Wow. You only met him yesterday."

"And I bonded with him." I smiled softly, remembering my awe when he first told me about bonding with Ollie. "With the biting and the foreverness."

His own expression softened, likely remembering the same conversation, and he nodded. "With the biting and the foreverness, yes."

"And I chose that, Beck. I knew it was an option and...I chose it."

I didn't need to tell him that that was where our pivotal difference was: all of this had fallen in his lap and had taken him by surprise when it had happened to him. I had grown up as a shifter and, after he and Ollie bonded, I understood that the magic wasn't just in stories anymore. While I had never imagined that I, as a beta, would ever be presented with the opportunity to bond with a mate, I had known what I was doing before I went with my instincts. I had *chosen* my fate.

It was that choice which made the sudden changes in my life seem so much easier to handle. I had known what I was signing up for. I had known, theoretically speaking, what to expect going forward.

"It's that easy for you?" Beck still sounded a little bewildered. "I know you chose it, but it's still happening so fast. This time yesterday, you hadn't even met the man. Now, you're bonded forever and are having triplets in, like, six months. How are you so calm?"

"Sandy asked you that same question, remember? Or at least something close to it. And you said that what was done was done and there was no sense losing your shit over something you couldn't go back and change."

"Well, yeah, but Ollie's pack had just tried to snatch him off the street, too, and that kind of put it into perspective for me."

Thankfully, my mate was not at risk of being kidnapped by a cult-like pack. Or, rather, I hoped he wasn't. At least, no more at risk than any other member of Shifters Sanctuary.

I clapped Beck on the shoulder and squeezed. "This is still kind of like that. Not with the life-endangerment, but Brandt was already pregnant either way. He was having my kids either way. And, honestly? Even if I could go back in time to change it, I wouldn't. Not just because of the whole thing where it might potentially help keep an entire species going, either."

The flash of guilt across Beck's face made me aware that my words might have struck a nerve, but he shook it off and asked, "No?"

"No. Brandt has wanted to be a dad for hundreds of years. This…this makes him *so* happy. Am I a little terrified of having kids with someone who is practically a complete stranger right now? Yeah, I am. But yesterday, while the bond was still settling in, I could *feel* his happiness inside me and there's no way I would want to take that from him." Pushing back to my feet, I added, "It's different to your situation. I know you and Ollie love the twins, but neither of you expected them and, on top of the alpha thing being a surprise, and the threat from his pack, you had a lot to deal with. For me? The only threat I'm facing is that my mom will want to move here and never leave when she finds out she's getting grandchildren."

Beckett laughed at that. "She's welcome here. Everyone is. That's kind of our thing."

"Don't tell her that," I joked back, then I groaned as the truth of what I was saying fully dawned on me. "She's going to be *impossible*. She's been wanting a grandbaby for a long time. Add to that the fact that she was right about coming back here…"

"Wait, what? What do you mean?"

Reaching for one of the t-shirts in the pile of clothes I still had to pack, I started to tell Beck everything about my feelings since I visited for his wedding, and the conversations I had had with my mother. My suitcase was fully packed by the time I was finished, and Beck appeared contemplative.

"Do you think there's something to it?" he asked. "To her connection with the universe, or whatever she calls it? Because

Sage and Dex are looking into the magical side of shifters and alphas and stuff...and maybe your mom can help with that?"

Didn't Brandt say something about it sounding like the old ways last night?

My thoughts swirled as I started to consider the fact that my mom's airy-fairy talk might actually be a bit more than just a quirk. What if she and her family before her had been passing down forgotten magic from the older generations of shifters? If something she knew could help the pack —my new pack, *Brandt's* pack— I couldn't risk not asking.

"I guess I'm calling Mom."

Chapter Thirteen

My intention to work was derailed the very moment I walked through the doors to the clinic. I should have anticipated that my friends would be just as eager to corner me as my brother had been.

Damon and Ollie looped their arms through mine and guided me into the soundproofed treatment room and closed the door behind us.

Damon pointed to one of the chairs next to the desk. "Sit and start talking, buster."

I did not sit.

"I thought we were easing into it," Ollie said with some amusement, but Day shook his head.

"We don't have time for the softly-softly approach." He looked at me. "Jazz has the kids. She's going to give them way too much sugar and then hand them back all hyped up."

"Is that not a reasonable consequence for abducting me?" I teased lightly.

"Payback's a bitch, Bran," Day shrugged. "You'll have three toddlers of your own soon enough." His smug expression fell into one of hurt. "I can't believe you didn't tell us. Tell me."

The guilt welled up inside me again and I looked at the floor. "I didn't tell anyone. I couldn't. What I did..."

"*Pssshhht,*" Damon waved his hand dismissively. "Forget the ethics for a minute—"

Ollie made a strangled sound at the back of his throat.

Damon ignored him. "Forget the ethics," he repeated. "For as long as I've known you, you've had baby fever. Don't deny it." He pointed his index finger at me. "I've watched you with the pack kids."

"Yes," I agreed, "but—"

"So *finally* getting to have your own is *huge,*" he cut me off before I could say anything about the actions I had taken.

Ollie nodded, adding, "And that's ignoring the species saving thing."

"So, yeah," Day cut back in easily. "We've got your back, Bran. And, y'know, we've been through it all if you want to bitch about the morning sickness, or the sore back, or the...other stuff." He made a face, clearly remembering the many complaints he had shared about his condition when he had been pregnant.

I looked between the two men, feeling overwhelmed by their support and continued friendship. "Thank you. I..." As I moved to once again apologize for my actions, I realized that they —and Micah— were right. I couldn't keep going around in circles. I had made my choices, and they were making theirs. Tears welled in my eyes and I managed to choke out another effusive, "Thank you."

Day lunged forward and wrapped me in a hug, and I tried not to focus on how much larger I was, comparatively speaking. Oliver followed suit moments later, making the hug more of a huddle, but the embrace helped heal my guilt in ways I couldn't articulate.

"So," Ollie asked as we pulled out of the three-way hug, "three babies. You're a brave man, Bran. I thought two was a handful!"

"Are you going to find out if you're having boys or girls or whatever mix of both?" Day asked before I could react to Ollie's comment.

"Oooh," Ollie nodded emphatically, "yes, are you? And have you started thinking about names?"

"Uh..." I blinked, stunned by their rabid enthusiasm and rapid-fire questions. Neither man was particularly prone to such excitable behavior...though, now that I thought about it, Oliver *had* been just as enthusiastic when Lena and Brandi had announced their twin pregnancy. I had assumed that had more to do with his friendship with the women than anything else and...*oh*.

The urge to cry hit me all over again.

I had known we were friends, but to be treated the same way as his closest friends...well, it meant a lot to me. I was more introverted than either of my brothers, but I still craved the closeness of pack and family. Having Ollie and Day treat me like family warmed me from the inside out.

"It's such a pity kids don't shift until they're school-aged," Day lamented, moving the conversation along despite my lack of a response. He turned to Ollie and crooned, "Could you imagine cute little baby dragons? The tiny wings!"

"The breathing fire when they're upset," Ollie laughed back at him. "I'm concerned about the impulse control of five-year-olds, let alone babies or toddlers. So, no, I think school-aged is best."

Day rolled his eyes and folded his arms across his chest. "Spoilsport," he accused playfully. Then he looked back at me. "Do you think they might be dragons?"

"I don't know," I answered, finally able to get a word in edgewise. "And, to be honest, it makes no difference to me whether they are boys, girls, non-binary...dragons, horses, human. I—"

"Will love them in any and all combination," Ollie finished with a gentle smile. "Yeah, we both know. But it's still fun to hypothesize. I used to imagine a set of twin boys who looked like Beck."

Day leaned back against the examination bed and tilted his head as he looked at the first of us to find an alpha. "Didn't Eric tell you their sexes when he was doing your ultrasounds?"

Ollie blushed and shook his head. "Beck and I decided we didn't want to know. Everything else had been a surprise to that point, so we decided that could be, too."

"I'd want to know," Day said after taking a moment to consider our other friend's reasoning. "If I ever had another one —which will *never* happen— I would want to find out."

"Never say never, Day," Ollie teased.

Day snorted. "This coming from the guy who is trusting untested birth control." He winced and shot me an apologetic glance. "No offence."

"None taken," I assured him. "I understand why you feel that doing so is a risk."

Ollie sat on the edge of Eric's desk and drummed his fingers on the wooden surface. "I've seen the science. I trust you and Eric. And, really, condoms don't mix well with knots and multiple orgasms during the whole heat and rut thing." He gnawed on his lower lip for a moment before telling Damon, "You'd be better off taking the meds and using condoms if you want to eliminate as much chance of getting pregnant as possible. But even then..." He shrugged.

"You may have a point," Day mused in return. Then, looking at me once more, he smirked, "Are we placing bets on how long it takes you to sing the song of my people?"

"The...song of your people?" I looked at Oliver in askance. He held up his hands and twisted his lips in the universal gesture for 'I have no fucking clue'.

Day snorted. "The 'no more kids for me' song."

"I *am* middle-aged, even for a dragon," I conceded, then looked down at my stomach as melancholy swept over me. Placing my hand over the soft bulge, which had been present prior to my test-tube conception, I sighed softly. "They may be the only chance I get."

"Well now I just feel mean," Day complained, which startled a laugh out of me. He pushed away from the exam bed and closed the distance between us to rub between my shoulder blades. "You're still a dragon. Middle-aged or not, I think you've still got at least another hundred years of baby making in you." His eyes went wide and he looked in Ollie's direction in horror. "A hundred years of heats. Can you imagine?"

Ollie shuddered. "No, thanks. Hard pass."

Head swiveling to look between one and then the other, I said, "I've never experienced heat. But is it not...a pleasurable thing?"

"It's...intense," Ollie answered. "I don't like how out of control I feel when I'm in heat."

"Yeah," Day agreed, rolling his shoulders as if experiencing physical discomfort. "And having to rely on my alpha to make the unbearable ache stop is frustrating as hell. If I could just sit on a dildo to make the feelings go away, I would."

"You *definitely* wouldn't get pregnant if you could do that," Ollie told him by way of agreement.

"I hate that I have to fight my biological instinct every few months," Day grumbled. "Like, you think my omega would get with the program, but *nooooo*. I think that makes my in-heat mood swings even worse, now that I think about it."

I was fascinated by all of this. It was somewhat new information to me. With Eric dealing with the majority of the people-facing roles in the clinic, most of my job had become research-based. I probably should have shown more interest in learning about how we truly functioned as omegas, but I had been too jealous of those lucky few who could experience mating heats to want to learn.

That, I realized belatedly, was a mistake.

"I am curious as to whether the birth control will assist with minimizing these symptoms of heat," I pondered, watching as Oliver's eyes lit up.

"It would be amazing if it does," he admitted. "The many, *many* orgasms are amazing, but they don't really outweigh the pain points."

"I'll make a note to discuss it with Eric," I decided. "If not the birth control, perhaps another hormone supplement..."

"And we've lost him," Day joked, referencing my tendency to hyperfixate on scientific theories.

Ollie checked his watch. "We should probably rescue Jazz from my little hellhounds," he said ruefully, but the words were underlaid with affection. His twins were a handful, I knew, but he adored them. "I really do hope she hasn't plied them with ice cream and milkshakes again." He shuddered.

"We'll take them out for a run in the fields if that's the case," Day suggested. "They love it when we shift for them."

"I don't love it when they pull my tail. Or my ears."

I snorted. "Which is worse: that or the sugar high?"

Day and Ollie exchanged glances and, in unison, replied, "The sugar high."

"So, apparently, I have to call my mom," Micah told me later, when he came to the clinic with Beckett in tow.

"I mean, that's usually what people do when they find out they're having kids, isn't it?" Damon interjected cheekily from the reception desk. Then he made a face. "I mean, not me, because my pack was a Moonmusic cult base, but most nice shifters do, don't they?"

Beside my mate, Beckett shrugged. "Don't ask me: I was a foster kid and thought shifters were practically a myth."

I snorted. "You were living with two."

"And with a human nose, couldn't scent either of them for what they were," he argued back. "I had no idea how many really did live among us."

It still boggled my mind that people like Rex, Beckett, and Brandi had lived entire lives as humans without any real understanding of the world to which they belonged. At least my alpha had known he was a shifter, even if that did make him the odd one out. An anomaly.

"Anyway," Micah closed the distance between us in a few long-legged strides and took my hand, squeezing it, "I should warn you that she will probably be, like, super excited."

The previous day, he had spoken about his parents. It sounded as though they had a good relationship and were generally supportive people. As such, hearing his declaration that his mother would react favorably to his news made me smile. "I am pleased that she will be happy about our children."

"And our bonding," he added firmly. "She's been nagging me to settle down for ages."

Unease itched down my spine and I shuffled my feet. "Even with an omega so much older than you? So...untraditional?" I gestured to my bulky frame. "So seemingly incompatible?"

He scoffed. "Sugar," he cooed, and we both ignored Day's emphatic 'aww', which Beckett shushed. "My parents are hippies. It's all about peace, love, and freedom with them. Plus, they believe in fate. Not only did the universe deem you my compatible mate, but Mom will also say that you're my fated mate. And she'll probably love you for that reason alone."

"Even if I am a dragon?"

"Hippies love dragons. All the mythology and imagery and stuff is right up their alley."

I arched my eyebrow and shared a questioning glance with Beck, who just shrugged. Meeting my mate's gaze again, I began, "I am not entirely sure that is correct."

He rolled his eyes. "Fine, I'm talking out of my ass, but they will love you."

"Even though I implanted our eggs without your knowledge or permission?"

"Mom's getting three grandbabies. If anything, she'll ask when we're going to have more."

"*Brrrr*," Day's exaggerated shudder interrupted us, and he muttered under his breath, "No thanks, hard pass."

"Anyway," Beckett gave our friend a pointed glare, which the young omega merely winked at, causing the pack Alpha to sigh before turning back to me and Micah, "sharing your news isn't the only reason I'm encouraging Micah to call his parents." He tilted his head. "Can we head into the lab and talk?"

Curiosity piqued, I nodded and led the way down the short hallway in the converted cottage and to the farthest door on the right. The former bedroom was a fully functioning little laboratory, and it was the room I affectionately considered my research cave. I sat on my rolling chair and, after following Micah and me inside, Beck closed the door and leaned against it. Micah situated himself at my desk, resting his hip against its surface.

Goosebumps pimpled my skin as the awareness that he was finally in the place where our children had been created settled over me. It didn't matter that it had been an unorthodox creation and conception, it truly felt as though things had come full circle.

Oblivious to my thoughts, Beck said, "To cut to the chase, I think Micah's mother might have some knowledge about traditional shifter magic. She might even be able to practice it...more than just the ability to shift, I mean."

I sat up straighter, looking up at Micah for confirmation. "Really?"

He shrugged. "I mean, I was telling Beck about her insistence that the universe guides her, or whatever..."

I tilted my head. "In what way?"

"I always thought it was just wishy-washy talk, you know? Like psychic abilities or whatever. But," he rubbed the back of his neck and grimaced, "she's always known just when to call me, and she was the one who told me to come back here. Said the universe willed it, or something like that."

"Which sounds to me," Beck took over, "like maybe there's something more to it all. I'm not an expert in shifter stuff —not even close— but I know you and Eric sent Sage and Dexter on some kind of magic research spree...and I thought maybe this might help, too?"

Nodding, I contemplated the fact that I had thought something similar about the old ways the night before. "It is certainly worth exploring." Removing my phone from my pocket, I brought up Sage's contact details to send him a message. "I will ask Sage when he and Dexter plan on returning. It would make the most sense to have their input."

"Aren't you the oldest?" Micah asked. "Wouldn't you remember more of the old magics?"

"They never interested me quite as much as science, I am afraid. Even though there was some crossover a few hundred years ago, my memory is not that efficient. Sage and Dexter have been traveling the world, looking for older dragons or even sorcerers who specialize in magical theory or, preferably, practice magic. If there are those with the ability to tap in to the magics, who knows what advances we can make for shifter kind."

My mate scrunched his nose adorably. "So, you're hoping that my mom might be able to help...what, exactly? Practice magic if they bring back the knowledge on how to do so?"

"Pretty much," Beck answered. "We don't know what possibilities are out there, but with Moonmusic still posing a threat, we're willing to look into all avenues to keep our pack and others like us safe."

It was an admirable sentiment, but I couldn't help thinking that if we eventually managed to bring back the magic of our elders, they might soon follow.

Still, that should not prevent us from researching.

Micah nudged my foot with his own and smiled down at me when I looked up at him. "Ready to meet my parents?"

<h1 style="text-align:center">Chapter Fourteen</h1>

Mom's squeal could be heard all the way from California, I was certain of it. I had asked to Facetime with her and Dad, and it was surprisingly easy to tell them that I was mated —no longer a beta, but an alpha— and that they were going to have grandchildren. Sitting on Brandt's couch, with my phone propped on the coffee table in front of us, we watched my dad wince as my mom shot out of her seat, still squealing at a pitch which I feared would damage all shifter and animal hearing within a hundred-mile radius of both her house and Brandt's.

"Mom," I laughed, "stop. You're hurting my ears." I jutted my chin at my screen. "I think you made Dad deaf."

"I'm sorry," she apologized, sitting back down so we could see her in the frame of the screen again. Her blue eyes were shiny with happy tears, and she clutched her hands to her chest, "I just never dreamed this day would actually happen. The universe told me it would, but—"

That was the perfect opening for my main reason for calling, and I leapt on it. "Actually, Mom, the universe thing…can we, uh, talk about that?"

"You want to talk about the voices in your mother's head and not about the fact that you're suddenly an alpha?" Dad asked with a hint of bewilderment. "Mike, really?"

My parents, for all that they were a pair of aging naturalists, were like apples and oranges sometimes. Mom was an eternal optimist who just expected that fate and karma would do their thing, but Dad could sometimes get hung up on concepts that threw him for a loop, even if he was easy going most of the time.

It was funny how I seemed to be a mix of the two of them, and not just physically. I didn't really look like either of my parents, even if I had inherited Mom's facial structure and a similar color of hair to Dad's, but personality-wise, I was a blend of the two of them. I went with the flow...until something came along for me to hyperfixate on.

I shifted in my seat. "Well, it's just that—"

"This is kind of a big deal," he continued. "I know your friend, Brett?"

"Beckett."

"Beckett, right," he nodded. "I know he was the first alpha known to exist in hundreds of years, but I remember you saying he was practically human before he met his omega. You are —were— a beta. You already had a designation. Does it feel different to be an alpha now?"

I considered the question seriously. It had only been a day since I had first popped a knot and bitten down on Brandt's neck, and I really hadn't felt any different outside of the bond itself, and the physical changes during sex.

"Not...really," I admitted slowly as I really thought about it.

"But changes could develop over time," Brandt cut in gently. He had been nervous to meet my parents, even if he had tried to hide his anxiety. Even now, he was sitting stiffly at my side, and only speaking if he absolutely had to. Of course, that could have also been because he could barely get a word in edgewise with my mother on the call. "The three other alphas all reported their shifter senses developing over time, though they were, as you said, starting from a human baseline. Still, I suspect we may see changes to Micah's senses and abilities over the coming days, perhaps even weeks."

"Oh, Mikey, he sounds so exotic," my mother told me, making me facepalm.

"Mom," I groaned, "that's not the compliment you think it is. It's actually offensive."

Her eyes widened and suddenly the tears didn't seem as happy anymore. I immediately felt guilty. "I'm sorry," she said, "I didn't mean—"

"I know," I told her softly. "It's just that it's kind of dehumanizing and also fetishizing and—"

"And I was not offended," Brandt placed his hand on my knee and squeezed. Under his voice he added, "But thank you for defending my honor, my alpha."

I stifled a groan of an entirely different kind. "Behave," I murmured back at him, enjoying the deep, dark chuckle my plea elicited.

Then he turned his attention back to the screen and said, "Thank you for the compliment, Mrs. Hawthorne."

Mom recovered from her own guilt at rapid speed and...was that a *blush*? Oh, God, did my mother think my bondmate was hot?

While I was grappling with those disturbing thoughts, she giggled, "Oh, no, sweetie, call me Hannah." After half a breath, she asked, "Where *are* you from originally, Brandt?"

"My clan traveled around Europa —what we now call Europe— quite a lot before we eventually settled in the New World, that is, America. I believe I spent most of my formative years in what you would now call Eastern Europe; Hungary, Ukraine, Romania..." He aimed a crooked smile at the screen which made my stomach flip with instant arousal. "I am aware my accent is somewhat mottled between that and spending a couple of hundred years here..."

"It's lovely," Mom assured him. She nudged Dad with her elbow. "Isn't it, Jeff?"

Dad nodded. "Sure is." Then he looked into the camera. "Do you have any theories on why your designation changed?"

While Mom was more of a hippy than Dad, it was a little out of character for him to ask about 'theories'.

"Not really." I narrowed my gaze and leaned forward, feeling mildly suspicious of the question. "Do *you* have any theories? Because, honestly, I didn't think there was anything that really set me apart from other betas at all. Aside from...y'know."

Dad winced and nodded, while Mom rolled her eyes the way she always did when I so much as alluded to my smaller-than-average size.

"I hardly think your body issues —which are *so* unfounded, baby; you're perfect as you are— anyway, I doubt they would have anything to do with being an alpha." She bobbed her head as if punctuating the statement.

Dad's expression twisted. It was hard to really read him through my phone screen, but I knew him well enough to tell that he disagreed with her.

"Dad?" I prompted, an irrational sensation of dread welling up inside me.

The sensation increased when he sighed heavily and gave the camera a baleful, apologetic look. He opened his mouth, but Mom interrupted him, pleading, "Jeff, no. Please."

He physically turned sideways in his seat on the patchwork couch inside their shabby-chic cabin and threw his hands into the air, "We should have told him years ago, Hannah. He's in his thirties now. Almost forty. Hell, he's an *alpha*. He can handle it."

"Handle what?" I leaned in closer to the phone, feeling Brandt's large, warm palm land on my back in a bracing, comforting gesture. "Should have told me what?"

"Mikey," Dad began, raising his voice over the top of Mom's protested "Jeff, don't!"

"Mikey," he repeated in the tone that told me I was not going to like his next words, "there's a chance —a strong chance— you're not my son."

I...what?!

I slumped back against the couch, feeling like the world was spinning.

There were so many certainties in my world. Things that kept me grounded. Truths I could rely on to maintain the chill outlook I was proud to possess. Things like 'grass is green', and 'the sun rises in the east and sets in the west', and 'Hannah and Jeff Hawthorne are ridiculously, stupidly in love with each other'.

Mom would never, ever cheat. Even if they were all about free love or whatever...their relationship was solid. And Dad...Dad was my dad. He had raised me from birth. He'd taken me for my first shift. He...he...

"What?" I heard my own voice croak while thoughts and emotions spiraled in my brain. "How is that...I mean...were you, like...swingers, or...?" Because *that* I could potentially stomach. If they'd participated consensually together and...*ugh*. I didn't want to think of my parents that way.

"Oh, no, baby," my mother's answer was firm and sweet all at once. "No, nothing like that. I...well, you know we tried for years to have a baby, don't you?"

Brandt rubbed my back as I nodded.

Mom smiled sadly at me from the phone screen. I didn't know whether I wanted to hug her, or throw the phone at the wall. "Well, we...*I*...got desperate after my third miscarriage. I...the universe directed me to a shaman..."

At my side, Brandt straightened, but he didn't stop rubbing my back. "Okay...?" I prompted.

Mom's expression shuttered. "He gave us —Jeff and me both— some potions and tonics. Rituals to perform at certain phases of the moon..." Licking her lips, she exhaled. "Then, after the final new moon in the cycle, we had to return to him. We...don't remember a lot from that night, but six weeks later, my pregnancy was confirmed. And it was perfect; I didn't even have morning sickness. Then you were here, and *you* were perfect. But...well." Her face fell. "You didn't really look anything like Jeff. Didn't scent like him, either."

"It didn't matter to us. You were ours, one hundred percent, even if you might not have been mine genetically," Dad took over. "But...with the tonics and potions and moon-magic rituals...I think you've always been different from the rest of the pack, Mike. And I think—"

"That that's why I'm an alpha," I finished for him. "*That's the difference.*"

I had always felt like an outsider in my pack, after all. Maybe there was something different inside me. Something at a molecular level. Something influenced by magic.

"I'm so sorry, baby," Mom sniffled. When I blinked and focused back on the screen, she appeared distraught. My heart panged. "It...we didn't see it as any different to using a sperm donor or having a mix up with IVF or something. You were our baby. Are still our baby, regardless of how you came to be."

My thoughts shifted to my own children — the trio of embryos I hadn't actually been involved in creating, unless masturbating into a cup counted as participation. I didn't feel like I would love them any less for not having come about the traditional way, and I certainly didn't resent Brandt for his desperation to bring them into the world, either.

"I'm not gonna freak out, Mom. I'm a little shellshocked," I admitted, "but...you're right. You both raised me. You both loved me. I'm not...I mean, I am a little upset that you didn't tell me, but...it doesn't change who I am. And I am who I am because of you two."

It might explain why I didn't look anything like Dad, though. But I still took after him in personality. There was something to be said about nature vs nurture, or whatever.

"This shaman," Brandt spoke into the awkward silence descending over the call, "do you recall anything else about him? His species? Whether he remained in the area? Anything?"

Mom shook her head. "No...he was only passing through. He just seemed to be in the right place when I was at my lowest point." Her lips quirked. "A gift from the universe. From fate."

"And his scent? His species?"

"I...he wore scent blockers," she answered, frowning. "I remember finding that odd and asking him about it, and he said it helped keep his clients calm if he maintained a neutral scent, so we couldn't see him as predator or prey. I thought that was a bit funny, because we're horses — we don't prey on anything, except maybe the occasional apple tree."

Whipping my head around to look at Brandt, I blurted, "You're thinking he was a dragon, aren't you? But then..." I frowned. "He'd have to have been an alpha."

"Yes," he agreed solemnly. "However, as far as we are aware, the last known dragon alpha was—"

"Your father." I felt supremely uncomfortable at what that might mean.

"Fate wouldn't do that to you," Mom's voice filtered towards us from the phone as we stared at each other in dawning horror. "To either of you. Besides," she sniffed, "Brandt, you said you ran tests on all the samples in your lab. That would have shown a DNA match between you, wouldn't it?"

Relief washed over Brandt's handsome face. "Yes," he breathed the word out and nodded at my phone. "Yes, of course. And it did not."

"So..." I locked eyes with Brandt again, unsure how to describe the maelstrom of feelings inside me. Shock, trepidation, hope, awe, sadness...they were all there. "That must mean there's another dragon alpha out there somewhere. Or, at least, there was thirty-seven years ago."

"And he is old," Brandt added, his dark eyebrows furrowing together. "Old enough to practice magic long-thought forgotten."

That...was an intimidating thought indeed.

"Speaking of," Dad spoke up again, and I didn't like the uncertain look on his face. Even though I had just told him that I didn't see him any differently, that he was still my dad, I guessed that he was still unsure that I really meant it. "Your lifespans are drastically different. How will being bonded affect that?"

"We are not sure," Brandt answered for me. "We are the first alpha-omega pairing of different species. I would like to take samples of Micah's blood and compare them to my own, and, yes," he added, directing the next words my way, "it would be helpful to locate someone well versed in the magic and history of the old ways. They might have the answers which we have not been able to find during our research."

My parents nodded, and the silence that fell between us, sitting on Brandt's comfy leather couch, and them on the other side of the call was awkward and strained.

Brandt cleared his throat, "Similarly," he admitted, sounding apologetic, "we're unsure which species of shifter our children will be. It does not matter to either of us, obviously, but there are many unknown variables in our situation."

He's a smart, smart dragon, I mused as Mom brightened at the reminder of her grandchildren. He had known exactly what he was doing by bringing the conversation back around to them.

I squeezed his thigh in gratitude.

He squeezed my knee right back.

Nothing more needed to be said.

"I still can't believe we're getting *three* grandbabies," Mom cooed. "Tell me, have you started thinking about names? Oh, and what about clothes? Toys? Oh, boys, I hope you'll allow us to come visit. We'd love to help you in those early days. Babies are hard work, you know."

And maybe my gratitude was too pre-emptive.

"We should shift," Brandt told me a few days after the call with my parents. I wasn't sure if it was a suggestion borne of scientific curiosity, or if he was attempting to distract me from the funk I'd fallen into.

Because, as much as I had told everyone that the bomb my parents had dropped on me didn't bother me...it kind of did.

I had spent my entire life feeling like an outsider in an otherwise accepting, supportive pack. For years, I had thought there was something wrong with me. They were nice people, *good* people, and I still hadn't felt right with them.

Was it because some part of me had always known I was different?

I understood why my parents hadn't told me. They didn't want to hurt or confuse me, and I appreciated that. But when I had packed up to leave —when I had explicitly told them it was because I knew I didn't belong— they should have said something.

No matter what happened with my kids, I vowed that I would always be honest and upfront with them.

And, Gods, I was having kids of my own.

I had no idea what I really was, genetically speaking, and I was having kids with a stranger.

Well, no. He wasn't really a stranger anymore. Brandt and I had spent days exploring our bond, and getting to know each other properly. From favorite foods and movies to our deepest dreams and wishes, we had been sharing as much information with each other as possible. And, thanks to the bond we shared, he felt like he was a part of me already.

So, I suspected Brandt's suggestion to shift was probably less about science and more about drawing me out of my mood.

It worked.

"You mean I *finally* get to see a real dragon?" I leapt from the couch and grinned, probably confusing him with my sudden enthusiasm.

He chuckled. "Yes. And I get to meet your horse."

"That seems a bit anti-climactic next to a fire-breathing dragon," I replied, then shrugged, "but you do you, sugar."

"Come on," he reached for my hand and tugged me towards the front door. "This is long overdue. You are my bondmate, and you deserve to be acquainted with every part of me, and I with you."

He made valid points, I had to give him that.

Brandt drove us to the clinic and parked in the parking lot in front of the building. "We will walk from here. I need space to shift."

"Just how big is your dragon?" I asked with awe as I followed him around the cottage which housed his lab.

"Well," he responded contemplatively, "when I am shifted, my claws are large enough to hold grown humans easily. And I could eat a fully grown human in a single bite, too."

My eyes widened. "Wow."

"However," he continued, "like all shifters, I am completely cognizant of my actions when I am in shifted form. You have no reason to fear me."

"Aww," I couldn't hold back the amused, fond sound. "That's really sweet, but I'm not going to be afraid of you. You're my mate. My omega. The only way you're going to eat me is if you eat my—"

"*Whoa*, little ears present," Rex's southern drawl cut me off with a laugh as we rounded the corner behind the cottage, heading towards the fields at the back of the property. The puma shifter smirked at me as I snapped my mouth shut. "Hi there, boys." He lifted the toddler on his hip. "Say hi to Uncle Bran, Cam."

"Ban!" the little guy said, and I watched my mate turn to mush.

Gasping, Brandt reached out to pluck the toddler from Rex's grasp. "Very good, little one!" he declared, then looked at Rex. "When did he learn my name?"

"Maybe yesterday? The day before? He's been saying Pa and Da for a while now, but Day's been tryin' to get more out of him. You're his fourth word." As an aside to me, Rex added, "His third was 'no'."

I snorted. I hadn't known Damon and Rex long, nor had I spent much time with them, but it wasn't a surprise that their son was learning to be stubborn and argumentative early on.

"Such a clever boy," Brandt fussed at the kid in his arms. He was beaming at him, and the smile made him look so much younger and lighter. Not that I didn't think he was super hot with the brooding smolder, mind you. "Can you say it again? Say Uncle Brandt?"

Cam giggled and nodded. "No!"

Inside me, my alpha radiated warmth and pride as I watched my mate continue to play with the toddler. It took me a long moment to understand that he —that *I*— was imagining the omega with our children.

Holy shit, we were going to have this for ourselves before too long.

Only, for us, there would be three of them.

"Ah, I know that feelin'," Rex patted my shoulder and gave me a knowing smile. "Is reality finally hitting you?"

It was one thing to know that my mate was pregnant, but something entirely different to witness him interacting with a baby. He was glowing with happiness as he continued to chatter with the boy, tickling the kid and making him squeal. It definitely reinforced my belief that I would never have refused him the chance to have kids of his own, but it also made my heart rate increase with mild panic.

Because —and I might not have mentioned this yet— we were having *three* of them.

Soon.

"You're okay," Rex patted my back. "They start off pretty small and helpless, and that makes it easier in a lot of ways."

"I'm not freaking out," I lied a little, then I sighed. "I mean, I am, but not because I don't want this. It's just...it's so soon, you know? And what if I'm not as good with kids as he is? Because look at him." I gestured towards Brandt, who was now laughing as he tossed Cam into the air and caught him again, much to the toddler's raucous delight. "He's a natural."

"He is, yeah," Rex agreed. "But Beck and Ollie both say you're awesome with the twins. And, really, it is easier when they're your own, too. You're the one setting the boundaries on how to interact with them, and your instincts kick in and you just know what's best for them. Or, at least, you *want* to do what's best for them." He shrugged. "Sometimes it doesn't always work out."

"That's ominous."

"That's parenthood."

Before I could respond, Brandt brought Cam back to his father. "I wish to continue playing, however Micah and I have plans to shift and meet each other in our shifted forms for the first time."

Rex grinned. "How'd you get that past Eric? He'd want to observe something that huge, wouldn't he?"

"He would," Eric himself appeared behind us and Brandt stifled a groan as his brother approached. "Especially because you're the first mixed-breed alpha-omega pairing. It only makes sense for someone to be there to document the occasion so we have a record of it."

"And on that note," Rex propped Cam on his hip and dipped his Stetson, "I'm out. I think this little guy's ready for a bath and a nap anyway. Say bye-bye to Uncle Brandt and Micah and Eric, sweetheart."

Cam waved and smiled. "No!"

Brandt chuckled.

"Seriously, though," Eric arched an eyebrow as he looked between us, "you weren't really planning on doing this without asking someone to take notes, were you?"

"I can take my own notes," Brandt responded almost petulantly.

Having grown up as an only child, I'd never experienced what it was like to have a sibling, and it was amusing to watch Brandt interact with his youngest brother. Even though they were hundreds of years old, they really did seem to behave like pre-teens when they were together.

Will our three be the same?

The thought reminded me that I hadn't even had a chance to see what adding the middle brother, Sage, into the mix did for their dynamic.

"Well, I'm coming with you," Eric declared in the same sort of tone. "You're too close to the situation to present an unbiased account."

Brandt scowled, but I placed a placating hand on his shoulder. "Just let him, sugar. I want to see you shift."

"Besides," Eric added cheerfully, "it will be interesting to see if you feel the same sort of lethargy in shifted form that the other omegas reported during their shifts. Of course, you're only just in the early stages of your second trimester, so we should definitely get you to shift at least once a week to monitor your energy levels across the rest of your pregnancy."

Brandt gave me a baleful look. "He never switches off."

"Maybe he needs an alpha of his own."

"*Gah,*" Eric shook his head, and if I wasn't mistaken, his already pale tone seemed to turn a little whiter. "No. Nope. Not for me. I'd rather just observe and record data. I don't need the lived experience."

Interesting.

I shared a glance with Brandt who winked back, then teased, "Are you afraid of mating, little brother?"

"Of course not," Eric turned his nose up, his mop of blonde hair flopping backwards with the movement. "But not every omega wants the whole 'picket fence with an alpha and two point three pups' lifestyle. They shouldn't *have* to want it to be taken seriously, either."

I felt a little guilty for being so amused at his refusal of a mate. "That's fair," I told him, nodding. "Your designation shouldn't determine your life goals or your dreams. If you don't want an alpha and kids, that's not a bad thing."

"But it is not wrong to want them, either," Brandt defended his own feelings, and I took his hand, bringing it to my lips so I could brush a soft kiss over the backs of his knuckles.

"Not at all, sugar."

"Anyway," Eric shook out his shoulders. "Are we doing this thing or not? I have appointments in an hour."

Brandt was magnificent. His dragon form was *huge*. At least the size of a small building, when you included his thick, scaled legs and his massive, spiked tail, not to mention his enormous head.

He had made me stand half a field away from him as he shifted, but as soon as his transformation was complete, I hurried towards him. The closer I got, the bigger he loomed.

His scales were a dark, blood red color. I had seen them before, of course, when they had framed his face during our mating, but to see the effect on the entire, massive dragon was something else. They glinted red in the sunlight, but would probably appear black at night time. His face was adorned with pearly-white spikes, running along his snout and in the space I would call his eyebrows. Larger versions of the same spikes traveled in parallel lines down his back, trailing into a singular line down his tail and clustering near the tip. His tail alone would be a deadly weapon.

As I approached, I noticed that his eyes were just giant versions of the eyes I was becoming so familiar with: deep, soulful brown orbs that I could drown in if I let myself. And then there were his wings, which he extended, presumably for me to properly see them.

The backs of his wings were scaled, but underneath was almost leathery. I wanted to run my hands over the smooth, inviting surface, but with his height and mass, I was way too short to reach.

One day, I told myself, running my palms over the scales I could reach on his arm.

When he dipped his head, bringing his eye down to my level, I realized that the diameter of his eyeball was only a little smaller than I was tall. I grinned at him and patted his muzzle.

"You are gorgeous, Bran," I murmured in awe, and I'm almost certain he purred. Then shifted his head and nudged me with his nose, pushing me backwards.

"What?" I asked him, even though he couldn't answer.

He snorted, and warm air blew up dust from the ground at my feet. Lifting his claw, Brandt pointed at his chest, then ran the same talon from the top of my head to my feet.

It still took me a moment to understand. "Oh! My turn to shift. Got it."

He snorted again and nodded.

"I'm telling you, my horse form is *way* less impressive." I repeated my earlier argument. "I probably should have gone first."

The dragon in front of me let out a grumbly, growly sound which I read as irritation. Some people might have thought it was scary, but I just thought it was adorable.

"Okay, okay," I whipped my shirt off, "I'm doing it."

I turned my back on Eric and removed the rest of my clothes, then forced my shift as quickly as possible.

It felt...strange.

When Brandt had shifted, I had focused on the sensations through the bond in awe. His form was so different to mine, and so feeling him grow and contort and sprout wings had been something completely new to me.

But my own shift, which I thought I knew better than the back of my hand, felt somewhat new, too. Not completely. My shape was still fundamentally the same. But...it kept going, tugging and contorting my back and, strangely, my forehead in ways that felt kind of reminiscent of Brandt's shift.

Through our bond, I felt a jolt of deep, intense shock, and it made me look up at my mate. His dragon eyes were wide with human levels of wonder, and he let out another huff of warm air as he took a couple of lumbering steps backward.

I brayed at him, wishing I could demand an answer for his intense surprise —surely he had seen a simple horse before— and I stomped my front hooves in the dirt, kicking up another cloud of dust.

"Holy shit," I turned at the sound of Eric's awed declaration. "Micah...do you feel anything different?"

I rolled my eyes as best I could and whinnied, because how the hell did he expect me to answer? Then I remembered I could still nod and if I'd been in my human form, I would have facepalmed. Chuffing, I nodded at him.

He grinned at me, and it seemed almost manic. "You're...actually, no, hang on." He pulled out his phone and took a photo of me, then hurried forward, tilting the screen so I could see it.

What the actual fuck?

I let out a startled squeal and reeled backwards, suddenly feeling uncoordinated in a way that I hadn't since my first childhood shifts. My long legs felt gangly as if I was a foal, and I stumbled away from the strange thing I had just seen.

"Whoa," Eric shoved his phone back into his pocket and held both hands up to placate me as I reared back onto my hindquarters, kicking at the air with my front legs. "Calm down. It's okay. Really. It's okay."

How? I wanted to demand, but I didn't have the ability to speak, what with being shifted and all. *How is it okay?*

Because the photo he had shown me hadn't been of my usual horse form. No: the creature in the photo had wings and a horn.

A unicorn.

What the hell was happening to me?

Chapter Fifteen

As I watched my beautiful mate rear back with confusion and fear —emotions which resonated deep inside my chest and took my breath away— I hurriedly shifted back into my human form and rushed to him.

As I neared, I took in every detail that I could. His coat was an almost metallic golden color, like the rarest of the Akhal-Teke breed of horses, and the color extended to the sleek wings tucked against his flank. He had long, elegant legs and what appeared to be a silky-smooth mane in a shimmering golden-white color. But it was the metallic gold unicorn horn in the middle of his forehead, perfectly twirled and tapered to a deadly sharp point at the end, which stood out the most.

"Darling," I soothed him, reaching out to stroke his soft, smooth flank as I approached from the side, "it's all right. You are magnificent."

He turned his head towards me, and I had the presence of mind to duck before his horn could make contact. His nostrils flared and he released a short snort of air rather forcefully.

"You are," I insisted, stroking the side of his neck. I marveled at how silky and smooth his coat was. It was almost iridescent in the sunlight. "I understand this is a shock, however you are breathtaking, Micah."

"A unicorn," Eric declared, sounding just as awed as I felt. He carefully walked towards me, also approaching from the side, though I was certain my mate would not kick out with his powerful hooves.

My brother glanced at me with wide eyes. "Have you heard of unicorn shifters?"

Aware that Micah was watching me, I shook my head slowly. "No. However, many believe that dragons are myths these days, too. Perhaps unicorns have concealed their existence better than us?"

Eric considered this and nodded, even as his eyes continued to travel over my mate's shifted form. "True," he said, in the distracted tone he often used when he was thinking. "So much knowledge has been lost to time...unicorns could be one of those things."

Micah's fright and panic had eased out of our bond and I smiled at him, reaching towards his horn. "May I?" I asked.

He let out a gentler chuff of breath and lowered his head carefully. When my fingertips brushed the glossy gold surface, I was momentarily surprised. "It's warm," I said out loud, more for Micah's benefit than for Eric's, though I knew he was taking notes. My brother was also likely dying of jealousy, but I just knew that Micah would not allow him the privilege of this kind of exploration. At least, not yet. When I stroked the gold ridges a little more firmly, Micah nickered. A rush of arousal traveled through the bond and I immediately understood.

He must feel the same way as I do when he strokes the scales on my face.

"Apologies, darling," I soothed.

"What? Why? Talk me through what's happening." Eric demanded with a hint of a whine. "Please, Bran."

"It's an erogenous zone," I murmured, removing my fingers and stroking the length of Micah's muzzle instead. "I felt similarly when I par-shifted during our mating, and he stroked the scales on my face. Instant arousal."

"Huh," from the corner of my eye, I watched my youngest brother tilt his head and cock his hip. "I've never experienced anything like that."

"Have your scales erupted during sex?"

"Well...no." He frowned at me. "Most men don't like it when you go lizard on them mid-coitus."

Micah snorted lightly, and I assumed he felt as amused as I did.

"Humans, no," I agreed with Eric's sentiments, "but shifters can surprise you."

"Yeah, well, it's not something I've ever done — spontaneously or otherwise." He frowned at me. "Have you always—*pppffft*?" he accompanied the odd sound with extended fingers gesturing at his face.

I chuckled. "No. It only happens when I am extremely...how do people phrase it now? Into it?"

"Don't strain yourself to sound young, Bran," he teased me in response, "and there's no need for euphemisms, either. It's a hyper-aroused thing, huh?"

"I suppose," I shrugged. "It has happened every time with my mate, though."

"Fascinating..."

I groaned. "Please do not tell me you wish to watch us mate. I draw the line at that."

Micah stamped his front hooves and whipped his nearly-white tail in what I assumed was agreement.

"Ew, no. Not even for science, big brother." Eric shuddered.

Rolling my eyes, I turned my complete attention back to my mate. "Should we test your wings?"

His body swayed as he stepped backwards, shaking his head.

"Darling," I pleaded, "I will shift and fly with you." Just speaking the promise filled me with anticipation and excitement. "Fate...the universe —however you wish to see it— has granted us the ability to fly together. Is that not a sign to you?"

Apprehension traveled between us and I tried to see this from his perspective. This was the first time he had shifted into this form. For his entire life, he had been a horse, comfortable on the ground. The ground was firm and stable and solid: the sky was unknown and fathomless. Then there was the risk of falling, of plummeting to certain death from unsurvivable heights.

"I will be with you," I told him gently. "I won't allow anything to happen to you."

On some level, a voice at the back of my head said that he had no reason to trust me. I had not yet earned his trust, not so soon at any rate. However, my mate proved that voice wrong, letting out a sigh before he bowed his head in obvious acquiescence.

"We will not go too high or too fast," I promised him, backing away so that I could shift in return.

He neighed at me and stamped his hooves again, stretching out his wings as he gave them what I could only describe as an experimental shake.

"It will come naturally," I told him, assuming he was making a point of not knowing how to fly. "I will attempt to share through the bond what I feel when I take flight, but your instincts should take over."

There were no more disgruntled sounds, so I backed away and then shifted back into my dragon form. I did not feel too drained, and I made a note to report as much to Eric, as much as it irritated me that I had become his lab rat. Still, it would help us to treat our pack's shifters, and to share the knowledge with others like us around the world.

With the shift completed, I looked down at my mate and purred with appreciation. My dragon had never seen anything as perfect. Even though our size difference was ridiculous, that was my alpha. My mate. And he was glorious.

Forcing myself to concentrate on what usually came naturally, I flexed my wings for flight. Leaping from the ground, I beat my wings to create thrust, working the muscles until I was soaring through the air, gliding and only flapping when necessary. I focused on sending the entire process through the connection I shared with Micah, and I paired it with encouragement.

Then I circled the field, watching with bated breath.

At first, Micah attempted to repeat my actions. His equine form reared back on its hind legs and leaped, beating its wings...only to land without any lift off. He gave it a few tries, all with the same results, before Eric moved towards him. I assumed my brother was giving my mate some kind of pep talk or advice, but from my altitude, I could not hear what he said.

But I felt a wave of determination emanating from the bond before Micah's golden form turned around and galloped through the field. I followed from above, and felt a surge of pride for him as he sprang forward during his run into the wind, spreading his wings and finally gaining the lift and thrust he had been missing before.

I swooped down to meet him, giving him space to get his bearings, but remaining close enough that I could intervene as promised should anything go wrong.

At first, the emotions that traveled through the bond were shock and awe, followed by fear as he rose higher and higher into the air, leaving the ground far behind us. But, as his wings slowed their frantic beating and began to glide and flap slowly in the same relaxed pattern as my own, the fear dissipated.

His coat and horn reflected the sun's rays as he experimented with dipping and diving along currents of air. Had I been human, I would have whooped as I joined him, twirling around his smaller form as he became more confident with his abilities.

Joy tinted with disbelief filtered through the bond, and I was certain he could feel my echoing enjoyment and amusement, too. Never in my wildest dreams had I dared to believe that my mate —my alpha— would have the capacity to join me in flight.

I lost track of time as we meandered through the sky above Beck's farmland, but movement below us caught my eye. Focusing, I smothered a dragonly sigh at the sight of my brother waving us down.

Making certain that Micah was following me, I began a lazy descent, then landed not far from where I had taken flight. I cast my gaze back up to the sky to watch as my mate also came in for a landing, his hooves touching the ground so he could canter then trot to a stop. He made the movement seem effortless, as though he had been flying his entire life.

"Sorry to cut that short," Eric apologized as we shifted back to our human forms. "But I really do have appointments to get to, and I have *so* many questions..."

"Yeah, well," Micah breathed heavily as he hastily tugged on his underwear, sounding as if he had been running a marathon, "you know where we, uh, where Brandt lives. You could have come knocking later. Or, better yet, texted."

Eric shrugged. "I could have, but this way I can take new blood samples." His eyes lit up. "I'd like to take them from you in shifted form, too, if possible."

"Does it have to be right now?" I asked him, which earned me a baleful glare.

"Aren't you itching to get answers too?"

I was actually itching to get my alpha back into bed, but I did not think Eric would appreciate that answer, so I sighed. "I suppose I would like to do some research on the existence of unicorns." I cast Micah an apologetic glance. "We are starting from scratch when it comes to knowledge of your kind."

"My kind," he repeated. "I'm a horse. That...the wings and the horn and the super shiny gold coat? That's not my usual form. I mean, I've always been a golden color...but not like that."

"Perhaps," Eric postulated, "you're not all that different to the other alphas after all. I mean, yeah, you knew you were a shifter...but your alpha is an entirely different breed which you never knew about, much like they didn't know they could shift at all." He pulled out his phone to type notes. "I wish we had some sort of baseline reading of the others' blood prior to their alphas making an appearance. I know we have yours," he looked up at Micah briefly before burying his nose in his screen again, "but, for obvious reasons, we don't have any of the others on file."

"And they can't contact their doctors from before they shifted?"

Eric's head shot up and he met my wide-eyed stare before slowly turning back to Micah. "I never even thought of that." Before Micah could say anything more, Eric flung himself into his arms and kissed his cheek. "You're brilliant!"

Pausing with my shorts halfway up my legs, I growled.

"Scales, sugar," Micah extricated himself from my brother's grasp and closed the space between us, cupping my jaw. I shuddered as he ran his thumb over the side of my face. "You're the only omega for me."

"Sorry," Eric sounded genuinely apologetic. "I keep forgetting how possessive pregnant omegas can be. Especially in the early days of their bond forming."

"You won't forget if I bite you," I grumbled back at him, and Micah chuckled as he resumed dressing.

"I think the growly, jealous vibes are hot, sugar."

I huffed, "I am not *jealous*. You are *mine*."

Eric snorted.

I rolled my eyes at my brother. "You can shut up."

"I didn't say anything," he protested, but he sounded amused.

Choosing to pointedly ignore him as we finished getting dressed, I accepted Micah's outstretched hand and fell into step with him as we made our way back towards the clinic. Eric trailed behind us, asking Micah questions about his shift and how it differed to his original form.

"Yeah, once I was in the air instinct just...took over, I guess," Micah answered when Eric asked him about his first flight. We approached the front door to the clinic and he opened the door, gesturing for me and Eric to precede him inside.

Chivalry is not yet dead, I thought as I smiled and walked inside.

"Well look who decided to come to work," Day teased from the receptionist desk.

"It is a tough life being one of your bosses," I sassed back, coming to a stop in front of him. I folded my arms across my chest. "When were you going to tell me your son was speaking, hmm?"

He had the grace to appear apologetic. "With the excitement of everything else happening, I forgot to brag," he admitted. "Sorry, Bran. Rex texted and said you got to hear it in person, though."

"I did." I grinned, feeling all warm and gooey at the memory of hearing the little voice speak a broken version of my name. "It is very exciting. He is growing up so fast."

"They do that," he agreed lightly, then gestured at my belly with his chin, the corner of his lips quirking. "It won't be long until yours are here and growing like weeds."

"Six months at most," I smoothed my palm over the soft bulge which I swore was more prominent than it had been only a few days earlier. "But with multiples, it will likely be sooner."

He grimaced. "I do not envy you having to push three of them out. I felt wrecked enough after one, and you both said it was such a quick and easy delivery." He shuddered as if reliving the experience. "Never again."

"But is it not worth it to have your son?"

Playfully, Day rolled his eyes. "Fine, bring up the reward at the end. Let's see if you're as cheerful after popping one of yours out, shall we?"

"I still reserve the right to complain about the pain."

"Too late," he turned away to tap at his computer keyboard. "*Think of the reward*, Bran."

I looked over at my mate, who was still patiently answering Eric's questions, and I imagined how patient he would be with our babies.

Think of the reward indeed.

Chapter Sixteen

Number three —four? fifty? whatever— on the list of things I had not been expecting when I planned my return to Shifters Sanctuary: no longer being a horse. I still *felt* like a horse, but I wasn't a horse.

I was a mythical flying horse with a horn in the middle of my forehead.

A unicorn.

I was a unicorn.

Days after that revelation, and I was still trying to process the change. Still trying to reconcile the me I had always known with the me I had become. The me I apparently had always been deep down inside.

My alpha was a preening, cocky asshole. From the moment I had shifted, I had felt his pride —my inner pride— warming my soul. I had felt *right* in ways I hadn't felt while shifted before. Was it any wonder I had never truly felt like I belonged in my original pack?

I wasn't one of them. I'd been an imposter and I hadn't known it.

Also, this pretty much cemented my parents' suspicion that my dad wasn't biologically my father. It didn't change how much I loved my dad, but I had to admit that I wish I had known earlier, that I could have researched, or tracked the shaman down, or…something.

Because being blindsided by being an entirely different breed or species of shifter was something else.

"Do you think you're the only one of your kind?" Beck asked me as we sat on his back porch, each nursing a bottle of beer as his kids ran around on the grassed area in front of us. "Or do you think there are more unicorns out there?" He snorted and shook his head. "Unicorns. Jesus, that sounds outrageous." He shot me an apologetic grimace. "Shit, sorry."

I waved him off as the sound of toddlers battling waged on in the background of our conversation. "Nah, I get it. It feels outrageous, even though I'm *definitely* a unicorn now."

I'd tried shifting twice more, just in case the first time was an anomaly or a shared hallucination. Both times, I had shifted into the golden-colored unicorn, wings and all.

"So…is this just a you thing, do you think?" Beck repeated his question, then leaned forward in his seat and called out, "Rory, we don't sit on our brother's head! Let Duke up, please!" After his daughter reluctantly complied, he slumped back in his seat. "They're little savages."

Case in point: as soon as he was able to get back to his feet, Duke roared and crash tackled his sister back down to the grass.

I laughed.

"Oh, sure, laugh it up," he sighed as Rory screamed and wrestled her twin with a vicious sort of energy that fascinated me. "Just remember, you're getting *three* of these. Good luck, I say."

"Yeah, well, maybe mine will be docile." I winced as Duke cried out when his sister sank her teeth into his arm.

"Shit," Beck sighed again and pushed to his feet. "Anyone who says they get easier as they get older is a lying liar who lies."

"Daddy!" Duke cried, shoving his sister to the ground and making a break for Beck. "My bited! My ouchie!"

"I know, bud," Beck scooped him up and kissed over the tiny toothy imprints in the otherwise soft, unblemished toddler's skin. "I've kissed it better."

"Awe-y mean!" From his perch on Beck's hip, Duke glared at his sister, who poked her tongue back out at him.

"Rory was a little mean, yes," Beck agreed, rubbing his son's back, "but you were both playing rough."

"Awe-y mean!" the kid repeated.

Beck nodded again, then looked my way. I didn't love the glint in his eyes before he adopted an excited tone, "I know what will make it better," he declared to his whimpering toddler. "Who wants to see a unicorn?"

Ten minutes later, I was cursing my new pack alpha and both of his hell spawn. They couldn't hear me, though, because I was in my shifted form, but if Beck didn't stop them from tugging at my tail and wings, I was going to run him through with the pointy weapon permanently fastened to my forehead.

"Ooh-nicown!" Rory shrieked happily, her pudgy little hands smacking down on my back, courtesy of the fact that her father —my *former* friend— had put both toddlers there like I was one of those pony rides.

The only one riding me like a pony is my mate, I grumbled to myself, immediately feeling better at the images the thought brought to mind.

"Yes, he is a unicorn," Beck responded to his daughter with the patience of a man not currently being treated like a fairground attraction, "and you have to be gentle with him."

"Pity," Duke added.

"He is very pretty," Beck agreed.

"What are you...*Beckett*," Oliver's exasperated voice came from the house and I turned to find Beck's omega scowling down at us, "did you even ask Micah if it was okay before you turned him into their latest distraction?"

I couldn't contain my nicker of amusement as Beck's shoulders slumped guiltily. "He loves them, though," he argued. "Plus, he's going to have triplets. Think of this as practice for his future."

"You're ridiculous," Ollie's response was accompanied by a shake of his head, but even I could hear the fondness in his tone. "It's nap time now, anyway" — he pointedly ignored the dual cries of 'No nap!' from my back— "so you can stop torturing your friend."

The kids cried and stomped their little feet as they were hauled away and up onto the porch, and I took the opportunity to shift back to my human form and hurriedly put my clothes back on. By the time Beck returned from handing his offspring to his mate, I was dressed again, standing in the middle of the expanse of yard space with my arms folded and an eyebrow raised.

Beck gave me a sheepish smile. "So...your unicorn form is awesome," he started, and I couldn't help but laugh.

"Thanks," I said as I chuckled. "But that's still the last time you volunteer me as your kids' pet for the day."

"Aww, but Brandt always goes dragon for them."

The mention of my mate made me smile. "He would."

"I thought you said you liked kids," Beck teased.

"I said I'd always wanted kids of my own. Your monsters are your problem, dude."

He snorted. "Oh, in that case, let's see if I'm sympathetic when you're getting negative three hours sleep a night." He shuddered exaggeratedly. "There's a reason they use sleep deprivation as a torture device."

"You're my Pack Alpha now," I reminded him, giving his shoulder a nudge with mine as we made our way back up onto the porch, collecting our lukewarm beers, "you have to be sympathetic to me."

He took a draw from his beer and made a face at the bottle before asking, "Are you okay with that? Me being your Alpha?"

"Why wouldn't I be?"

I followed him inside and he took my beer from me as we entered the kitchen, replacing it with a cold bottle from the refrigerator. "Well," he replied, then gestured for me to head through to the living room, "we were roommates. Equals. Friends. I wasn't even a shifter. And now I'm the official leader of the pack you've moved into and that...well, it might make things awkward. Especially with you being another alpha, and one of such a unique breed…Like, I mean, I haven't learned all the rules yet, but you could probably challenge me for my spot here."

Only just having sat down on the couch, I almost choked on the mouthful of cold, crisp alcohol I had just taken. Coughing and spluttering, I shook my head. "Challenge you?" I asked incredulously. "Dude, no. I don't want that kind of responsibility. It's enough coming to terms with being an alpha at all, *and* there's the 'gonna be a dad' thing on top of that. My dance card is full, your position as the pack's boss is safe."

"I'm not your boss," he protested, then groaned and rolled his eyes when he realized I was teasing him. "Dick."

I shrugged. "You're the one making a big deal out of the Pack Alpha thing. I just want to settle down with my baby mama and live the life that makes my inner alpha content."

"Oh, please let me be there when you call Brandt your baby mama in front of him."

"You don't think he'd find it endearing? He likes my nicknames and sweet talking."

It was Beck's turn to cough over a mouthful of beer. "Dude," he complained, "I don't need to hear that."

"I didn't mean in a sex way…but he does like that, too, I guess."

"*Anyway,*" he pushed on, ignoring my childish attempts to make him uncomfortable. "You never got a chance to answer earlier: do you think you're the only unicorn out there? Some sort of…magical anomaly?"

"Honestly, I have no idea. Eric and Brandt seem to think that's unlikely, as surprised as they both were by my new form, but seeing as they can't find any records of unicorn shifters at all…" I shrugged. "Who knows?"

"Have they reached out to Sage and Dex? Asked them to add 'find unicorns' to their 'find magic' mission?" He paused and screwed up his nose, leaning his head against the headrest of his faded armchair. "Listen to the words coming out of my mouth. This sounds surreal."

"Yeah," I bobbed my head and took another sip of my drink, then leaned forward and let the bottle dangle from my fingertips between my spread knees. Tilting my head in his direction, I added, "I grew up as a shifter and this all sounds far-fetched to me, too." Taking a breath, I continued, "As for Sage and Dexter...yeah. Eric called them the day I shifted. We're all working blind here at the moment."

Snorting, Beck brought his bottle to his lips again, "Story of my life, man."

Chapter Seventeen

In the following weeks, Eric, Ollie and I continued to research, searching old records for any mentions of unicorns or the old magics. Word traveled through the pack about the existence of unicorns, specifically the unicorn living in Shifters Sanctuary, and Micah spent a substantial amount of time meeting our neighbors and other members of the town and patiently promised that he would attend the next pack run if only to sate their curiosity. (And, when he followed through on the promise, there was no chance of him and I having any alone time until we took flight.)

Meanwhile, Sage and Dexter checked in from various international locations, where they were presumably meeting with other dragons who might be hording old texts or, better still, personal knowledge of the magic or old ways.

In my personal life, Micah and I grew closer. He returned to New York for a few days to retrieve his clothes and personal belongings, organized the termination of his lease (apologizing to his roommates for the sudden and short notice), and then formally moved into my home.

My omega preened at the knowledge that our alpha —*my* alpha— was staking his claim so officially and publicly. After hundreds of years without alphas, I considered myself an independent omega, but there was still something comforting on a cellular level in feeling so wanted by my alpha that he would restructure his entire life for me and our pups.

Speaking of our pups, I woke one morning, roughly a month following our bonding, to a much rounder belly than the one I had gone to sleep with. It was mind boggling to experience, but I had most certainly 'popped' overnight. At almost eighteen weeks pregnant with triplets, I was surprised that it had not happened earlier...but then, my belly had been soft and rounded to begin with.

My mate and I had fallen into a routine where he would wake early, go for a jog in human form, return and shower, then crawl back into bed with me. On this particular morning, I woke while he was still showering, and he emerged from the ensuite bathroom in a billow of steam with his towel cinched around his waist.

"What's wrong?" he demanded, closing the distance between the bathroom door and the bed. "I felt surprise from the bond and—oh, *wow*."

I was rubbing the pronounced swell of my belly, still awed by my sudden overnight change of physiology. We slept naked, but I did not bother to cover up. My mate probably knew my body better than I did by that point.

I had yet to feel the babies move, but now it felt so much more real just seeing the evidence of their existence. Looking up at Micah, I blinked back tears of awe and happiness. "It feels very real now."

"I'll bet," he sank to his knees on the carpeted floor, bringing his face in line with the side of my rounded abdomen, "can I…"

"You never need permission with me, darling," I murmured, feeling his awe and trepidation trickle through the link connecting us. "I trust you."

It honestly ran much deeper than simple trust and affection, but I was aware that I had already piled a lot onto the man's plate already. Springing big words like 'I love you' on him when he was still coming to terms with everything else did not seem fair.

Nevertheless, I was certain that he could feel how I felt about him, and it had not yet sent him running for the hills.

His hand shook before he placed it ever so gently beside mine, and then he dropped a whisper soft kiss on the stretching skin, too. A lump developed in my throat at the tender gesture, making it hard to swallow.

"Pretty much halfway," he murmured, rubbing over the distention in a swooping circle. "That's" —he glanced up, his smile fading— "hey, sugar, what's wrong?"

I shook my head, trying —and failing— to swallow around the emotion. "You are a good man…a good alpha," I told him. "This is all hormones, but seeing you just now, imagining the father you will be…Fate has been kind to me. Kinder than I deserve."

"We're not—"

"No, no," I acknowledged, "there is no need to circle back to the things I did wrong, I know. But I still feel incredibly lucky that you are my mate, Micah. My alpha."

Pushing to his feet, he removed his towel, throwing it in the direction of the bathroom. He crawled onto his side of the bed, pressing his long, lean body along the length of mine. "I feel just as lucky to have you," he said, nuzzling his smooth cheek against my goatee. "You're giving me a life I could only dream about. A pack where I don't feel like an outsider," he placed his hand on my belly again, "a family —children— of my own. A future where I don't feel like I'm constantly scrambling to have a purpose. That's all because you accepted me as your mate, Bran. As your alpha. And that's to say nothing of the fact that I don't feel like I'm physically disappointing anymore, because you're kind of perfect for me."

Love flickered through the bond between us: an emotion so pure and so layered that I couldn't quite describe it. Nor could I tell you which of us it started with. We both felt it, both looped it back to one another.

I chuckled wetly, feeling overwhelmed all over again. "Only kind of perfect?"

Instead of answering, Micah hummed and kissed my jaw, then down my neck, then over my chest. My nipples were still sensitive, but ripples of intense pleasure shot across my nerve endings as he nibbled gently over one pebbled nub and then the other. His hand stroked my rapidly swelling cock as he continued to toy with my chest. I became slick, and I writhed under his attentions, gasping when he released my erection and slid two fingers inside me without warning.

"Oh, fuck, Micah..." I all but purred, rocking my hips to match the rhythm of his fingers. "Gods, *yes.*"

"You get so wet for me, sugar," he crooned into my ear before biting down gently on my lobe. "I love the way you feel on my fingers, so hot and ready for me."

"*Nnngh.*"

He was rocking his hips as well, and I felt the sticky, wet head of his hard cock leaving trails of precum on the side of my belly. I wanted to beg for him to slip inside me, to fill me up with his perfect dick and his amazing knot, but his fingers felt too good.

"I love feeling how turned on you get," he whispered hotly, his face still plastered to the side of mine, "with your slick, and your perfect cock, and through the bond. I'm surrounded by your pleasure, sweetheart. I love it so much."

Every thrust of his wrist took me closer and closer to the edge of release. With the way my hormones had been, I felt like I was perpetually aroused, but it was an entirely different level once Micah encouraged it.

"I want to feel you wrapped around my knot so badly, Bran," he continued with his beautiful, filthy and somehow still so sweet monologue, "want you to squeeze every drop of cum from my dick until I can't give even a tiny bit more."

I felt my scales break out around my temples and over my forehead, and I was unable to hold them back.

Micah's smile teased at my cheek, and satisfaction rumbled across our mystical connection. "That's it," his voice dipped low with additional lust, "that's what I want. Lose yourself, sugar. Give in to how good this feels. Let me take care of you."

His nose brushed over the scales along my temple and I groaned at the burst of pure bliss I felt from him doing so.

"M-Micah..." I pleaded his name, but I had no idea what I was pleading for.

"Fuck, sweetheart, you really like it when I touch your scales, don't you? You get even wetter for me" —as if to test his theory, he pressed a kiss to the scales along my hairline and I could feel my slick increase— "*yes*, baby, like that. Just like that."

My neglected cock throbbed in time with my erratic heartbeat. However, I was too lost to the pleasure to take care of it myself. I was panting as I writhed. I needed...*something*. Anything. I wanted to come, but I wanted the moment to last forever. I wanted my mate inside me, but I also never wanted him to stop fucking me with his fingers. I wanted him to keep saying those decadent, naughty things. I wanted...I wanted...

"Bran, sugar, fuck yes...keep spilling over my fingers...God, I'm just imagining being inside your perfect hole again, filling you all up, *breeding* you so you're always full of my pups."

"Fuck!" I roared and arched from the bed, clamping around his fingers as I came, cock untouched, all over the underside of my swollen belly. The orgasm was short, but intense.

Micah groaned and swore as the feelings of it through the bond pushed him to orgasm as well, coating my side with his release even as I felt his pleasure ricochet back to me, making me come again, however weakly.

"Shit," he fought to catch his breath as he flopped onto his back, then winced as the movement jostled his knot, sending jolts of pleasure through the bond again, "I didn't mean to come, too."

Laughing softly, I shook my head and rolled carefully onto my side to face him, heedless of the mess I was making on the bedding. "I will never get used to how good bonded sex is," I informed him. "It is like you know exactly what to do and say to make every experience..." I searched for the right word.

"Mind-blowing?" he offered playfully. "World-rocking? Life-changing?"

Snorting, I nodded, already feeling sleepy from the effects of a strong orgasm. "All of the above."

"I'm gonna need another shower," he said, running his fingers through my hair.

My eyes shut of their own accord, and I leaned into the touch. "Mmhmm."

He chuckled, and his fingers continued to stroke over my scalp. "Sleep, sweetheart. We'll clean up later."

"At what point was someone going to tell me we were researching unicorns because my big brother got knocked up by one?" Sage's voice demanded from the lab's doorway.

I dropped the report I was working on and swiveled my chair around to face him. My younger brother, the middle child between Eric and I, smiled broadly at me. He was as physically different to me as Eric, but he looked nothing like our youngest sibling, either. Tall, almost lanky in his leanness, and with long, vibrant red hair, Sage was the most stereotypical omega of the three of us, appearance wise. His eyes were a piercing bright blue, and he must have been spending more time in the sun than usual, because his skin was almost brown with the covering of freckles over his arms and face.

"Sage," I greeted with a wide smile, "it is good to see you."

It had been months since he and Dexter had left on their last magic-finding mission. I hadn't realized how close we had become since moving to Shifters Sanctuary until he was no longer here. We kept in touch via text messages and the occasional phone call, but that did not compare to being able to speak to him in person.

"So, we're just not going to address the elephant-sized baby bump in the room, then?" he teased.

"We are," I assured him, and pushed out of my chair with a muffled groan. Ever since my belly had 'popped' two weeks earlier, it felt as though it had doubled in size. The strain the distention was putting on my back was almost ridiculous. "However, let me say hello properly first."

He eyed my belly with caution as I crossed the space between us, then made a soft 'oh' sound as I wrapped my arms around him and brought him in for a hug.

"Jesus," he muttered as we pulled apart, looking down at my stomach with equal parts awe and horror, "you're *huge*, Bran."

"Be thankful that my hormones are behaving today. Yesterday, that comment would have set off a stupid amount of tears." I cocked my head and sighed. "And I might have thrown a chair at you, too."

"Consider me warned, then," he smiled, still looking down between us. "Eric said you're having triplets?"

"It was nice of him to deliver all my news for me," I griped with no small degree of sarcasm.

Sage snorted. "You know Eric; he always has to be the center of attention."

"Youngest child syndrome," I sighed. "He's such a brat."

"Still, I kind of appreciated the head's up. If I'd walked in here and seen you without the warning, I might have had a heart attack." Sage accompanied the gentle rebuke with a push to my shoulder. "What's with not telling me before now?"

"I wanted to tell you in person."

"Okay...but you're, what, five months in? What would you have done if I didn't come back before they were born? Waited to throw three babies at me and be all 'congratulations, Sage, you're an uncle!'?"

"And you call Eric the dramatic one," I grumbled, rubbing at my aching back. Then I shrugged and exhaled. "Honestly? I do not know. It wasn't the most traditional conception and...I suppose I was trying to avoid your disappointment for as long as possible."

"Yeah," he guided me back to my desk and helped me into my seat, the corners of his lips lifting at my sigh of relief, "Eric told me you helped yourself to research materials." He leaned his bony ass on the edge of my desk and crossed his long legs at the ankle, gripping the edge of the desk with his palms as he drummed out a random beat on the underside with his fingertips. "I asked him if he could blame you."

"You...what? Really?"

"Come on, Bee. It's me. I want kids as badly as you do. I would have done the same thing, given half a chance." He chewed his bottom lip. "Could you..." Pausing, he cleared his throat and leaned down to whisper. "If my eggs ever do their thing in your petri dishes, can you tell me? Please?"

I blinked back at him, stunned. "Eric would kill me."

Sage cast his gaze to my belly again. I recognized the longing and heartache on his face. It matched my own, or at least the way I had felt before Micah's sperm had fertilized my eggs. How could I deny him the happiness that I had found, even hypothetically?

"Of course," I said softly, without needing to hear him beg. "I will tell you."

"This is why you're my favorite brother," he replied, straightening back up from his stooped position. Despite the playfulness of his tone, he wiped at his eyes with the knuckle of his index finger, and I had to swallow back tears of my own.

I blamed hormones.

"So," Sage broke the strangely emotional mood, "tell me more about this alpha of yours. Eric said he's a unicorn. I'm guessing that's why Dex and I have been on a wild goose —or, I guess, horse— chase?"

I drooped, losing hope that Sage had brought back vital information. "Yes. And he is magnificent."

"So Eric said. I'm a little jealous that I haven't seen him in shifted form. But we did meet briefly earlier." He winked. "He's pretty, Bee."

"He is," I agreed, once again allowing my adoration for my mate to run through me and into the bond. I received an answering wave of bewildered amusement for my efforts, and I chuckled.

"You lucked out. Babies and an alpha..." Sage sighed. "What I'd give to have that."

I couldn't assure him that it was in the cards for him, so I did not bother trying to placate him. "I know," I said instead. "Which is why we are hoping you and Dexter can find someone who can help us with the magic of the old ways, or some texts that might be able to explain why some people have hidden alpha syndrome and what we can do to locate them and unlock their alpha sides without requiring an omega and a mating to occur."

"Well, I had no luck. Dex called me from Madrid about a week ago and said he'd found a lead, though. Haven't heard anything from him since."

I frowned. There was something off about the way he spoke about his best friend. I knew they had been estranged for a hundred years or so, but I didn't know the backstory there, either. At the time, I hadn't been bothered, but now that I was close to my brothers again, I found that I did care.

"Is everything all right between the two of you?" I asked carefully. "Things seem strained again."

Sage shook his head before I even finished asking. "It's all good. You know Dex — he's also a bit of a drama llama."

"He has seemed oddly subdued since he came to live here."

"Yeah, well, he'll get over it or he won't."

There was definitely something happening there, but I knew better than to push Sage. If he did not want to discuss it, I would leave him be.

Clearing my throat, I took the conversation back to safer ground. "So," I began, "No luck on the magic front. What about unicorns?"

"I did find a super old journal which mentioned them," Sage admitted, and I sat up straighter, ignoring the twinge in my back.

"Go on..."

"The dragon who owned it wouldn't let me bring it with me," he scowled, "but I did borrow it and scanned every damn page of the thing. I gave the file to Eric before I came in here, and he's going to go through it and see if there's anything useful in there."

"Well," I slumped again, immediately feeling the pressure in my back release, "that is still a good sign that Micah is not the first of his kind."

"Yeah, that's what I thought." Sage grinned at me. "Now, be a good big brother and tell me *everything* about him. Not the science-y shit: the fun stuff. How is the whole being mated and bonded thing working out? Are you in *luuuurve*?"

I laughed. "It is going well. We work very well together, which is not a surprise, considering our theories on fate and compatibility. As for love," I lowered my voice and felt heat rise to my cheeks. "We have not said anything to each other, but...I believe so. Still, it has only been seven or so weeks. We are not rushing anything."

"Uh huh. Not rushing anything," he repeated drily. "Because bonding the day you met, moving in together, and having three babies together in a handful of months is totally taking it slow, right?"

"I think I preferred it when you were almost unreachable," I pouted, though the twitching of my lips gave my amusement away. "And you are correct, of course. Things between us are quite serious and permanent...but, somehow, saying the words out loud is daunting."

Sage smirked knowingly. "Ah, but you've still told each other silently, huh?"

"Through the bond, yes. We share feelings across the connection between us. It is...something else, Sage." I rubbed the center of my chest. "Truly. I wish more than anything for you to be able to experience this."

"I live in hope, big brother."

I reached out and squeezed his knee. "I do as well."

Who knew? Perhaps Dexter's lead would bring us one step closer to finding the answers we all wanted so desperately.

Chapter Eighteen

Dexter Burnside —and, man, did I find the dragons' surnames kind of hilarious, or what?— was a whirlwind of a man. He burst into Eric and Brandt's clinic in a dramatic flourish, heralding his own arrival with a loud, British accented, "Your savior has arrived!"

Considering I was just about to walk into the exam room with Brandt so we could see our babies on Eric's ultrasound machine, I turned to face the new dragon with amusement and irritation in equal measures. He stopped short when he saw me, and I could see that he was sizing me up, his sharp gaze traveling from my feet to the top of my head, while Brandt exasperatedly greeted, "Hello, Dexter."

I made no secret of the way I eyed him over in kind. He wasn't quite as tall as the others, but the way he stood —shoulders back, chin raised— told me he thought highly of himself. I supposed he had every reason to: he was attractive. Slender, wearing a tailored suit, with an angular face and perfectly styled blonde hair.

"Bran," he practically purred at my mate, smiling toothily as he oozed smarm, "you naughty boy; you should have said that you found yourself an alpha." He dropped his gaze to Brandt's belly. "There's something in the water in this Podunk town, isn't there?"

From the reception desk, I was almost certain I heard Damon growl, and that suspicion was confirmed when Dexter turned to face the desk and said, "Now now, kitty. Behave."

"Dex," Eric cut in with a bite of authority, "leave Day alone. Go wait in my office. I've got an appointment to finish first, then you can tell me everything you've discovered."

"Spoilsport," Dexter sighed dramatically, but he headed past us and down the short hallway to Eric's clinic office.

"He's a handful, isn't he?" I asked, watching him disappear into the room in question.

"He is, but he's all bark, no bite." Eric said. "Now," he beamed and practically bounced on his heels with excitement, "let's go see your babies."

"Oh my God," I muttered as the first of three humanoid forms appeared on the black and white computer monitor. It was curled up, but there was no denying the slope of its spine, the shape of its head and face, nor the tiny little hand flexing in the black space above a rounded little belly. "That's a baby."

"What did you think was in here?" Brandt asked. "Eggs? Dragons? *Winged-foals*?"

"Shut up," I replied without heat, unable to tear my gaze away from the screen. "I just...this is..." Stopping to take a steadying breath, I tried to calm my suddenly frantic heartbeat.

That was a baby.

A real baby.

Hard proof that in a few months' time, I really was going to be a dad.

"And here's number two," Eric said cheerfully, moving the transducer across Brandt's belly and showing another curled up humanoid form on the screen. This one was kicking a little foot in the black area surrounding it.

"Oh my God," I repeated, with only a tiny bit more panic in my voice.

I had missed the twelve-week ultrasound, and with everything else that had happened in the couple of months since, neither Brandt or Eric had organized another one until his scheduled twenty-week scan. It was my understanding that, because he was carrying multiples, there would be a few additional scans in the leadup to their due date, just to stay on top of any potential issues that might pop up.

"This one's looking good, too," Eric told us, "so let's visit baby number three."

As the wand moved again, I watched the screen. Sure enough, a third little body appeared within seconds.

"Is it...smaller than the others?" I asked quietly, finally shifting my gaze away to observe Eric's face.

He was frowning a little, which I didn't think was a great sign. I watched as he used his other hand to take screenshots and measurements, little yellow numbers appearing on the screen as he worked.

"Yeah," he eventually answered, sounding distracted. "This one's a bit smaller than their siblings...but it's not unusual in multiples for one or two to be undersized."

"*Undersized*?!" I repeated with concern, then I looked down at Brandt for reassurance.

He was frowning at his brother. "Is it still within a healthy developmental range?"

My gaze swung back to Eric, catching the minute downturn of his lips. "...Yes. But only just, Bee."

"What...what does that mean?" I demanded of both of them, not liking the unspoken conversation that seemed to be taking place between the two men of science and medicine. I didn't have that background. "Can we fix it somehow?"

"We just need to monitor them all a bit more closely," Eric answered me in a tone that felt almost like practiced reassurance. "We can't really treat them from outside the womb."

"So, what does that mean, exactly?"

"We would be looking at an early delivery," Brandt answered calmly. He looked at his brother. "We should buy incubators, just in case. And—"

"I know," Eric's tone was the most serious and soothing I had ever heard it in relation to either of his siblings. "And we will. As soon as we wrap up here, I will arrange it."

Dread settled in the pit of my stomach. The panic which had been welling up in the face of my looming fatherhood was nothing in comparison to the fear of something going wrong. Of my babies needing medical intervention before they were even born.

I grasped Brandt's hand and squeezed it. He squeezed back. Neither of us said a word.

"Like I said," Eric resumed taking his measurements, "baby three is still within an acceptable size range for their twenty-weeks gestation. We don't have to panic, but we do need to be aware that there *might* be complications, and it's better to prepare for the worst-case scenarios early."

I didn't want to think the words 'worst-case scenario' in relation to my children or my mate.

"Let's hear the heartbeats," Eric offered when neither of us responded to his attempt to reassure us. "I promise you; this little one is looking super strong."

That *did* actually make me feel a bit better. "Okay."

Eric flipped a little switch on the machine and then pressed the transducer down on Brandt's belly. Brandt bitched a little, reminding his brother that his bladder was full, but he stopped complaining as the fast, loud *whoosh-whoosh-whoosh*-ing filled the air.

"See?" Eric grinned. "Baby three's heartbeat is perfect."

Tears spilled over Brandt's cheeks, and I felt my own eyes mist over.

"Wanna know their sex?" Eric asked. "Three's decided to be an exhibitionist."

I let out a startled laugh and I looked to Brandt for his decision. "It might make deciding on names and stuff easier?" I suggested. "But I don't mind if you want the surprise."

He shook his head. "I would like to know."

"Then we find out."

"So, that's a yes?" Eric confirmed, and we nodded. He smiled. "Three's a girl, guys. Congratulations."

I honestly hadn't given a thought to what their biological sex would be, but finding out still hit me hard in the solar plexus. "Oh, wow," I choked out. "That's...wow."

Brandt nodded, his Adam's apple bobbing.

"Shall we see if One and Two are just as cooperative?" Eric offered.

"Please," Brandt asked, his voice gravelly and strained with emotion.

I committed the image of our daughter to memory as best I could before the transducer moved back to the baby flexing their hand.

"Okay, number one is being a little shy right now, but..." Eric moved the wand, trying to view the baby from a different angle. He contorted himself around Brandt's belly and then— "Ah ha! Gotcha!" He took a screenshot, then pointed at the screen. "Number One is also a girl."

As elation filled me once more, I couldn't help noticing the flicker of disappointment on Brandt's face as I turned to smile widely at him. It was only there for a moment, blinked away and replaced by a blinding smile that looked and felt genuine, but it was there nonetheless.

"Sugar?" I whispered, not quite sure why I was bothering, considering I knew Eric's shifter hearing would hear me anyway. "What's wrong?"

Brandt shook his head and cleared his throat. "Number Two," he demanded of his brother. "Please."

Eric swung the wand back to the second baby and did his contortionist act again. He cast his brother a brief, concerned glance, asking, "Are you sure you want to know?" He smiled, but it didn't quite reach his eyes. There was an understanding there which I didn't get. I was out of the loop, and I didn't like it. "Don't want a wildcard?"

Brandt shook his head.

Eric nodded, then smiled again. The same dull smile as moments earlier, not completely genuine.

"Congrats, guys. Another girl. The complete trifecta."

"Sweetheart, please talk to me."

Brandt hadn't spoken since the ultrasound. I couldn't feel any spikes of emotion through the bond, but I knew he was unhappy. Some part of that hurt me, though I was careful not to tell him so.

I hadn't been a complete potato since I had moved to Shifters Sanctuary. I had been reading up on kids and parenting, preparing myself for the changes that were heading my way. Part of that had included reading articles about gender disappointment, even though Brandt and I had both agreed we didn't care what sex our kids were.

It was only because I had read those articles that I knew Brandt might be feeling some kind of way about only having girls, and that his feelings were completely outside of his control. Still, would it be so bad to have girls? Ultimately, babies were babies, weren't they? They all ate, slept, and pooped the same.

After hours of silence and feeling blocked out from our bond, I was beginning to feel frustrated. Not at the way he had reacted to the news of three girls, but to being deliberately shut out by the man I had been falling in love with.

From his curled-up position on the bed, Brandt finally spoke. His pained words were muffled by the pillow, but I heard them anyway. "I can't, Micah."

Carefully sitting on the edge of the mattress, I rubbed his back. "You can. I'm not going to judge you for feeling any particular way. I just...I don't want you to shut me out."

"I am a terrible person," he lamented after another stretch of silence.

"You're not."

"I am!" I don't think either of us was expecting the vehemence in his tone, and he shook his head again, softly repeating, "I am."

"How? Explain it to me, Brandt, because what you're feeling is valid."

My mate rolled onto his back but kept his red-rimmed gaze directed at the wall. I supposed that was still an improvement, though I really wished he would look at me.

"Is it?" he demanded. "After everything I did...after knowing that there were no guarantees...is it truly fair of me to be disappointed that not one of our children will be a dragon? That my species still dies with those of us remaining scattered and miserable around the world?"

"But they're not even born yet. We don't know—"

"Dragons are an all-male race," his voice hitched. "And I truly believed that I did not care what breed of shifter our children were...but..."

My heart sank. "Oh, *sugar*..."

"No. It is wrong of me to feel this way. I do not understand *why* I feel this way when I am still so excited to be having children at all. I *love* our daughters. I do not...I *hate* this irrational, awful feeling."

"It's not irrational," I tried to soothe him. "You're not saying you don't want our girls. You're not even disappointed that they are girls."

He snorted derisively.

"No, sweetheart, you're not. I know you're not. The bond doesn't lie, remember?" I reached for his hand and squeezed. "I think you're upset because so much of your original justification for implanting the embryos revolved around potentially saving the dragons. Finding out that it hasn't happened this time hurts. It's allowed to hurt. We all want to make sure dragons survive, but you put your ethics and body on the line for it..."

Brandt burst into tears and moved to bury his face in his pillow again, but I didn't want him to hide from me. Climbing over him so I could stretch out beside him, I tugged him in for a hug, not caring that his tears and snot were messing up my shirt.

"Let it out," I murmured, pressing kisses to the top of his head. "I'm here, I've got you."

"I love them," he repeated once he calmed down. "I love them so much and I feel guilty for...for this..."

"It's okay to be sad about the situation with the dragons," I assured him. "It is. It doesn't mean that you love our kids any less."

I listened to the quick inhalations as he fought to regain control of his emotions and I held him until he went lax and calm. "We're going to find a way to save the dragons eventually," I promised. "Dexter and Sage might find something to help. Or

I'll just have to live up to my promise to breed you over and over again."

I meant the last bit as a joke, and I was relieved when Brandt chuckled wetly against my chest.

"Don't make promises you cannot keep," he muttered, but there was a hint of arousal and amusement accompanying the words.

"Like getting to fuck you into oblivion is such a hardship for me."

He snorted, and the silence that fell between us felt comfortable again. After another minute or so, he said, "Thank you."

"For what?"

"For not thinking me a monster. For working through this ridiculous episode instead of running away. For—"

"It wasn't ridiculous," I insisted, then gently cradled his chin between my thumb and index finger so I could make sure he was looking at me. "Bran, sweetheart, I can't imagine how frustrating it must feel to not be able to hold onto your emotions as much as you'd like to, but it's going to take a lot more than that to scare me away."

"Still," he sighed, "thank you."

Kissing his forehead again, I replied, "Always, sugar."

Chapter Nineteen

Brandt

The guilt I felt over my reaction to learning that none of my children would be dragons was difficult to shake off. Even though Micah assured me that my feelings were valid, it still felt wrong to feel any kind of disappointment regarding my babies. My daughters.

I was going to have three daughters.

Three unicorn daughters.

At least, I could only assume they would be unicorns. It was unlikely that they would be horses when Micah was clearly not really a horse shifter. Not that I understood quite how that worked, though, considering he had thought himself a horse for his entire life prior to releasing the mystical hold on his alpha and its abilities.

I did not enjoy not understanding the fundamentals of what had kept his unicorn form hidden, just as I did not like that we were still in the dark about how to unlock or release someone's alpha side without the presence of a compatible mate. I understood that it was a mixture of science and magic, but the fact that it had been three years since Beckett and Oliver had accidentally unlocked Beck's alpha and we were no closer to having answers was frustrating.

Cuddled up in my alpha's arms, I grumbled when my phone rang, disturbing the peaceful silence. However, my disappointment and irritation melted away when Eric started speaking when I answered the call, not even waiting for me to say 'hello'.

"Bran, get back to the clinic. Dex found something."

"Does this say what I think it says?" my brother demanded the moment I stepped into his office. He pointed at the computer monitor and I leaned over his shoulder to read the scanned page on the screen.

It was handwritten, in spiky, cursive writing that, at first, seemed to be little more than scribbling. But then words began to jump out at me from the jumble in an unexpected mixture of Hungarian and Romanian. I let my greedy eyes scan the page from the start once my brain knew what it was looking at, and I felt my heart rate increasing as I read.

"Holy shit," I breathed, and Eric sat back in his seat with a wide, satisfied smile.

"So it does?" he prodded, "My language skills are a bit rusty when it comes to reading. But...it basically affirms our theory, doesn't it? That there's a spell we can perform to unlock an alpha who hasn't yet presented as one?"

"Yes, and there is mention of pheromones...well, what we know now to be pheromones," I pointed at a sentence which essentially referred to unexplained scent signals between potential mates, "which appears to be key in the spellcasting."

"Do you think we could replicate the pheromones synthetically? Rather than having to find an alpha's potential or compatible mate, could we replicate a generic attraction pheromone to trigger them?" Eric started taking notes on his phone as he was talking, his eyes bright with excitement.

I did not blame him; I felt just as invigorated and eager to learn.

"Possibly," I answered, considering the science behind his idea. I leaned in closer to the screen. "Are there more pages?" I asked. "More information than just the confirmation of our theories?"

"Yes, but nothing on the specifics of the magic," Eric sounded disappointed. "It's more an account of watching the spell cast on an infant born to shifter parents, without a mark and without the scent of a shifter."

He looked up at me and I immediately understood. "Beck, Rex, and Brandi," I nodded. "It does not explain Micah, though."

"No," Eric agreed, "but what if, like anything, the...let's call it a gene? What if it has mutated...er, or evolved over time? What if it's the same thing, only because he was born to mixed species of shifters, it presented differently due to different biological makeup?"

"How would we determine if that is the case?"

"Well, we've been testing their blood for DNA connections and chromosome anomalies...but maybe..." he started typing on his phone screen again, "I think we should invest in a mass spectrometer."

"Oh, of course," I wanted to facepalm. "A mass spectrometer would isolate known and unknown compounds, whereas the karyotype testing is performed under microscope..." I groaned. "How have we not considered this before?"

"We were too focused on the magic component itself. One of those 'can't see the forest for the trees' things, I guess." Eric sounded rueful. "But with a mass spec, we might also be able to isolate the shifter gene...maybe even genes for our specific breeds..."

"What, so we could attempt to genetically engineer dragons?" I asked, attempting to ignore the renewed swirling emotions over the babies I carried. Giving my head a quick shake, I pinned my brother with a pointed stare. "Eugenics is a dangerous path to travel down, Eric."

"It's just a theory," he defended, then turned his chair to face me fully, causing me to take a couple of steps back. "But, while we're on the topic, how are you feeling? And I mean really."

"I am fine."

His blonde eyebrows tilted inwards as his eyes narrowed. "Bran, come on. I know you're going to love your kids no matter what, but some part of you was desperately hoping for a dragon and, unless our species has evolved significantly..."

"Perhaps it has," I mused, considering all the other changes we had become aware of over time. "Female alphas exist now, where we have no record of them doing so before. Perhaps the magic itself has changed and evolved."

Sitting back in his chair, Eric observed me in silence for a moment. "That is a valid point. But, Bee, the likelihood—"

"I am aware." Swiftly cutting him off, I sat in the armchair beside his desk; the one he had his patients sit in during their appointments. "And I will admit I was irrationally upset at first. I feel terrible for it. These babies" —I placed my hand over the gravid swell of my abdomen— "are a dream come true for me regardless of their breed of shifter. I momentarily lost sight of that, and I am struggling to forgive myself for the lapse."

"We all want to save our kind," Eric told me softly. "It's okay to want both the kids *and* to bring more dragons into the world. You're not a bad person because you're only getting half of that this time around."

"The most selfish half," I muttered, then cocked my head. "This time?"

Eric snorted and fiddled with the edge of the notepad sitting on the desk in front of him. "Please. Tell me that you and that alpha of yours aren't going to be taking advantage of every single heat you have once these babies are born. You're going to overrun this town with your babies."

"I am going to enjoy trying," I agreed, a thrum of arousal traveling through my veins. "But I am middle-aged. Who knows how many viable heat cycles I even have left in me. I met Micah after I had implanted the embryos, so I have not even experienced *one* yet."

"It's a good thing we're both men of science, then," my brother grinned. "We'll work it out, Bran, I promise. This is the most hope and advancement we've had in hundreds of years, and I think we're onto something with our new theories."

"I do, too," I glanced around his little office, with its examination bed, desk and computer, posters of anatomy and a bookshelf containing pull apart models of various organs, and I sighed. "We are going to have to move the clinic if you want to get a mass spectrometer in here."

"I think we've outgrown this place anyway," Eric agreed. "I've asked Sage to reach out to some of his friends in the building industry. If we manage to crack the code on this magic and pheromones thing, we're going to need a dedicated hospital space and more housing. Plus," his gaze softened and dropped to my belly again, "we need to get those incubators ready just in case."

That was a sobering reminder that I had more important things to worry about than my babies' species.

"When can we break ground on a new facility?"

Chapter Twenty

"**D**arling, come quick!"

At Brandt's excited call from the couch in the living room, I just about dropped the glasses I had pulled from the dishwasher to put away in their proper place. Hastily placing the glasses on the counter, I rushed across the open-living-style space and practically skidded to a stop in front of him.

"What's up?"

Without speaking, my mate reached for my hand and yanked it to his belly. I felt the movement —the gentle, almost bubbling tapping— beneath my palm almost instantly.

"Oh my god," I exhaled, my gaze glued to my hand, as if I could see through it and Brandt's skin and to the babies themselves. "Oh, *wow*."

Brandt had been feeling them move around inside him for a few weeks, but this was the first time they had been detectable from the outside. I was thrilled that their timing meant I got to be the first person to experience it, and I was also...kind of terrified.

It was yet more proof that we were going to be parents. That *I* was going to be a parent. The weeks were speeding forward, time passing so fast that it felt like all I had to do was blink and our girls would be here.

It wasn't that I wasn't excited about them, because I was. I had zero regrets about bonding with Brandt and locking myself into the future he had tried to give me a free pass from. But as the reality of what was coming started to dawn on me, *three* babies felt like a scary undertaking.

We had set up their nursery in the spare room across the hall from the main bedroom, and as I had put the cribs together (while Brandt had grumped from the plush rocking chair because I had insisted that the manual labor be my domain), it had started to dawn on me how much work they would be.

Those three white cribs, in a room painted in pastel shades of the rainbow, were a symbol of the sleepless nights coming our way. Of countless diaper changes. Of crying, and spit-up...and all the other not-so-fun stuff Beck grizzled about.

Brandt and I were still probably going to hire help, because we were in the fortunate position that he was a dragon with hundreds of years of savings and investments behind him, but that didn't mean we weren't going to be hands-on dads.

It was just that, as their arrival loomed closer, I was starting to worry that I had no actual idea what I was doing.

Hanging out with Lena and Brandi's newborn twins —boys they had named Peter and Benjamin, which the rest of the pack teased them about on account of being rabbit shifters— only made my insecurities about my abilities increase. It turned out that newborns were so much smaller than any other babies I had previously held. Their little bodies were solid, but tiny and squirmy and, oh Gods, what if I dropped one? And changing them? Yeah...I hadn't been prepared for newborn diapers.

The movement beneath my palm faded away and I tried not to feel too disappointed, but Brandt grabbed my wrist and moved my hand to the other side of his belly. The tapping there felt a little stronger. I grinned and looked up at him. "Do you think they're having a dance party in there?"

He chuckled and nodded. "Or perhaps fighting like Beck and Ollie's children."

I grimaced. "I hope they're not as violent with each other. I love Beck's kids, but they're little demons unless you keep them separated."

"Two little alphas." Brandt said, adding, "Not that I truly believe there is a personality difference between alphas, betas, and omegas, just as I do not believe boys are inherently more rough and tumble than girls. It just amuses me that they are both such dominant little creatures."

"No wonder Beck's so afraid of having more kids," I laughed. "Those two are going to turn him prematurely gray."

"Hey," Brandt pouted down at me, "what is wrong with turning gray?" He turned his head to the side and gestured at the silver streaks that never failed to make my stomach flip and my cock twitch.

"Absolutely nothing," I replied, my tone low with lust.

Brandt snorted. "You are insatiable, aren't you?"

Rubbing my hand in slow, sensual circles over his bump, I smirked. "Only with you, sugar."

And, just like that, my trepidation for my impending fatherhood faded away, replaced with a surge of answering arousal through our bond.

"Micah..." Brandt purred, winding his fingers into my hair.

Despite his growing belly —and the growing list of complaints about his discomfort— over the weeks, Brandt's second trimester hormones had continued to make him increasingly horny. I loved every second of it. It didn't matter where we were or what we were doing, stopping everything to indulge his body's demands was no hardship for me.

This moment was no exception. I pushed his shirt up, exposing the taut skin of his belly, and I pressed kisses all over it, murmuring, "Close your eyes and block your ears, kids."

Brandt groaned and chuckled all at once. "You are ridiculous."

"You love it," I smirked into his skin.

"I love *you.*"

I froze for only a moment before I was pushing up from my crouched position and dropping onto the couch beside him. I yanked his mouth to mine in a bruising, possessive kiss, certain that he could feel the spike of elation and adoration I felt for him through both the bond and also the action itself.

"I love you," I told him when we parted for air.

"Good," he nodded, then arched his hips from the couch. "Now, I believe you were about to defile me?"

I laughed, pressed another quick kiss to his lips, then returned to my knees on the rug between his spread legs. His fingers wove into my hair again, and, with a bit of maneuvering, I managed to pull his sweatpants out from under him and off.

With my hands at his thighs, I spread his knees wider, exposing every inch of him for my viewing pleasure. His big cock was straining towards his belly, his balls already drawn up in anticipation, but it was his entrance, slick and furled, which had my full attention.

"*Micah...*" he spoke my name as a plea, whispered and breathy, and it made me ache for him, but I left my own cock alone. Even after months of practice, I knew that I was probably going to come far too soon when the arousal bouncing between us via our connection was so intense.

I leaned in teasingly, so close that he could probably feel my breath tickling his hole, before I averted course and pressed a kiss to the inside of his thigh.

"*Nnngh,*" he complained, and I grinned, then nipped at the flesh under my mouth. "You are *terrible.*"

"Uh-uh," I practically crooned, rubbing my nose over the spot I had just bitten, "be nice, or I won't give you what you want."

"Fuck," his entire body rocked with the petulant way he threw his head back against the headrest. "Don't tease me, alpha."

Inside my shorts, my cock twitched. I bit at the inside of his thigh again, a bit harder than before. As he mewled, I reprimanded, "No playing dirty."

The fingers in my hair tightened their grip and tugged. "Please," he begged. "I need..."

"Need...?"

"Your mouth. Your fingers. Your cock. *Everything.*"

I loved the desperation I could hear in his voice, and even though we had been learning to shield our emotions from one another, I could feel hints of how intense his need was through the bond. Pulling back from his thigh, I found his previously slick hole actually dripping, and that alone shattered my resolve to draw out his begging.

Flattening my tongue, I licked the trickle of thick, sweet-ish liquid from where it was running down the underside of his perfect ass. Brandt cried out and arched into the contact, but I lapped slowly at my prize, savoring every burst on my tastebuds as I followed the lines of liquid to the source.

His grip on my hair was almost painful, and I relished it. I loved when he lost control, when he writhed under my ministrations. It was a heady feeling to see this powerful man brought to a whimpering, pleading, thrashing mess by my tongue alone.

"Please," he murmured as I finally began to tease at his rim, "please, Micah. Alpha. Please." He rocked his hips in short, sharp movements with every repeat of the word. "Please, please, *please.*"

When I finally speared him with my tongue and wriggled it inside, he almost sobbed. "Yes, darling. *Yes.* Just like that. More. More, please, *more.*"

I was going to come untouched if he kept going.

His heavy breathing, the musky scent of his skin, the sweet and salty taste of his slick...it was a feast of sensation.

Unable to stop myself, I reached up to stroke his neglected dick in time with the thrusts and curls of my tongue. "Fuck!" he yelled, no; damn near roared. "Oh, fuck, your mouth...Darling, your mouth...I—*fuck!*"

If I had thought it was a sensory overload before, it had nothing on feeling his orgasm slam through the bond we shared as warm wetness coated my hand and his channel clenched around my tongue, spilling more delicious slick into my waiting mouth. I licked and sucked and slurped and did everything in my power to keep my answering orgasm at bay, even as he fed the aftershocks of his bliss to me through our connection.

He whined when I drew back to breathe and calm myself, and I glanced up, wanting to see how debauched he looked.

I was not disappointed. His hair was sweaty and messed, as though he had been thrashing against the back of the couch. His skin was flushed pink, and his dark eyes glazed over. His shirt was bunched up beneath his softening pecs, and the skin of his rounded belly was shiny with perspiration, too.

Even though I hadn't come, I was beyond satisfied at seeing him so thoroughly wrecked.

"You good, sugar?" I asked him while I pushed to my feet, watching as his hooded, sleepy gaze focused in on my hand —the one covered in his cum— as I raised it to my mouth and proceeded to lick it clean.

"Jesus Christ," he cursed breathily, his eyes darkening with lust even though he sounded, and looked, completely wrung-out. "That is hot." His gaze traveled down the length of my body. When we locked eyes again, he beckoned me closer with a crooked finger. "Come here."

I smirked at the double entendre and couldn't let it go. "That's my intention."

He blinked at me, then groaned as I stepped in between his still-spread thighs, bringing my cock to his face level. "Really?"

"You should know better than to leave those opportunities open to me."

"Gods help us, you will be the king of the dad jokes," he bemoaned, but he was smiling as he popped the button above my fly and then lowered the zipper.

"One of us has to be the embarrassing dad."

"Fuck," he muttered and palmed his cock, "you have no idea how sexy that is."

"Me being embarr—*Jesus*, Brandt...I'm warning you; I'm on a hair trigger right now." I didn't feel any shame in admitting it as he wrapped his big hand around my not-so-big dick and stroked. I was proud of myself for not coming the second his orgasm rocked through the bond. It had been a close call.

"Mmm," his lips quirked, "*good*. I have little patience, and I have missed your taste."

And in retribution for my teasing him, he left me no time to respond before taking my aching, leaking cock into his mouth and sucking.

I lasted thirty seconds in the perfection of his mouth before I was curling over the top of his head and coming hard down the back of his throat. I started to pull away as I felt the tingling that signaled my knot inflating, but he grabbed my ass and sucked me in deeper, gagging as my cock grew to accommodate the knot.

"B-Brandt," I tried to pull back, afraid of hurting him, or suffocating him, or getting stuck in this position, with his jaw unable to release my knot.

A wave of reassurance traveled through the bond and he hummed, which made me curse and spurt down his throat again. When he swallowed that, the stimulation to my cock head and my knot restarted the process.

"Fuck, fuck, fuck..." I hissed, hoping I wasn't going to choke him, while simultaneously riding out the intense pleasure/pain of the multiple orgasms and knot stimulation. "If I have to call your brother because we get stuck like this..."

My mate snorted, which set the whole cycle off again.

Breathing heavily, I tried to think unsexy thoughts, attempting to encourage my knot to deflate. "You're going to pay for —*unghh*— this."

All I felt was a spike of amusement and arousal through our connection, which did not help in my bid to will the knot away.

Glaring down at him, I demanded, "Don't. Move."

He winked, then hummed his agreement.

My knees threatened to buckle.

As soon as my knot went down, I was going to kill him...well, if I hadn't died from overstimulation already.

I assumed he felt my fatigue and the increase of pain in the pain-to-pleasure balance, because a few moments later I watched, mildly horrified, as he partially shifted, his jaw literally morphing as scales erupted all over his body and he grew in size. He was still humanoid, but bigger. Big enough, and reptile enough, that he was able to unhinge his jaw and release my knot.

While I stared at him and caught my breath, recovering from almost orgasming to death, Brandt shifted back to his usual form. He gave me a smug smile. "Did you forget that I can partially shift at will?"

"I didn't know it went beyond the scales around your face thing."

"Oh," the smugness turned to sheepishness. "Then, surprise?"

I blinked at him for a moment before chuckling and carefully easing down onto the couch beside him, not wanting to set my knot off again. "You're *so* lucky I love you."

His expression softened out and he nodded. "Yes, I am."

Time continued to pass. I picked up occasional jobs out of town, but nothing that would keep me from my mate for more than a night or two at most. As his due date loomed closer and closer, I found myself feeling increasingly more protective and possessive. Plus, his mobility was greatly impacted by the three babies throwing off his balance and putting strain on his back. I preferred being able to look after him, massaging his back and rubbing his feet.

Yeah, I was a sap. But he was my omega, and he was pregnant with my children, and it made me happy to look after him.

Eric continued to monitor him closely, which I was grateful for, even if Brandt and I both complained at having become Eric's favorite new lab rats. But our third baby was still measuring on the small side, and watching her health was more important than anything else.

"Have you tried shifting recently?" Eric asked during one of our weekly appointments.

Brandt groaned and closed his eyes, splaying one of his large hands over his belly and wincing. I assumed one of our miniature cage fighters was attempting to box their way out of his abdomen, so I reached over to rub soothingly at the spot while Brandt answered, "I barely have the energy to put on my shoes of a morning. I can not imagine attempting to shift."

"Well," Eric cocked his head, "I think we should try it. It might give your little ones more room to grow."

"Your logic is flawed," my mate grumbled. "Every other pregnant shifter has mentioned feeling even more ungainly in their shifted form."

Eric shrugged. "Yeah, well, none of them have been dragons, have they?"

"But—"

"Brandt, please. For our research. For *science*." Eric's voice took on a placating lilt which reminded me of Beck trying to get his kids to eat vegetables. "You love science."

I tuned them out as they bickered, focusing instead on the foot currently stretching my mate's belly into a strange, lumpy shape. I was still kind of mystified every time I felt our kids roughhousing inside him. It somehow felt surreal and *too* real all at once.

Before I knew it, those babies would be out in the world, and I would be responsible for looking after them.

Maybe my mom was right: maybe it would be best if she and Dad came to visit for a while once the girls were born. Brandt and I were in the middle of interviewing shifters to be our live-in nanny, but I suddenly felt the desperate need to be with my family. My entire family. Mom, Dad, Brandt, our babies...I wanted them all in one place. I wanted them all in the pack I'd claimed as my home. My inner horse (and, yeah, I still called him a horse, even if he did have wings and a horn) blew out a burst of air through his lips and stamped his hooves. He was getting anxious, too.

I came back to the conversation as my hand was dislodged from Brandt's belly as he struggled to get to his feet. Helping him up, I supported his back as he explained that Eric had convinced him to try shifting.

"If nothing else, I can curl up in my dragon form and sleep for a short while," he muttered as he waddled (I would never use that phrase within his earshot) down the clinic's short hallway. "That should alleviate some of the pain in my back as well."

"I'll shift and cuddle with you," I said. "We're getting better at communicating through the bond, so maybe we can use it as a chance to practice in shifted form."

After Beck and Ollie had told us that they had learned to send focused sensations and feelings to one another —and the pink slashes across my friend's cheeks had told me exactly what they used that discovery for— Brandt had been determined to master the skill himself. It took a lot of concentration, and I still wished we could send each other actual thoughts instead of feelings or phantom touches, but it was still pretty cool that we could silently communicate at all.

"I want to hear about how that goes," Eric chirped behind us. "You haven't tried while shifted yet, have you?"

"Not yet," I answered, guessing that my mate was close to turning around and snapping at his brother again. The further he progressed in his pregnancy, the more volatile his mood swings became. "And I'm interested to see if we can do it, and from how far a distance."

Not that I had plans to be separated from Brandt at all. He was thirty-two weeks pregnant and, even though Eric hadn't said anything, I was under the impression that he thought the babies could arrive at any time. My own research had confirmed my suspicions: on average, triplet pregnancies only really made it between thirty-two and thirty-five weeks.

I really needed to call my mom.

When we got to the fields behind the clinic, I helped Brandt out of his shirt and sweatpants. He toed off his slip-on shoes and Eric and I stepped back to watch him shift. Even his transition into his dragon form seemed to take longer than the last couple of times I had watched him, as if even the magic that thrummed through our veins was struggling to find the energy to complete its task.

The magnificent, hulking, dark red form of my mate finally materialized in front of us. Even in his state, his belly seemed swollen beyond belief.

"Fascinating," Eric murmured, eyeing his brother before typing on the ever-present notes app on his phone.

"Do you think his body is struggling because the girls are unicorns, not dragons?" I asked.

"Doubtful," Eric didn't look up from his phone screen. "Considering our young don't shift for the first time until they're five or so."

I scrunched my nose and thought back to when Lena was pregnant with her twins. She was a rabbit, which obviously couldn't accommodate two human-sized fetuses in her shifted form. "So...the babies just grow —or shrink— proportionally to the shifter in question?" I looked back at my giant mate and his gravid belly and shuddered at the idea of a humanoid fetus the size of a small car. "Weird."

"You know, I've never actually tried to use the ultrasound machine on a shifter before..." Eric mused.

Brandt let out a dragony growl.

I snorted. "I don't think starting with Bran is a great idea."

"No," he replied sarcastically, "you don't say."

I couldn't contain my amusement, and my inner horse nickered happily as well. It turned out, he felt like Eric met the family criteria as well. In many ways, I supposed that the dragon did.

He was my bonded mate's brother, after all. That essentially made him my brother-in-law. And, with all the time Brandt and

I had spent with Eric, I had actually come to see him as a pseudo sibling. Even Sage and I had started joking with each other, though I didn't feel quite as close to him yet. I supposed that was because he was off scouring the world for more information about the old ways and the magic, so we hadn't really gotten much of a chance to properly bond as in-laws.

Turning my back on Eric, I stripped and shifted, still not completely comfortable with my wings and horn. In the months since discovering the change to my shifted form, I had gone on a couple of runs with the pack, and that had gone a long way in helping me embrace the changes...but it was still weird.

No weirder than the knotting thing, though, I supposed. Or being able to communicate emotions and concepts through the magical bond I shared with Brandt.

I guessed I was just sad that it was one more thing to set me apart from the family I had grown up with, even though my parents seemed just as excited about my new form as they had been about my being an alpha.

Shaking the musings from my head, I trotted over to my large, grumpy mate and rubbed the side of my face along his muzzle. His jaws were large enough that, if he opened them wide, he could probably swallow me with one bite, but he let out a sound which I could only describe as a purr when I greeted him affectionately.

And that was the other issue I had with my updated form: I couldn't nuzzle him the way I craved. Not without the weapon jutting out from the middle of my forehead gouging him, anyway.

Stupid horn, I thought irritably. Then I sighed.

In all likelihood, our daughters would be unicorns like me. I didn't want them feeling self-conscious of their forms, so I knew I had to work on the issues I had with my own.

A warm puff of air ruffled my mane and I concentrated on trying to send feelings through the bond. It was harder when we were both shifted, especially when I was practicing sending an actual message instead of spikes of random, deeply felt emotions.

I focused on sending calm, vividly imagining Brandt curling up on the ground like an oversized, scale-covered cat, and then added the image of me curling up against him. I focused on how warm and safe that would feel, and a jolt of surprise came traveling through the connection we shared.

Immediately concerned, I took a few steps back, staring into his huge, dark eye. He huffed, sending up a cloud of dust and dirt from the ground. Then he closed his eyes and I wasn't sure if it was just that he was tired, or—

Holy shit, I thought as I felt the warmth of his scales along my flank, despite not being pressed up against him. *Okay, yeah, I get it now.*

With enough concentration, we could send each other physical manifestations of what we were imagining.

No wonder Beck and Ollie use this for sex...

I wanted to experiment with that idea myself, but Brandt had been too uncomfortable and too exhausted, and I wasn't the kind of alpha who would demand sex from his heavily pregnant mate just because he was horny.

Instead, I had been getting reacquainted with my hand and my toys, and had taught myself how to shield my orgasms from traveling through the bond when I got myself off in the shower or after Brandt had gone to bed at night.

Maybe that was why I was able to accidentally send him that mental image, or sensations, or whatever — I was getting better with my control over my end of the connection we shared.

By unspoken agreement, we practiced with it some more before Brandt's large eyes began to droop. I felt his side of our bond dimming with his drift into sleep —a familiar sensation which no longer startled me— and I used the side of my face to nuzzle the end of his muzzle again, willing him to rest.

Once he drifted off, and the bond went dark (for lack of a better description), I made my way to his side and lay down on the grass by his side, folding my long, golden legs underneath me. The warmth emanating from his scaled belly was almost enough to lull me off to sleep as well...until something inside him moved, thumping at my side.

Our giant babies, I realized, snorting with amusement. I assumed his dragon form had thicker skin, plus the shield of scales, which meant our girls couldn't stretch his shape out quite so easily. But I could feel at least one of them giving it a red-hot go.

Be good for Papa, girls, I thought, unable to voice the words I had spoken so many times by that stage. *We'll get to meet you soon.*

Chapter Twenty-One

A fter shifting back to my human form following an extended nap, I had to admit that I felt better for it. In fact, I felt *good*. It was actually strange to feel energized after weeks of lethargy and discomfort, but as Micah helped me climb back into my sweatpants and stretched-out t-shirt, I straightened up and grinned salaciously at him.

"What?" he asked, smiling back at me.

"You are going to so much effort to dress me when all I can think about is getting us both undressed again as soon as possible."

I felt his surprise, sudden and sharp, roll through our bond before he followed it with simmering arousal. "I'm totally on board for that, sugar."

Even though the verbal confirmation was unnecessary, I still melted at the endearment. Opening my mouth to suggest we just undress where we stood, my plans were foiled by my brother's exasperated "I'm still here."

Micah and I turned to find Eric sitting on the grass maybe fifteen feet away, his knees raised and his arms folded atop them. He gave me a sardonic smile. "Shifting helped?"

"The nap helped," I corrected him. "I felt even more exhausted and ungainly while shifted. It was not a pleasant sensation. However," I cast a quick glance towards my alpha before looking back at my brother, "we can share sensations and even mental images through the bond while shifted."

Eric sat up straighter and brushed his unruly blonde hair back from his face. "Really?" His blue eyes gleamed with interest. "Is it easier to do in shifted form than your human form?"

"You realize you just put an end to our sexy fun times, right?" Micah muttered at my side. "We're back to being lab rats again."

"We can always sneak away to my lab," I informed him with a playful waggle of my eyebrows.

"Nope. Nuh-uh. No." Eric interrupted, getting to his feet and dusting his hands over his denim-covered thighs. "You're not defiling my labs. Take your hormones back to your place. I'll take notes later."

Winking at Micah, I replied over my shoulder with a distracted "If you insist." Then I took my mate by the hand and practically dragged him towards the clinic's parking lot.

I had no idea why I was so extremely horny so suddenly, but I didn't particularly care. It had been too long since I had last felt his knot, and I did not wish to wait any longer if I could help it.

The need built during the few minutes' drive between the clinic and our home. I hadn't felt so overwhelmingly desperate since before Micah and I had bonded. It felt as though my body —my omega — was trying to tell me something, but I had no idea what.

All I knew was I needed my mate inside me immediately.

As soon as we were inside the house, I slammed the front door and shoved Micah against the cool, painted surface, slanting my mouth over his. He kissed me back with the same intensity, likely feeling my desperation through our connection and mirroring it, and the sensation of his tongue twining with mine momentarily cooled some of the burning need.

It was only a short reprieve.

I could feel my slick pooling in my underwear, and my veins felt as though they were on fire. My skin was flushed and heated, and my heart hammered.

"I've got you, sugar," he murmured, running his hands down my sides, "let's get you somewhere comfortable so we can take care of this" —he slid one hand beneath the ridiculously protruding mound of my belly and rubbed at my erection through my sweatpants— "okay?"

I whimpered and nodded. Even at my most insatiable point during this pregnancy, I had never felt so out of control of my body. There was horny and then there was...whatever the hell this was. "Please, alpha."

"Aww, baby, come on." Gently pushing me backwards, Micah guided me to the bedroom with a hand on the curve of my spine. We paused at the foot of the bed and he asked, "How do you want to do this?"

It had been a few weeks since he had last fucked me and my belly had grown much more cumbersome in that time. Despite my desperation, I did not think I had the stamina to ride him, nor did I think my back would withstand the ordeal. If I was careful not to put weight on my stomach, I could get on my hands and knees, but my back twinged at that idea, too.

Following that, I shielded Micah from the guilt I felt at mentally dismissing the idea of attempting to lie on our sides. For the first time since we had met, I couldn't help thinking that he wasn't quite endowed enough to give me what I needed in that position, at least, not until he grew and knotted. I ached to think it, and I would never say the words out loud, but that was the reality of the moment.

"A pillow beneath my hips might help if I'm on my back," I eventually decided. "It might be easier for you if I am near the edge of the mattress, too."

He nodded and moved to gather pillows, then stopped and dropped them in a pile. "Wait," he told me, smiling softly, "I have a better idea. Do you trust me?"

"Always," I answered without hesitation.

Then he turned on his heel and slipped into the ensuite bathroom. Moments later, the sound of running water met my ears and Micah reappeared in the doorway. "What if you ride me in the tub?" he asked. "The water will take the weight off your back, and you've got enough slick happening that I don't think the water causing friction will be an issue." He shrugged, adding, "We might get water everywhere, but I can clean that up afterwards."

It was so thoughtful of him. My eyes welled with appreciative tears and a lump formed in my throat. "Perfect," I told him, unable to say more.

"C'mere," he extended his arms. "Let's get you out of those clothes again."

He undressed me with care, tossing my slick and precum soiled underwear and sweatpants into the hamper. Then he peeled off his own jeans and shirt, revealing his unblemished skin and long limbs. Though neither of us could see it beneath my gravid belly, my cock jumped and strained at the sight of my mate on display for me.

He was such a beautiful man, inside and out.

It still boggled my mind at times that he hadn't loathed me for my actions, that he hadn't turned tail and run away, that he had wanted the future I had paved without his consent. Setting aside the mystical aspects —the bonding, the knotting, the shifting and the fact that I was a dragon and he was a unicorn— it still seemed unbelievable that a beautiful younger man like him would want an older, chubbier man like me.

But he did, and I would thank fate and my lucky stars for eternity.

"Okay," Micah said, pulling me from my emotional musings, "I think the bath is good to go. Let me help you in." He followed through by taking my hand and steadying me as I awkwardly swung my leg over the tub's side.

The water inside was just shy of hot, and I knew it would ease the constant ache in my muscles even while I planned on bouncing in Micah's lap. Never had I been happier to have insisted on a comically large tub when I had remodeled the bathroom. Being a large man to begin with, I hadn't wanted to feel cramped in it. Now, there was enough space for both of us, and I was excited to be taking advantage of the fact.

Micah climbed in and settled with his back against the enameled side of the tub, stretching his long legs out beneath the water. He held my hands as I lowered myself on top of him, crossing my ankles behind his ass. With my belly in the way, it took some maneuvering before we found the right angle and positions for me to sink down on his cock but the moment he was inside of me felt like a revelation. Like coming home after an extended time away. I wanted to weep with relief and happiness.

"Gods, sugar, this feels incredible," Micah panted as I started to bounce gently in place. Water sloshed over the sides of the tub and slapped on the tiled floor, but I did not care. It only added to the ambiance of the moment — the soundtrack of our lovemaking as our heavy breaths and moans echoed off the walls.

I had to admit, being submerged in the bath changed the sensations I had become so used to. Because the water was not lubricating, I swore I could feel the veins and ridges of Micah's cock inside me, even though I was producing so much slick. I was surrounded by warmth, and I felt lighter and more agile than I had in months. When his hand slid from my hip and into the gap formed by my distended abdomen, I moaned with unrestrained pleasure, feeling his fingers close around my neglected cock.

"Oh, *fuck*," he growled out, "keep clenching around me like that and I'm going to come before you do."

"Do it," I demanded, deliberately squeezing around him this time. I delighted in the way his expression contorted. "Come for me, darling. I need it. I need you to fill me up."

I couldn't explain why I needed it so badly, but my omega would not be satisfied until he came. I felt as though I was on fire and, idly, I wondered whether this was akin to being in heat…though that made very little sense as I was already heavily pregnant and unable to conceive.

"Oh, Jesus-fuck, Bran…your scales…"

Wet fingertips came up from my other hip and brushed my temple, setting off renewed jolts of pleasure through my body and I let out a guttural, "*Nnnngh.*"

The bliss I felt must have shot through the bond because that was enough to set my alpha off. His grip on my cock tightened as his hips convulsed and I felt his cock swell.

"Fuck, sugar. I'm coming," he warned me, his voice strained and low. "Fuck, *uuunnngh.*"

I allowed his orgasm to consume me. The pleasure of it raced through the bond and into my own nerve endings as I also relished the feeling of his cock growing and swelling and locking his seed inside me. His knot put pressure on my prostate and I was done. My back arched and I came with a cry, barely riding out my own orgasm before he was coming again. The sensation of him filling me did exactly as I had anticipated, cooling the heat that had been devouring me from the inside.

With my heart racing from the come down, I slumped and gripped the edges of the tub to keep myself upright, grinning lazily at the feeling of Micah's cock jerking inside me, the jolts of pleasure through the bond matching each twitch.

"Don't move," he demanded, sounding wrecked. His usually glorious hair was wet and stringy around his face, and his forehead and pink cheeks glistened with perspiration.

He had never looked more gorgeous.

"I...*oh.*" My hand flew to my belly as it tightened with a cramp.

Micah's grimace and annoyance at my movement immediately morphed into concern. "What's wrong?" He attempted to sit up straighter, yelping at the tugging to his knot.

"Most likely Braxton Hicks contractions," I replied, frowning down at my belly as I rubbed my hand over the area, ignoring the phantom, lingering pain. "Orgasms can sometimes trigger them."

"And you didn't think to warn me—*ah, fuck.*" He cursed and came again when I tensed and groaned through another mild cramp. "Shit," he caught his breath, "are you okay? Are they supposed to come so quickly together?"

I bit my lip. "They can be erratic," I answered, but my brain was already leaping through other potential scenarios. Scenarios where these were not Braxton Hicks contractions but the onset of labor.

Because, I realized after the fog of my heat-like desperation faded, semen contained prostaglandins. In pregnancies, when deposited near the cervix, prostaglandins helped soften the cervix to prepare for dilation. Additionally, oxytocin was the hormone produced by the body during orgasms, and oxytocin was also the natural form of the synthetic hormone, Pitocin, which is often given to patients via drip for formal inductions of labor.

While I didn't have the same physiology as most pregnant people, I was still an omega. I had a sneaking suspicion that the science of labor worked similarly, though my body would develop a birth canal for the actual event. After all, magic and shifter biology still had *some* science working in the background.

So, I was heavily pregnant. and I had just had a lot of prostaglandins and oxytocin introduced to my system, and I was cramping at what might just be fairly regular intervals.

The signs all pointed to early labor.

Not wanting to panic my mate unnecessarily, I attempted to keep my suspicions to myself. Carefully shielding my feelings was harder when we were intimately connected, but not impossible. So, I did my best to remain calm and nonchalant, even when another cramp tightened my belly. I even managed not to clench around Micah's knot, though that took effort I wasn't certain I would be able to maintain if the cramps continued to increase in strength and rhythm.

Five more cramps later, and I was certain a pattern had established itself, and I was no longer able to conceal the pain from the bond, or from my expression.

Thankfully, though, Micah's knot had begun to deflate enough that he could pull out of me. I heaved a sigh of relief and eased myself backwards until I was resting against the other end of the tub.

Micah watched me for a moment, then, more calmly than I had expected, asked, "They're not Braxton Hicks contractions, are they? I mean...those last couple came through the bond..."

Taking a wobbly breath, I shook my head slowly. "I...do not think they are, no."

He steeled his jaw and nodded. "Okay." I could see his anxiety written plainly on his face, but I didn't feel it through our connection. I assumed he was shielding his concern from me, and I appreciated it. I had enough of my own. Licking his lips, he asked, "What do you need me to do?"

Chapter Twenty-Two

When I had silently told my girls that I would meet them soon, I hadn't actually meant that I would meet them that same day. We weren't ready. It was too soon. They would be *so* premature and one of them was already too small, and—

I stopped and took a breath, the pain on Brandt's face a sharp reminder that I had to keep my shit together.

"Call Eric," he replied after riding out another contraction. I couldn't feel his pain through the bond, and I wasn't sure if that was because he was shielding me from it, or because something in the magic knew not to incapacitate us both. "Let him know to prep the incubators."

I didn't understand how he could be so calm about it. About knowing that our girls would need special care for some unknown amount of time. About knowing that they probably wouldn't be coming home with us for days, if not weeks.

At least being in the incubators will keep them safe and healthy, I reminded myself.

It hadn't been that long since Eric and Brandt had purchased the supplies for a neonatal nursery in the lab. A handful of weeks, really. Eric had spoken to the staff at the two nearest hospitals, too, letting them know that we may request assistance in order to properly care for three premature infants. For all that Brandt and Eric were both doctors, neither of them had that level of experience or knowledge in pediatric medicine. As far as we knew, Eric's promises to make healthy donations to the hospitals in question ensured that, when he put in the call for help, we would receive it.

Now that Brandt was in labor, I really hoped that help would arrive.

I climbed out of the tub and headed over to our pile of discarded clothes, digging through them in search of either one of our phones. I grabbed my jeans first and found my phone, bringing Eric's contact information up before pressing the green call icon.

"Come on," I huffed into the sound of the call ringing, "come on, come o—oh, thank God," I cut Eric off as he answered, barely getting out the 'he' part of 'hello'. "Brandt's in labor."

I didn't know whether to be relieved or irritated when Eric barely reacted. "Okay. I'm assuming it's only the early stages, so we have some time to get organized."

"He...he said you should get the incubators ready. And, uh, maybe call those doctors or nurses or whoever was on standby to help out with the girls."

"I'm already on it," he assured me. "How is he doing? Is he feeling contractions? How far apart are they? Has his birth canal started—"

"How about I put him on the line?" I felt out of my depth and kind of useless as an alpha, but I didn't want to get the answers wrong. This was my mate and children's health we were talking about, and I wasn't a medical professional. I was a makeup artist, for fuck's sake. Trying not to panic, I thrust the phone in front of Brandt and hit the speaker phone icon on the screen. "You're on speaker."

For his part, Brandt gave me an almost amused raise of his eyebrow before he calmly answered Eric's questions, wincing and rubbing his belly midway through the call.

"Because this is a higher risk pregnancy than the others have been, I think you should come down here as soon as you're able," Eric advised, making my pulse spike. "We need to get some steroids into you for their lungs. We can also monitor your progress more closely and can intervene if there are any complications. Are you good with that?"

"Of course," Brandt agreed readily. "I am currently in the bath, but Micah will help me out and we will be there soon."

"Yeah, maybe we'll aim for a water birth next time," Eric joked, and I felt myself go pale. Oblivious, he said, "See you soon," and ended the call.

"Micah…" Brandt gently pushed my hand, holding the phone, towards my chest. "I am fine. *We* are fine."

No thanks to me, I thought with derision, but I shooed the thoughts away and nodded. "I know. But, they're still so early…"

"We knew that would be likely," he soothed. "Multiples usually are. And there are three of them sharing very limited space in here," he rubbed his bump. "They will do better with space to grow and develop further with adequate medical care. And I" —he paused to grimace— "I will do better once my body is my own again."

I was still anxious, but I understood that he knew better than me when it came to these things. "Let's get you out of there, then."

"I take it back," Brandt complained hours later, bent over the side of the hospital bed as another contraction wracked his body, "I take it all back. This is torture."

I rubbed his back, unsure what to say or what to do to help him.

"I cannot even blame you," he continued to complain, "because I did this to myself."

"You can blame him for the next one," Eric informed him with an easy shrug. "And potentially for inducing your labor, too."

"Eric!" Brandt snapped his head up and glared at his brother.

"Wait," I looked between them, "what? This is my fault?"

"No." My mate's voice was forceful.

Simultaneously, Eric repeated, "Potentially."

"How?" I asked.

Eric grinned, clearly happy to have a captive audience for a medical lecture. "Well, sex can induce labor due to a number of reasons, including the hormones released during orgasm, and the lipid compounds in semen can—"

"*Aaargh*," Brandt interrupted, his fists gripping the sheets so tightly that his knuckles turned white, "could you perhaps focus on your patient, brother?"

"You're grumpy when you're in pain, Bee," Eric's reply was blithe.

Brandt growled. "I am going to shift and eat you."

"Then who will deliver your babies?"

Brandt panted and whined, widening his stance. "M-Micah could do it," he said with a confidence I definitely didn't agree with. "He is my a-alp-*fuck*!"

Inside me, my horse whined and stamped his hooves uneasily. I was right there with him. Seeing our mate in so much discomfort was unbearable.

"He is my alpha," Brandt continued, as if he hadn't just been close to giving me an aneurism with how much pain he was in, "and instinct would guide —*oh, Gods, fuck*— I need to push."

Eric smirked. "The magic words," he declared, then dropped to his knees behind Brandt, who was still braced over the lowered hospital bed. He lowered it further still. "Let's get this party started, hmm?"

"I am going to destroy you," Brandt muttered at him.

"Yeah, well, before you do...could you move back a little and bend your knees. More of a squat...that's it, good." Eric looked up at me, as if sensing how completely useless I felt. "I need you to stay close in case you have to hand me supplies, but rub his back and hold his hands...whatever he needs you to do to get through this, okay?"

I just nodded.

My mate gripped my hand as soon as I offered it to him, and I used my other hand to continue to rub his back and his shoulders while he panted and whined. Eric told him to push when the next contraction crested, and he grunted and growled, squeezing my fingers as he followed the instruction.

"That's it," Eric encouraged him, positioned awkwardly where Brandt was squatting so he could keep an eye where it needed to be, "just like that on the next one, too."

I was surprised when Brandt chose this as his preferred birthing position, having assumed it would be just like in the movies, with the laboring partner reclining on a hospital bed. But he had explained that this was preferable because gravity would work with the babies, not against them, and with three to push out...well, it made more sense to take every advantage he could get.

Still, it didn't look like the easiest position for Eric to be in, having to watch from an awkward, crouched position on the ground, with a mirror on the floor between Brandt's spread feet for additional guidance.

Eric didn't complain, though. For all that he and Brandt (and Sage, when he was around), argued and stirred each other up, they loved and supported each other. This was just another example of that. Eric encouraged Brandt and praised him for every contraction and every push, even while Brandt bitched at him to stop being so patronizing. He just chuckled and kept at it, and I backed him up.

"You're doing so good, sugar," I murmured, pressing a kiss to the top of Brandt's sweaty head. "You're so strong, and we're going to meet our girls soon because of you."

"*Uuugggghh,*" he groaned, "it *burns.* I cannot...*oh God,* it's too much."

"Baby One is crowning, Bee," Eric said, "that's why it's burning. This is the hard part. Push as hard as you can on the next contraction, okay?"

Brandt let out a strangled sob and shook his head. "I can't."

"You *can*," I insisted, squeezing his hand. "You're a fucking *dragon*, baby. You can do anything."

He yowled, not having the time to offer any kind of argument to my words before the next contraction built and crested. "Push, Bran," I urged. "You've got this, and I've got you."

"Almost there," Eric added. "The next one will do it."

Brandt was shaking his head in denial, and it broke something inside me to see tears rolling down his cheeks. "It's too much. Too—" He cut himself off with a sound that was somewhere between a scream and a growl, then he slumped forward, his shoulders going lax.

At the same time, Eric declared, "Head's out." He looked up at me and smiled. "I think she looks like you."

"Of course she does," Brandt sighed. "I do all the work and she comes out looking like him."

"She's one of three," I reminded him, glad that his humor seemed to be returning to him, "you might have the dominant genes in the other two."

"Come watch," Eric told me, and I was torn between holding Brandt's hand and comforting him, and watching our firstborn enter the world.

Compromising, I kept hold of Brandt's hand, but tugged it across the narrow, plastic mattress so I could lean around and— "Oh my god." I was equal parts horrified and enraptured. It was a surreal sight to see a tiny head emerging from my mate's body. Especially when it was out of an orifice which hadn't existed until a couple of hours earlier.

I couldn't tear my gaze away, squeezing Brandt's hand as Eric coached him through delivering her shoulders. Then, all of a sudden, she was out, in Eric's hands, taking her first breaths as she let out a warbling cry.

"Oh my god," I repeated, hearing my own voice wobble. She was so tiny. Smaller than even Lena and Brandi's babies had been. Like a delicate, porcelain doll...covered in blood and vernix and who knew what the hell else. But she was perfect.

"Congrats, guys, your eldest daughter is here," Eric said, more for Brandt's benefit than mine. "Micah, take off your shirt. Skin-to-skin contact is encouraged right now. Sit on the bed and hold her."

He passed her to me after I was shirtless and helped me position her tiny frame in my far-too-gangly arms. I was convinced I would squish her or drop her.

"Say hi to Papa," I heard myself say, turning my body and tilting forward so Brandt could see the perfection he had brought into the world. "You made this, sugar," I told him as he rolled onto his side and reached out a hand to stroke over her soft newborn skin.

Tears blurred my vision watching him and I blinked, not knowing when I had started to cry.

"You've only got to do that twice more," Eric told him, and he turned to level a scowl at his brother.

"You could not let me enjoy the reprieve from the contractions for even a minute, could you?"

Eric just rolled his eyes.

I snickered to myself and silently wondered if this girl in my arms would have the same kind of relationship with her sisters.

The first of the support nurses arrived midway through Brandt birthing our second daughter. The redhaired, human woman blinked in shocked surprise before she beamed brightly at us and scrubbed in, stepping to Eric's side to help with the birth.

She earned major points for that, as far as I was concerned. Even though she scented as human, and seeing a man giving birth in the middle of rural Iowa must have thrown her for a loop, her professionalism and obvious joy to be a part of the moment instantly made her trustworthy to my alpha.

"And here's Baby Two," Eric beamed up at me, supporting our second daughter in his arms. She looked bigger than our firstborn, slightly plumper in the cheeks and belly, though still a scrawny-looking preemie, which was to be expected. The tuft of hair on her head was thicker and darker than the hair on the baby I was still cradling against my chest, and I smirked and leaned forward to kiss Brandt's cheek.

"Baby Two is all you, sugar," I told him. "So I told you so."

My exhausted mate snorted and rolled onto his side again to watch as Eric transferred the baby to my other arm. As with our eldest, Brandt reached up and stroked his index finger down her flailing arm in greeting.

"Hello, precious," he murmured, and I lost myself to tears again.

"Oh, that's just too sweet," the feminine voice startled both me and Brandt, and we looked to the nurse who cringed and held her hands in surrender. "Sorry. I'm so sorry. You're just such a gorgeous family, you know?"

Brandt raised an eyebrow and looked at me in askance. I shrugged.

Eric chuckled. "You must be Tammy, right? Thanks for just jumping in."

"It's my pleasure," she nodded. "And I am. Tammy, I mean. Hi."

Her awkward wave and friendly smile only made her seem more endearing. She looked to be roughly my age, with thick red hair like Sage's tied in a ponytail at the nape of her neck. Her eyes were bright blue, and she had a perfect hourglass figure. I imagined a number of the women in the town might feel threatened by her, if not for her easy smile and genuinely friendly personality. Or maybe even more so because of those things.

"If this is not the most awkward way to meet someone, I do not know what is," Brandt muttered, then grimaced. "And I believe break time is over."

Our third daughter came into the world far more quickly than her elder sisters. She was tiny —smaller than the others— and Eric and Tammy seemed to speed up as they worked to get her into an incubator before either Brandt or I could hold her.

My heart broke a little to see our tiny girl with oxygen tubes and a heart rate monitor and various other wires and tubes attached to her frail-looking body, but I knew that this was what was best for her.

With wobbly legs, Brandt climbed onto the bed and Eric guided him through passing the afterbirth while Tammy took our two other daughters and checked their oxygen levels and heart rates, then took their measurements, noting everything down before she smiled apologetically in my direction.

At the same time, with Brandt's labor ending, whatever magic had closed off the bond eased away, and I was able to feel his emotions again. I forced myself to pay attention to Tammy first.

"Their oxygen isn't quite where it should be, so I think we should get them in their incubators as well. But I'll defer to you, Doctor Weldman," she added in Eric's direction, and he shook his head.

"I trust your judgement on this. I don't have as much neonatal experience."

"But...Brandt didn't get to hold them," I protested, feeling my heart break all over again. It didn't seem fair that my mate had gone through that entire ordeal and hadn't held even one of his daughters.

"Two minutes," Tammy said, bustling over with both babies in her arms. Brandt accepted them greedily, ignoring whatever Eric was doing to tidy him up post birth.

"Thank you," Brandt's voice was choked with emotion, and I felt the overwhelming love come rushing through our recently re-opened bond. I gasped and only barely managed to hold back my own sob as the cascade of feelings seemed to double my own.

Instead, I wrapped my arm around his shoulders and leaned in, pressing my cheek to his as we looked down at two of our babies together. He murmured low greetings to our girls, telling them how much we loved them and that we were so excited for them to meet everyone.

Then our daughters were whisked away by their uncle and his new assistant, and I felt Brandt's despair slam into me with such force that it took my breath away.

<h1 style="text-align:center">Chapter Twenty-Three</h1>

"**Y**ou can't live in the clinic, Bran."

Despite hearing Day's words, I did not look up from my seat in between two of our girls' incubators. Instead, I kept my eyes glued to the barely noticeable rise and fall of our youngest's chest. I was still aware of the silent conversation taking place between my mate and my young friend, though.

It had been three days since I'd given birth. Three agonizing days of not having free access to my children. Of having to watch machines and tubes support their growth, while I fought with the torture device better known as an electric breast pump.

I felt like a failure as a father.

Not only had I not been able to carry them long enough to be able to take them home with me, I was also unable to provide enough milk to properly nurture them. Eric, Tammy, and Casey (the other neonatal expert Eric had brought in from a local hospital), had all tried to reason with me, reminding me that most chestfeeding parents' milk supply didn't come in until at least day three, but I was determined to at least provide colostrum to my newborns in their first days.

It was a blow to my pride and my confidence when they suggested that, until my supply came in, we supplement with formula.

I knew it was a wise decision, and I had never bought into the formula vs breastmilk debate, but I had envisioned bonding with my babies through chestfeeding and having those dreams dashed hurt. A lot.

As did being unable to hold my girls at all.

To overcompensate, I had sat myself in the hospital-grade neonatal unit Eric had commissioned and built for the clinic, and I had insisted on keeping vigil over my children. I only left the room to use the bathroom, becoming increasingly upset every time I was confronted by the evidence of my postpartum bleeding. It was a reminder of everything I was going through, and I hated it.

"You can leave," I told them both, still not taking my eyes off my baby. She needed a name. All three did. But I refused to name them until I could hold them. "But I am staying here."

"Sugar," Micah's voice was tinged with sadness and an edge of frustration, "you need to rest and recover properly. You've barely eaten, barely stayed hydrated...Your dark circles have circles."

"I will eat when—"

"No." While he didn't raise his voice, the hairs on the back of my neck tingled. I had never heard my alpha use his alpha power before, and it made my stomach turn to think he was using it on me. "You *will* take care of yourself." When I tore my gaze from our daughter and looked at him —really, truly looked at him for the first time in days— I saw my own heartache radiating back at me. His expression softened and he crouched at my feet, squeezing my knee. "Baby, I know this sucks, but wasting away next to them isn't going to help them. They need you to take care of yourself so, when it's time to bring them home, you will be there for them one hundred percent." He swallowed roughly. "I've been doing research, and I think...I think maybe some of the problems you're having with the pump can be attributed to dehydration and not eating enough. How are you supposed to make food if your body doesn't have the energy to keep itself going, you know? And the stress and pressure you're putting on yourself..."

My eyes stung and I looked away, knowing that he was right. But as my gaze landed on our tiniest child, the urge to stay and protect them welled up inside me again.

"They're safe here," Day assured me from the doorway. I had forgotten that he was there at all, and I cringed internally at how disconnected from my surroundings I had become. "If Eric isn't here keeping an eye on things, I am. Or Ollie is. Or, hell, even Beck. Not one member of our pack is going to leave the girls unattended with outsiders, no matter how nice they might seem."

Considering Damon's son had almost been kidnapped by our cult-like adversaries, I knew that his vehement protective instinct was coming from personal experience, not just our friendship or connection through the pack. Still, the thought of going home —to the place where our daughters had cribs and clothing waiting for them— and not bringing them with me was upsetting.

"Your babies are safe here," Day repeated himself. "They're thriving and getting stronger every day. But you're not."

"Come home with me, sugar," Micah practically begged. "Come home, have a shower, eat something substantial...and then tomorrow morning I will bring you back here myself, okay? We can sit with our girls all day. We'll do it every day until they come home. But you have to take care of yourself or let me take care of you, too. That's non-negotiable."

I wasn't going to win this battle. Deep inside, I knew that if it had been any other omega in my place, I would have been insisting on the same things that my mate and friend were.

Sighing, I nodded. "Fine. But I will return as soon as the sun rises."

Micah squeezed my knee again. "And I'll be right here with you."

Walking across the threshold of my home without my babies in my arms hurt. It felt *wrong*. My stretched, flabby abdomen was barren, and my nest was empty. Inside me, my omega whined — not a sound I would have associated with dragonkind, but he whined nonetheless.

I knew that there were parents who had lost children. I knew that there were parents of children with health issues so severe, they may never leave the hospital. In the grand scheme of things, I knew what I was experiencing did not compare to the pain other families had experienced and would continue to experience once this trying time in my life had passed. Nevertheless, knowing as much did not mean I could simply snap out of my sadness over my situation.

I wished that I could.

I had not expected to feel this way. Though my pregnancy had not been all rainbows and lollipops, I had generally been happy and excited. I had even known that there was every likelihood our triplets would require a lengthy hospital stay as most triplet births were quite premature. I had thought I had braced myself for it.

I had been wrong.

"Come on," Micah took my hand and led me down the short hallway to our bedroom. The door across from our primary suite was closed, and I was thankful that my mate had had the foresight to ensure as much. I didn't think my heart could handle the sight of the empty cribs and other untouched items. "Let's get you showered properly, sugar."

It was his polite way of saying I stank. I hadn't washed since he had assisted me into Eric's shower in the early hours of the morning, shortly after the girls had been taken away to the neonatal nursery room. I had been mostly numb at the time, trying to process the night's events. He had carefully washed away the blood and other remnants from the birth, had dried me and manhandled me into the first pair of maternity underwear (a horror no living soul should have to experience), and then into soft pajamas which had seemingly materialized out of nowhere.

It was those same pajamas he peeled off my body in our ensuite bathroom, and I cringed away from them when I saw the spots where the maternity pads had not held up. Embarrassment squeezed my insides, and unpleasant heat infused my cheeks, even though my beautiful mate said nothing about the stains.

"Eric said showers are better than baths while you're still healing up," he explained softly as he ushered me in to the large shower cavity. "But as soon as you're cleared for it, I'll run you a relaxing bubble bath."

Tears slid down my cheeks, poorly disguised by the warm water cascading over my tender body.

"I..." I paused to clear my throat, my voice sounding gravelly and strange from the days spent in mostly silence. "I am sorry, darling," I finally choked out, hating how unhinged and out of control I felt. I was a man of science. I prided myself on being rational. However, at that moment, I felt far removed from rational thought or behavior. "I have been—"

"Stop," he interrupted me, pulling me into his embrace and holding me as I battled the urge to break down entirely. "You have nothing to apologize for. You gave birth to *three* babies only a few days ago. Not only was that a hell of a thing to go through, you've got all sorts of hormones in your system, you're exhausted, and you don't even get to cuddle your babies or bring them home. You're allowed to hate that. You're allowed to grieve the experience you wish you'd had."

It was becoming increasingly difficult to keep my emotions in check. "But I knew this would be the likely outcome...and all three of our daughters are thriving with care. It is selfish of me when other people in similar circumstances have not been so lucky."

I knew, logically, that my feelings for my situation did not invalidate anyone else's, but my emotional state was deteriorating, and I felt as though I was spiraling.

"I think you know you're not being selfish," my mate murmured into my ear as the warm water continued to cascade over us. "And I think if anyone else said those words to you, you would tell them they're allowed to be upset at the situation, wouldn't you?"

I considered Day and Ollie and Lena, and I nodded, choking back a sob.

"Honey, just let it out," Micah insisted. "Bottling it all up is going to make it worse. And," he swallowed, and I felt his throat working as he did, seeing as I had my face buried in the crook of his neck, "I'm hurting, too, Bran. Don't shut me out. Please."

The softly spoken admission and plaintive request were my undoing. I clutched at him as the gut-wrenching sobs broke free and I allowed myself to howl out the pain I was feeling. I had no idea how long we stood there under the shower's spray, while I cried in a way I could never recall doing before.

Micah held me through it, but as I slowly began to calm, I realized that he was crying, too. Guilt threatened to overwhelm me, but he squeezed me tightly, denying the feelings I had to assume had transferred through our bond.

"You have nothing to feel guilty for," he rasped out and nuzzled the top of my head with his cheek. "This is hard for both of us, and the bond is making the feelings more intense...but I appreciate it, because we're going through it together, you know? And we are. In this together, I mean. I'm not going anywhere, Brandt. You're not alone in this. I love you, and I love our girls."

A rush of conflicting emotions washed over me. I was still upset that my children were not yet able to come home with me, but I was also flooded with warmth and love for my mate. His support and the reminder that I was not alone in this experience were bracing.

"I love you, too," I said, realizing that I had not said those words since our daughters were born. "I am sorry that I—"

"Nuh-uh," he interrupted my apology again, "nothing to be sorry for, sugar." He gently pushed me back and cast his gaze over my face. I assumed I looked like a wreck, but he smiled softly and asked, "How are you feeling now?"

I had to admit that my emotional release had been cathartic. "Better," I admitted. "Still sad, but...better."

"Let's get washed up and go snuggle on the couch, then. I'll call in a favor with Beck and see if he can swing by the diner and grab us some burgers and fries. I think we could both do with something a bit greasy and carb-y."

My stomach growled and, for the first time in days, I acknowledged that I felt hungry. "That sounds wonderful, darling."

And, as we settled in on the couch a handful of minutes later, with the television playing a documentary about sea life, I finally felt myself beginning to relax. The sadness was still there, but it did not feel quite as unbearable with my alpha's arms around me. I knew that I would still have my ups and downs, but for the first time in days, I began to believe that everything would be okay.

The day the girls were declared stable enough to be held was easily the best day of my life. They still had various wires and tubes connected to their tiny, wriggly bodies, but their lungs were strong enough for them to breathe on their own, and their vitals were good.

Micah and I both cried as we cradled them in our arms, each of us agreeing that we felt far too large and clunky for their fragile little frames.

"They're like dolls," he whispered, staring down at our middle child with love hearts in his eyes. Those same eyes rose to meet mine, shining with emotion and more tears. "We need to name them, sugar."

I nodded and looked down at my firstborn and youngest, one carefully supported in the crook of each of my arms.

Gazing at my firstborn, the daughter who looked more and more like Micah as her wrinkled skin smoothed out and she slowly plumped up, I said, "Lucia." Licking my lips, I added, "It means light."

"Perfect," he agreed. "And this little lady?"

I smiled as he carefully lifted our second daughter for emphasis. "You should have the honor."

Micah grinned. "Belle," his answer came quickly and definitively. "Because she's beautiful."

"They are all beautiful," I rebuked gently, but I nodded anyway. "Belle it is." My lips quirked. "You are going to purchase all the Disney themed toys and clothing, aren't you?"

He nodded. "And I'll do their hair up in all the princess styles, too."

I sent affection and amusement his way as I sighed and answered, "Of course you will." Then I looked back down at our third daughter, still so much smaller than her sisters. "What do you think of Rita? From memory, it can mean pearl or brave…" I trailed off, not feeling the need to explain why I thought those fitting meanings.

Still holding Belle —and it was such a surreal feeling to suddenly have names for our daughters— Micah crouched carefully at my side and peered down at our tiniest of tiny ones.

"Hi, Rita," he whispered, making a hushed 'aww' sound as she cracked open a dark blue eye. "Yeah," his voice was thick with emotion, "that's the one."

It felt too easy. I knew we had discussed names on and off for weeks, but to just decide like that, without argument or debate, felt…strange. Then again, we were a bonded pair; it made some sense that we would be compatible on even this.

"If all goes well, they should be able to go home with you in a few more weeks," Casey's voice cut into my musings. I turned my head to find him leaning against the doorframe, wearing his powder blue nursing scrubs.

He was also human, but, like Tammy, did not seem at all fazed to be surrounded by shifters and talk of magic and dragons and unicorns. If anything, he seemed excited by it, his dark brown eyes lighting up any time the topics were mentioned within his earshot. Also like Tammy, he was extremely proficient in his work, and he truly seemed to love working with the babies as much as she did. I was thankful that Eric had managed to find two people who I felt I could trust with my children, not that I believed he had had much sway in the matter.

"I do hope so," I said in response to Casey's optimism.

He smiled and stepped further into the room. "Did you want to try chestfeeding today? Or were you going to switch to formula completely? Zero judgment," he held his hands up in surrender, "fed is best as far as I'm concerned. And you've got three little mouths to feed, so I'd probably recommend supplementing with formula anyway, if only to give yourself a breather every now and then."

We had already been supplementing my pumped milk with formula, and seeing my girls growing was enough to convince me that it had most certainly been the right choice for us. "I would like to try," I answered, "however, I read that, being premature, they may struggle to latch."

"They might," he nodded. "But we can work on that if it happens to be the case. I'm not qualified as a lactation consultant, but I've worked with a few in my time." He offered me a rueful smile.

Where Tammy was young, Casey was inching closer to what humans considered middle-aged. His brown hair had a few tiny glints of silver peeking out, and I saw similar hints of the grey on his stubbled jaw. Still, he wasn't that much older than Micah, and I didn't think he had any reason to worry about his age just yet.

"I would appreciate any advice you can give me," I replied. "I will admit that in my many years practicing medicine, lactation support is not something I have studied."

Casey shrugged. "Well, you never practiced in obstetrics or postnatal care, so it makes sense that it wasn't on your radar."

I appreciated his pragmatism and lack of judgement. Even Tammy had been surprised that, in hundreds of years, I had not taken the opportunity to branch out with my medical training. I supposed I was, at heart, a creature of habit.

Casey helped shift Rita from my arms to Micah's. Then, after I lifted one side of my shirt, he guided me through the process of assisting Lucia to latch on for her first feeding. Through whatever shifter magic ran through my veins, my body had been changing during the pregnancy to prepare for this ability, changing the shape of my already somewhat soft pectorals, but also shedding —for lack of a better word— any chest hair around my nipples. The changes had been so gradual that I had almost forgotten what I had looked like prior to the pregnancy, but gazing down at my nursing newborn, I was suddenly struck by how surreal the situation was.

"Wow," I murmured, the connection to my daughter soothing some of the lingering emotional pain of weeks spent unable to hold her or take her home. She brought up a tiny hand, as if kneading my pec, and it melted my heart.

"Looks like she knows what to do," Casey grinned. "When she's had her fill, we'll switch her out with Belle and switch sides when we do."

I nodded, transfixed by the rhythmic movement at my chest, the gentle pull as she nursed and the relief—both emotional and physical— of feeding her directly.

"Uh, sugar?" I looked up to find Micah biting his lip. He gestured with his chin towards my other side and...*oh*.

"Ah, your body has just gone into let down mode," Casey didn't seem at all fazed to see the wet patch forming on the other side of my shirt. "It's perfectly normal. You can use nursing pads to prevent it from happening...but, uh, I'm not entirely sure how you'd wear them...maybe fixed on with some medical tape? Anyway," he shrugged, "you might get to a point where you can feed two at once and it won't be an issue."

The thought was somewhat overwhelming, but I nodded. "We will make it work."

I was just thrilled with the strides forward we had taken already. For the first time in weeks, I began to see the light at the end of the tunnel. Through the bond, I felt my mate's love and affection, and I knew that he felt just as optimistic as I did.

Chapter Twenty-Four

"**A**ww, I don't think ours were ever this small," Ollie cooed down at Rita, rocking her in his arms.

Beck and Sandy had asked if they could throw us a 'Welcome Home' party in lieu of the baby shower we had never had (or wanted), and neither Brandt nor I could bear to say no to our pack.

"Remember the colic," Beck said, "and focus on how hard the potty training is." He shot me a pleading look. "Tell him how hard newborns are. Please?"

Beside me, Brandt snorted. "Our faithful leader is afraid of children."

"No," Beck corrected him primly, throwing his shoulders back and raising his chin, "I am afraid of going *all* the way back to sleepless nights and diaper explosions."

"But look at her," Ollie snuggled into Beck's side and lifted Rita higher. She snuffled in her sleep and curled further into his hold. "Isn't she precious?"

Beck's expression softened and he nodded. "She is. All three of them are. Really. But we have our hands full with the twins, don't we?"

Ollie pouted and sighed as he looked back down at my baby, crooking his index finger on his free hand before running it over her soft cheek. "I just miss this feeling, you know? Rory and Duke are three now, and they're getting so big and independent..."

"Independent?" Beck repeated incredulously, but he was smiling. "Did you miss the part where we are still trying to potty train them? Or where they still wake up and call out for us *right* when we're trying to enjoy some *alone time*?"

I had to smother a laugh as I leaned in to Brandt's side, murmuring, "Five bucks says he caves soon."

Brandt nodded.

Beck chuckled. "You know I can hear you."

"And you're not denying it," Sandy cut in, wandering over with Lucia cradled in the crook of her elbow. "I think our house could definitely use the pitter patter of more baby feet. It's been kind of boring since Brandi moved in with Lena."

"Maybe you should be voluntold to babysit more often," Beck argued. "Rory and Duke *love* their Aunt Sandy."

"Oh, it really is *such* a pity that I have to travel back to New York to work so often," Sandy widened her eyes with faux innocence. "You know I would love to look after the little monsters —I mean, sweethearts— more."

Beck's chuckle turned into a laugh as he shook his head. "You just said we should have more, but agree that the first two are too much to handle sometimes."

"Maybe they need siblings to entertain them? Little buddies to love on?" Sandy suggested, and I knew her well enough to understand that she was just trying to stir Beck up. They had been foster siblings, after all. We all knew she didn't actually think 'as entertainment for older kids' was a valid reason for Beck to have more children.

"Micah and Brandt have just made three little buddies for them to play with," Beck argued back. "And the bonus there is that we don't have to deal with the not fun side of their babies." He shrugged at me and Brandt. "No offence to your girls."

"Dude, I've babysat your hellhounds," I replied with a smirk. "I'm aware of the not fun side of kids."

"Where are the twins, anyway?" Brandt looked around our living room cautiously.

"Lena and Brandi are babysitting so we can visit you guys without distraction," Ollie answered. "It is nice to have a break."

I shook my head at Beck when he opened his mouth, probably with the intention of using Ollie's enjoyment of some kid-free time as proof that they shouldn't give in to his cluckiness. Even I knew that would land him in the dog house. Wolf house? Whatever.

"Well, that's nice of them," Sandy ran her hand through her purple pixie cut and grinned at Beck. "You'll have to thank them for sparing Micah and Brandt's house from certain destruction."

"Okay, stop, they're not *that* bad," Beck grumbled, taking the bait.

Sandy winked at Ollie, before saying, "Then there's no reason not to give in and have another one, right? Look at how sweet this baby is..."

"I hate you all," Beck sighed, but he couldn't hide his amusement.

I sat back and hugged Brandt closer, enjoying how right this felt. Being with my pack, seeing them welcome and faun over my babies, snuggling with my mate...I could hardly imagine what life had been like before I gave into the instinct to return to Shifters Sanctuary.

And, despite the pack's unrelenting vigilance against newcomers or passers-through the town, nothing scary or dramatic had happened since I had been there. Beck and Rex still spoke in low tones about the Moonmusic organization and their leader's ongoing campaign against us and 'our kind', but there hadn't been any attacks or kidnap attempts. Not since prior to Beck and Ollie's wedding, anyway.

When I mentioned as much to Beck, though, after the party had died down and he and I were seated on my back porch, each nursing a beer, he shook his head. "The rumblings and dissent are definitely still escalating," he told me. "One of the frat house guys," —he explained, referencing the large homestead housing people who had come to Shifters Sanctuary in the hopes they might be potential alphas themselves— "Matthew, is like a hacker or something. I didn't ask many questions about that. But we pay him to trawl the web and keep an eye on everything Morstein is up to...and we know he's keeping a close eye on us. Every time a new alpha pops up, he panics."

"But I've been here for months now and nothing's happened."

"Well, he's aware we have three dragons and that even bringing rocket launchers—yeah, I know, that sounds farfetched, but it doesn't make it any less true," he cut himself off at my wide-eyed stare. "Even bringing them didn't work in his favor. So now he's trying to convince his following that he's still got all the power and that we are the freaks."

"And the old-school packs really don't see how much better off they'd be without him? Like...what, exactly, do they get out of handing over their tithes and following his arbitrary rules?"

Beck shrugged. "Who the fuck knows? Ollie says that his pack firmly believe that their life is better because that's all they've ever known. Day agreed that his old pack didn't trust anyone who wanted an external education...and why would they? Leaders like that Morstein guy are scared of their followers having critical thinking skills, or of seeing how different things could be if they tried things another way. A way that doesn't financially and socially benefit him."

"That's why he's scared of you. Of this pack. Because you're —*we're*— proving that it can be done."

"Yeah. Of course, we have three centuries-old dragons with deep pockets which makes it easier, too," Beck sighed, "but it can be done. Look at your old pack: they're not Moonmusic fanatics."

"True." I thought of the pack I had grown up in back in California. "But we also were heavily influenced by human communities, I guess. Morstein and his crew are all about keeping shifter society insular"

"Yeah, so they can control it. If we all had packs like this one —or like your family's pack— where everyone is treated equally regardless of their secondary designation, or of their shifted species, and where town councils get to vote for what's best for the pack...that takes away the ultimate control. Morstein and his cronies don't want to give up that kind of power. And he's probably afraid that we, as alphas, outrank him in his system, too."

"And we can't, like, use that against him? We can't use the alpha powers and rank or whatever to stop him?"

"That's what I personally think he's most afraid of. That's why he wants to end us. Right now, he's still trying to convince his followers that we're not true alphas because we weren't born alphas. That because those of us he knows about grew up human, and that our human-influenced way of life is a threat to theirs. He has stopped trying to nab one of us for now, but that only makes me think he'd rather eradicate us at this point."

My stomach turned. "Eradicate?"

The word made me think of horrible historic events, both in human history and shifter history. Once upon a time, humans had hunted shifters into what they thought was extinction because they were threatened by our existence. Then they had turned on themselves, also driven by power and greed and fearmongering.

"Which is why we can't let our guards down. Especially while we still don't know how to determine who has an alpha side locked away behind a human or beta façade."

Years earlier, I never would have imagined my completely human roommate, a man who suffered from anxiety and claustrophobia when he was in too-large a crowd, would be an alpha. But now, hearing him speak so passionately about protecting a species he had never even known he was a part of, was humbling. Beck might have been uncomfortable accepting his role as pack Alpha, but he was born to lead. This conversation completely cemented that for me.

"I think Sage and Dex might be getting closer to finding more answers. Brandt was helping Eric go over some pictures from old journals a little while back...before the girls were born, I mean. But he said something the other day about Dex emailing more through from...wherever the hell he's traveled to now."

"Yeah, Eric's keeping me informed on that. We'll see what the new translations bring."

In the end, while the translations were a bust, the entire person Sage and Dex brought back to the pack was not.

At first glance, he seemed to be an older man, possibly in his sixties or early seventies, with a thick head of silver hair and a perfectly trimmed matching beard. But his scent reminded me of my girls, and he was in fantastic physical shape for a man of his apparent age. He was tall and long-limbed, kind of lanky like me, but seemed to exude the same sort of grace as Brandt, rather than my clumsiness.

Still, it blew me away when Brandt stiffened at my side and scented the air, murmuring, "Another unicorn."

I hadn't put two and two together until that moment.

"Micah," Dex smirked at me as he led the man further into the meeting room in Beck's house (a room which would always make me smile when I considered what Brandt and I had done there), "please allow me to introduce you to Sergio."

I rose from my seat to shake Sergio's hand, the hairs on the back of my neck spiking as I felt a tickle of recognition somewhere in the back of my brain. But that was weird, because I had never met this man before.

"You know what's fascinating about Sergio?" Dexter continued blithely, with that irritatingly smug tone of his. I kept my eyes on the pale blue pair in front of me, though, unable to look away. "Sergio," Dex answered himself, "spent a great deal of time in California roughly thirty-something years ago."

My heart rate increased and my mouth went dry.

"And Sergio," Dexter was on a roll, "just so happens to be one of the last true magic wielders on earth, don't you, Surge?"

Releasing the man's hand, I took a step backwards, right into Brandt's warm, steadying embrace.

"Dex," Sage sighed, "we talked about this..."

"I apologize," Sergio finally spoke, preventing Dexter from defending his actions. The older man hadn't taken his eyes off me, either, but his expression was carefully blank. He made me uneasy, but that was probably because I was ninety-nine percent sure this was the shaman my mother had visited in order to get pregnant. This was my biological father. "I never intended to cause a scene."

He seemed genuine enough, and his surprisingly American accented voice was low and calming.

"Dexter caused the scene, not you," Damon muttered from further down the table.

Dexter sighed. "Who invited the kitty cat anyway? Shouldn't you be playing receptionist at Eric's clinic?"

"Eric and Brandt are both here," Sage cut in, sounding surprisingly irritated with his best friend. "And Rex is Day's mate. Being one of only a few bonded pairs, it makes sense for them to be here."

"Welcome to bedlam," I offered the newcomer, my momentary shock rendering me numb as the others bickered around me. In that moment, I tried to remind myself that I still thought of my parents as my parents. Even if this guy was responsible for half of my genetic makeup, he wasn't anything to me but a stranger who had helped my parents out. Trying not to give the troublemaking dragon the satisfaction of watching me freak out, I forced a weak smile. "It's nice to meet you."

Brandt squeezed my hip and offered his own greeting, then suggested we all take our seats. I leaned into the reassurance he sent through the bond. I would process this latest mindfuck later. In private. Potentially over a Facetime call with my parents.

Dexter pouted as he took one beside Sergio, with Eric rolling his eyes and taking the seat next to me and across the table from both of them. Beck sat at the head of the long, timber table, tugging Ollie into his lap. Brandi and Lena were further down the table, across from Damon and Rex.

Because we had been told this meeting was important, most of the kids were being taken care of by other pack members — people Beck and Ollie had vouched for, though Ollie had winced and muttered something about Jazz giving the twins too much sugar. Brandt and I had our babies with us, though. They were sleeping in their strollers by the window at our backs, and they'd only need to be fed and changed when they woke up. (Unlike Beck's kids, who would probably attempt to scale the curtains in their boredom.)

"So," Beck clapped his hands together and looked towards Eric for guidance, "where do we begin?"

Chapter Twenty-Five

"I hear you have located information to unbind a shifter's repressed designation and abilities," Sergio said not long after our meeting began. His eyes drifted casually over Beckett, then Micah, then Rex and Brandi. "And I can see that you have already begun doing so."

"Actually, no," Beck told him with a slightly sheepish smile. "We, uh, we didn't control this. It kind of just happened naturally for us."

Sergio's eyes —set in a face so similar to my alpha's, it was almost as if we were seeing into the future— widened.

It was difficult not to pull Micah into my embrace and help him process the shock of meeting this man —this unicorn, his *biological father*— without warning, but he seemed just as eager for answers about the magic as the rest of us. Later, I would force the issue with him but, for the moment, we would focus on the task at hand. I would most certainly be having words with Dexter and Sage later, though. It was unlike my brother to allow his friend to be quite so chaotic.

"Naturally?" Sergio questioned.

Beck nodded. "Yeah. Rex, Brandi and I...we all thought we were human. Then we met our omegas and," he cleared his throat, glossing over the mating ruts which led to their knots forming, "suddenly, we weren't really human anymore."

"Fascinating." Sergio shifted his gaze to Micah. "And you?"

Micah shrugged. "I thought I was a beta. But then Brandt...uh, well, we felt drawn to each other and we put the pieces together and made a conscious choice to bond and draw out my knot and my alpha. At least, with the way we felt sounding so similar to what everyone else had experienced...it was an educated guess that it would happen."

I was surprised that Micah did not mention that he also believed that he was a horse until after our mating and bonding, but then, we had no idea about Sergio's intentions. It was likely wise to withhold any unnecessary information until after he reciprocated in kind.

The older unicorn nodded slowly and scratched his bearded jaw thoughtfully. "It does seem conveniently coincidental that it has happened to a cluster of people in such a small geographical area."

"To be fair, we were in New York, and Rex and Day were in Texas..." Ollie interjected.

Sergio's lips lifted in a little smile. "But to all be in the United States and all around the same time...it is still odd that we haven't heard of this happening anywhere else in the world, isn't it?"

"I agree," I told him, tilting my head genially. "Unless others are keeping it extremely well hidden, it does seem strange that it has all happened here with us."

"I think part of that can be attributed to the magic itself," Sergio said. Eric and I both straightened in our seats.

"How so?" Eric asked him, then gestured between himself and me. "We don't know a lot about the old ways, I'm afraid. They were dying out before we were born."

"Well, it's sort of like the way your parents' pack sees it," he replied, gesturing genially towards Micah with an upturned palm. "The magic —or fate, or the universe, however you wish to name it— generally blesses those it believes are worthy. The theory I and the other remaining mages and shamen believe is that magic itself began shielding alphas from their abilities until such time as we, as a species, respected each other enough to use the abilities correctly." He looked back over to where Oliver was seated on Beckett's lap and smiled. "You were chosen by magic first, correct?"

"Yeah..." Beck answered slowly, while Ollie nodded.

"The magic must have sensed that you would treat your mate and others as equals." He sighed. "The shifter community has lost its way. The mistreatment of omegas has been appalling. Perhaps the magic saw something in you...a potential to change the world and restore balance."

Beck snorted. "I was a nobody. I'm still—"

"You're a born leader," Micah cut him off. "The way you talk about this pack, about protecting everyone here and omegas in general...Beck, you're kind of made for this."

Sergio shot Micah a smile before he continued. "And once you settled here, so did the magic. It likely drew the others here as well," he waved a hand over the table, "ensuring that you had the support you needed to start bringing order and balance back to our world."

Eric slumped back in his seat. "So you're saying there's still no way to know who might have an alpha side locked away? Not until the magic springs their mate on them and —bam— instant family?" He pulled out his phone, scrolling through his notes. "The journals suggested there were spells…"

"With the magic cooperating, there are, yes." Sergio nodded, completely unruffled by my brother's intensity. "However, the spells themselves were hidden away. When the magic became erratic and uncooperative, the spells no longer worked."

"And so shifters began to forget the old ways," I finished for him solemnly. "How is it you are still able to wield magic?"

"I am old," he admitted, then looked at Micah with an unreadable expression. "We unicorns live as long as the dragons. We are mystical creatures tied to magic itself. It is a blessing and a curse." His gaze drifted past us, to the strollers parked against the wall. "Our numbers have dwindled without alphas. Even our betas have had declining fertility." He met my gaze. "We have been going the way of the dragons. Losing hope. There are not many of us left in the world. But with magic on our side…" Once more, he looked towards the strollers, smiling softly. "Balance is being restored, and so is hope."

"That doesn't answer—*ouch*." Eric jumped in his seat and then frowned at my mate. "Did you just kick me?"

"Be patient," Micah told him, "and *listen*." He turned back to Sergio. "Please continue."

"Take, for example, your existence," Sergio said, speaking directly to Micah. "Your parents came to me and pleaded for the magic —for me— to help them conceive and carry a child to term. They were pure, loving people and, through my connection to the magic, I knew I could assist them. However, please understand that I believed my entire contribution mystical by nature. I hadn't realized that I...well." His expression turned rueful. "I believe that was also fate at play."

Micah snorted. "You didn't think that —I can't believe I'm going to say this— sleeping with my mother might have meant she conceived your kid and not her husband's?"

Sergio shrugged. "As I said, the fertility of unicorns has been dwindling. I had no reason to assume..." he stopped and sighed, shaking his head. "Everything that occurred that night was consensual, and I believed the magic's insistence on my presence was to use me as a conduit and nothing more. I was obviously wrong. The magic tends to do as it wishes sometimes. It has its reasons. However, there is a different energy here in this place. I can feel it. And, to answer your question," he turned his attention back to Eric, "I believe, if we locate the information about the spells, we could begin the process of isolating those with shielded alpha abilities and we could unbind them without the necessity of matings and bondings. However," his gaze traveled around the entire table again, "that could change things for the omegas living in the proximity of unbound alphas."

Eric was all ears again, leaning forward eagerly. "Change things how?"

"My personal theory is that once alphas become unleashed en masse, the magic will balance that out by restoring omegas' reproductive cycles. Regular heats, even for unmated and unbonded omegas, were a common occurrence prior to alphas becoming extinct. Bear in mind it is just a theory, but it is a risk we run."

"Ugh, I hate heats," Day complained. "But imagine going through it without an alpha. Blergh."

"We would need to find a way to mass produce the omega contraceptives, too," Ollie added. Then he frowned. "Could betas get an omega in heat pregnant?"

"In the past? No," Sergio shook his head, but then he gestured towards Lena and Brandi. "However, in the past, female alphas were unheard of."

"What about betas becoming alphas?" Micah asked him with a hint of challenge. "Because I lived my life as a beta. A *horse* beta. It wasn't until I met Brandt that I changed."

Sergio's lips twitched. "As with the others, I suspect the magic was shielding your hidden alpha and true breed until such a time that it saw fit to unleash them." He held weathered hands at his sides with his palms up. "It's just a theory, but I believe the magic has changed things, presumably because times have changed. The world has changed. And magic is evolving to create true balance."

As a man of science, I felt uncomfortable with all the talk of magic...however, I knew that, as a dragon mated to a unicorn, my unease really was unfounded.

"Then, yeah," Ollie leaned forward and addressed Eric, "I'd say birth control is number one on the list before we go unlocking everyone's alpha sides."

"Well, that makes sense," Sage cut in from where he and Dexter had been suspiciously silent, "but don't we need to find the spells first anyway?"

Dexter cleared his throat. "I don't think that will be an issue. All those journals I have been sending photos of?" Eric and I nodded. "They belong to the same collection in rural France. The owner is quite...possessive. However," he smirked at Sergio, "maybe now that we have a magic wielder on hand, we can persuade the old man to..." he rolled his wrist in the air, "*donate* them to our cause."

Eric's gaze darted between Sergio and Dexter, before he pulled out his phone. "Where in France? Let's get you on the next flights over."

Life became a whirlwind of looking after our babies, research, and manufacturing omega-specific birth control. Micah's parents visited (to meet their grandchildren, and to provide emotional support for Micah as he dealt with the appearance of his biological father) and they were a great help with the girls. When they left, Micah and I knew we needed to hire a nanny after all.

Our relationship was still solid, but we hadn't spent any time alone as a couple in months. I was horrified to realize that the last time we had exchanged more than a hurried hand job was the night I had gone into labor. However, three newborns truly did interrupt any and all opportunities to do more together, and Micah and I were both constantly exhausted.

That had to change.

After weeks of interviewing candidates from the town, we eventually agreed on Carson, a young man who had been living in the homestead known affectionately as Frat House. I had been surprised when Carson said he suspected he had a hidden alpha side. If anything, the petite twenty-seven-year-old human seemed much more likely to be an omega. However, he explained that he was born to shifter parents but, obviously, scented completely human from birth and had never once shifted.

His parents had never shunned him, but when they heard about Shifters Sanctuary and Beckett's backstory, they encouraged him to come to us and try his luck.

Carson had been working at the town's daycare part time and picking up odd jobs at the local farms. With childcare experience and a naturally sweet disposition, it made sense for Micah and I to hire him, and he seemed thrilled to move into our guest room and out of the communal lodgings.

"They really do act like a frat house," he lamented with a sigh during his first night in our home. "They're all nice guys, but...I guess I didn't fit in there, either."

"Well, please treat our home as your own," I told him. "We do not expect you to take care of the girls overnight every night, only three out of seven nights a week. Enough to give us a chance to recharge. During the day, you won't have to watch them often, either. However, your room and board is covered here, and you should socialize...date...settle in properly."

And he did.

The first few nights leaving him in charge of the girls were treated as a trial run. Micah and I hovered, making sure Carson could handle them, but we needn't have worried. He was sweet and efficient, and he seemed to enjoy taking care of our babies, who were no longer quite so tiny or fragile.

"We lucked out with him," Micah said on Carson's first official night on duty.

"We did," I agreed.

It felt strange not to be tending to our daughters, to not be waiting with bated breath for the first wails during the night. The urge to leave our bedroom suite and assist him was fierce, but so was the desperate need to reconnect with my mate.

In fact, it was a need which had been building since early in the day, as though my brain had sent signals to my body, letting it know that tonight we were free and uninhibited.

I led Micah into our bedroom and closed the door, then slammed him bodily against its painted surface. He barely had time to let out a stunned "oof" before my mouth was slanted over his, my lips demanding he open for me.

I couldn't recall ever feeling so needy, not even when we had bonded, or the night I had gone into labor. As soon as our mouths connected, it was as though my veins were filled with lava. Arousal simmered in my blood and heated my skin. My cock surged to life, and I felt my slick spilling from me and into my underwear.

I tore at his clothes, not caring if I destroyed the fabric. I had endless resources: I would buy him more and tear those from his body as well.

"Whoa, sugar," he pulled his mouth from mine, turning his face to breathe. I attacked his neck, sucking at the smooth, flawless skin, leaving marks in my wake. "I know it's been a while, but..."

I whined and rubbed my erection into his thigh. "I...I need..." My brain was scrambled, thoughts pushed aside for primal urges. The ache inside me was becoming painful. I whined again.

Even though I could feel his answering arousal, through the bond and through his pants, Micah's concern broke through the fog of lust enveloping me.

"This isn't just pent-up horniness, Bran," he said, bringing a hand up to gently stroke my face, his fingers brushing over scales which I had not realized had erupted over my skin. "You're warm to touch —warmer than usual— and..." he chuckled, then removed his hand from my face, gripping at my hips instead, "baby, you're still rubbing off on my leg."

Sure enough, I had been grinding into him, seeking friction while my body begged to be filled and knotted and—*oh.*

"I...I think I may be in heat," I admitted. The frantic desire inside me, the fire in my veins and infusing my skin, the insane amount of slick I was producing; it all added up.

Gently pushing me to take a step back, Micah frowned. "That's soon, isn't it? You only gave birth a few months ago."

"There are not any set rules for these things," I fought to think rationally, struggling against the burning and the now painful urge to submit to my alpha. "For Ollie, it took almost a year before his first post-natal heat. For Day...maybe six months?" I frowned back at my mate. "Why...why are you not affected? To hear the others tell it, their alphas fall into rut with them. But you..."

Was I somehow defective? Were the pheromones I was sending out not actually compatible with my alpha after all?

"No, sugar, I am. I'm struggling here." To punctuate his point, he adjusted himself, and his sinfully long eyelashes fluttered closed as he allowed himself the moment of relief. "But I'm trying to shield it from you because..." He paused and licked his lips, swallowing roughly before he met my gaze. His eyes were blown wide with the same level of lust coursing through me. "Because we need to talk about this."

I did not want to talk. I wanted to fuck.

I whined.

"I know," he placated, reaching for me, and the touch of his hand on my skin was simultaneously a soothing balm and a jolt to my nerves, "but you're not on the pill, and we don't have condoms. If we do this...if we give in to the heat and the rut..."

I bit back another whine. My omega wanted nothing more than to bend over and be bred by his alpha. My alpha. *Our* alpha.

But it would not be fair to take that choice from him a second time.

Wrestling for control of my urges, I nodded. "You are correct," the words almost hurt to say, clashing with the instincts building in my gut and in my psyche, "I...I won't force you..."

"What? No," Micah gathered me into his arms and I breathed in his scent. The electric alpha buzz was tempered by the near sweetness of his breed. It tugged at my desperation, but I refused to give in. I still had free will, and so did he. "Sugar, you've barely recovered from having the girls. I'm not stalling because I don't want more kids. I'm stalling because I'm worried it's too soon to put your body through all of that again."

"Oh." Relief washed over me, causing my knees to buckle. "I...Micah, I am fine. More than fine. I..." Brushing my hand over my stomach, I sighed. "I am *softer* than I was prior to the girls. And there are stretch marks, and...well, my body is not as aesthetically pleasing, but I am perfectly healthy. Perhaps even healthier than I was when I implanted their embryos, because I am more physically active and I am more conscious of nutrition now, but...it would be okay. I could..." I licked my lips, still trying to ignore the raging inferno inside me. It was not easy, especially not with the topic of conversation mirroring my body's demands. "Another pregnancy...another baby...it would be okay."

"Yeah?" his tone was breathless. *Awed.*

Was it possible he wanted the same things I did? Not just because of the heat and rut telling us we did, but because we truly envisioned the same future together?

And why wouldn't we? I wondered. *He is my fated mate.*

"With my age, and the fact that I am still chestfeeding, there is a possibility the heat won't take," I told him. "But...yes. My body could handle it. And my heart..." I swallowed, my breathing hitching as I confessed, "my heart wants it, Micah."

"So does mine." I barely had a moment to process his reply before he was guiding me onto our bed, his mouth possessing mine in such an alpha display of dominance, it took my breath away.

Our clothes went flying, and the simple press of his naked skin over mine eased the pain of my heat.

"Jesus," he whispered against my mouth when his fingers sought out my entrance, "you really need my cock, don't you, sugar?"

I was certain my slick was making a mess of the bedding, but I did not care. We would do worse before my heat eased up, I was certain of it.

"Please, alpha," I arched my back, silently willing him to fill me up and fuck me, "*please.*"

I felt so empty that it hurt.

"You're so wet, baby," he nipped at my jaw, the scrape of his teeth over stubble and scales making me tremble with little shocks of bliss, "you're going to feel so fucking good around my dick."

I cried out as he slid two fingers inside me, teasing me instead of giving me the one thing my body craved more than anything else.

"M-Micah, *please.*"

"God, I love hearing you beg for me. Watching you writhe on my fingers. And, *fuck*, you're even hotter inside than I remember."

Later, I would consider just how far we had come from the first time we were together. When he was self-conscious and almost timid. I loved my alpha's submissive side, too —I loved to fuck him every bit as much as I loved feeling him inside me— but, in that moment, he was giving my omega side everything I needed.

"I-it is the heat," I managed to stammer, rolling my hips, trying to find some kind of relief for the intense need building inside me. "I...I feel like I will combust..."

"I've got you," he crooned, pressing kisses down my neck and over my shoulders. The cool moisture felt as though it sizzled with every brush of his lips on my heated flesh. "I'm going to breed you so good, Bran. Gonna put another baby in you."

"*Fuck,*" I bit the curse out, clamping around his probing digits, my body tensing for orgasm at the very thought. My cock strained and wept over the pooch of my belly, even though it hadn't received any actual attention. "A-alpha, *please.*"

"You want that, don't you?" He continued, pushing all of my buttons...except for the one inside me, as if he knew doing so would be too much. "You want me to make you all round with another one of our babies. Want to fill this whole house with them. The whole town, even."

"Y-yes…" My mate's words were ridiculous, but my yearning for children of my own had spanned centuries. Add to that my first ever heat and a breeding kink which had quite obviously been slowly festering away in the back of my subconscious for a while, and I was a babbling mess. There was nothing hotter than the very idea that my alpha would breed me over and over again. "M-Micah, *now*. I need…*nooo*." I voiced my complaint as he pulled his fingers from me, but he silenced me with a gentle tap to the side of my thigh.

"On your hands and knees, sugar. Facing the headboard."

I scrambled to do exactly as he had asked, moaning with delight when his long, lithe form stretched over my back and his cock slid inside me.

Instantly, the churning, aching feeling in my belly seemed to ease. It was a strange, almost mystical phenomenon, and I would wonder later on about the science behind it. Was it his precum? Did it cause a chemical reaction somehow?

"Fuck," Micah panted, grinding his pelvis into the fleshy globes of my ass, "fuck, I was right. You're *so* hot, sugar. And so wet. This…*ungh*," he pulled out and pushed back in, and his voice turned ragged, "this is going to be fast, baby."

I bent forward, pressing my face into the pillow, aiming to give him more access, or a better angle, or…I had no idea what. "*Yes*," I moaned obscenely as he thrust again, then repeated the word with every increasing slam of his hips, "yes, yes, yes."

"Oh, shit," he hissed, "don't…don't squeeze…"

I couldn't help it. My instincts had taken over. I wanted him to come. I wanted his knot. I wanted him to fuck me into the damn mattress. I wanted— "Oh, Gods, *alpha*." He'd found my prostate and the pleasure shot through me and, I assumed, through the bond as well.

Suddenly, whatever tenuous control he had held over his side of our connection crumbled, and I wailed at the onslaught of his pleasure and arousal combining with mine. On his next thrust, I saw stars. I convulsed beneath him, my cock erupting even as I felt what had to be a torrent of slick spill over his cock and between our bodies, trickling down the inside of my thighs.

"*Holy shit*," Micah's fingers dug into my hips, "fuck, Bran. Fuck, that feels...*oh God*." His words were barely comprehensible, lost as they were in his groan.

I felt his orgasm through the bond almost as clearly as if it were my own, and my body shuddered through coming again as his cock swelled and released inside me.

Once again, the heat in my veins seemed to subside, easing away even further as Micah's knot inflated and locked us together. He continued to pant and issue low curses through his resulting knotted releases, and I relished in the sensations bouncing through to me via our connection.

Boneless, sweaty, and covered in cum and slick, Micah and I eased down onto our sides, spooning together in the afterglow. Flashes of heat and need surprised me, but my alpha sensed them and ground into me, stimulating his knot and coming again and again until those bursts of desperation dissipated.

"That was...*wow*," he said after kissing the back of my neck. "How are you feeling?"

Opening my mouth to respond, I yawned. He chuckled, then groaned as his own movement bumped his knot. Jolts of pleasure bordering on pain came through the bond. My cock twitched in answer, but I was utterly spent.

"*Fuck*," he muttered, his fingers flexing on my thigh. "I forgot what this felt like, too."

"Mmm," I agreed, feeling my eyelids droop as the afterglow faded into exhausted satisfaction. "I have missed this."

"Sleep, sugar," he murmured, kissing the top of my head. "I've got you."

Yes, I thought to myself as the tug towards dreamland drew me closer, *he does*.

I did not know what was in store for us, for our personal future or for the future of the pack, or even for shifter kind in general. But I did know that, regardless, my unicorn alpha —a man so perfect, I worried I might have just dreamed him up— would always be by my side.

And perhaps, if fate really shone down on us, this heat would take, and hope for dragon kind would be on the horizon as well.

Epilogue

"We're *ba-ack*," Sage sing-songed as he sauntered into Eric and Brandt's clinic. He dropped his bag in the doorway and zeroed in on me, plucking Lucia from my arms without asking permission. "Hey, Princess Lucy-Loo," he cooed at her, beaming as she smiled and rewarded him with a sweet baby giggle, "did you miss your favorite uncle?"

"You're only saying that because you know Eric can't hear you in his office," Day sniggered from his spot at the reception desk. His smile fell as Dexter came through the doorway with Sergio on his heels. With a sigh, he glanced back up at my red-haired brother-in-law. "You couldn't have lost him in a forest in France?"

"You love me, really," Dex told him with a sharp smile. "Just admit it."

"Ugh," Day pushed his chair back, rising fluidly with Belle still held to his shoulder. She was fast asleep on him, which wasn't a surprise. He had always been one of her favorite honorary uncles. "I'll see if Eric and Bran are still busy."

Rita grizzled from the stroller, and I rocked it forwards and back to see if she'd settle back down. With Carson on a day off, and Brandt back to working full-time in the clinic, I was entertaining the girls (and myself) by bringing them out for a walk. After visiting my mate, we were going to go and annoy Uncle Beck for a little while.

However, with Sage, Dex and Sergio back from their travels through France, I suspected my plans were about to change. Both Eric and Brandt were champing at the bit to know whether the little expedition had been successful. I understood why: if we were able to unbind —or unlock, or reveal, or however you wanted to say it— a potential alpha's abilities without the need for a fated mate to trigger them, shifter dynamics would change worldwide.

It was scary to think of anyone holding that kind of power, but I didn't think that the Shifters Sanctuary pack would allow it to corrupt them. If anything, I knew that Beck hoped to attempt exactly what Sergio said the magic wanted — he wanted to restore balance and equality for shifters the world over.

Still, if Shifters Sanctuary did have the ability to reverse what Eric called Hidden Alpha Syndrome, word would eventually get back to the Moonmusic people...and I hated to think about what that might mean for us, considering the group's past actions.

I didn't want to think about my girls being in danger because of that. Or my mate.

My once-again pregnant mate.

Eric had confirmed Brandt's pregnancy only a week earlier, after staring at his brother with bewilderment for a few long moments, and neither one of us was surprised to see the two little bean shapes on the ultrasound screen, even if Eric was still grappling with the concept.

Brandt's first heat had taken days to break. Days we had spent curled around each other in bed, riding out the waves of desperate lust until we were too exhausted to move. Instinctively, we had known that it had been a successful mating. The fact that he was pregnant with twins did panic me for a few moments, but I knew we had Carson to help out, and we could always hire another nanny, too.

I couldn't wait to see the look on Beck's face when we broke the news to our friends. As far as I knew, he and Ollie were still debating when —if ever— they would have more of their own.

My friend might have a heart attack on my behalf.

"And now I think you can go back to your daddy," Sage declared out of nowhere, handing Lucia back to me, his nose scrunched. "You might want to take care of that."

I snorted but bent to rifle through the trusty diaper bag slung over the handles of the stroller. "I thought you wanted kids, too?" I asked him, fishing out the items I needed. I was a pro at doing things one-handed by this stage. "This would be practice for that. I'm assuming by how cheerful you are, your trip was a success. So, who knows? Maybe you'll be the next to find an alpha and settle down and have a herd of little dragons."

Dex made a funny strangled sound at the back of his throat, but Sage seemed to ignore him, just shrugging.

"In the unlikely event of that happening, I'll learn to change a diaper, but that day is not today," Sage took an exaggerated step out of my orbit. "You go have fun, though."

I rolled my eyes at him and nudged the stroller towards him. "At least keep her rocking so she stays asleep. I'll be back."

Eric's personal bedroom was down the end of the hall, so I headed in there to take care of my squirming, whimpering daughter. By the time I came out, the door to Eric's office was open and multiple voices were talking over each other in excitement.

"...testing it?" Eric asked as I entered, bouncing Lucia on my hip.

Day made grabby hands and took her from me, announcing that he would look after all three babies in the reception area because Eric's little office was crammed with people. Even Beck and Ollie were here, though Ollie followed Day out the door, swiping the stroller from Sage so he could take the other two girls with him.

"We would need volunteers for testing," Brandt said from where he was leaning against the exam bed. I moved over to his side and he slung his arm around my shoulder. "And we would need to ensure it happens in a controlled environment. Some of the journal entries suggested that the sudden release of one's alpha abilities brings on an extreme rut-like state. We would not want to risk it occurring where it cannot be contained."

"Even in rut, though, we have control over ourselves. We don't just leap on the nearest omega and do the unthinkable," Beck argued with a frown. "Unless you're saying that the synthetic pheromones might trigger something like a rabid rut."

"Synthetic pheromones?" I asked. It hadn't taken me *that* long to change the baby, had it? I mean, okay, I might have played with her tiny little toes and sung a couple of nursery rhymes to her, but...had I really missed that much of the conversation?

"To simulate the presence of a fated or compatible mate," Eric explained. "We think it will help spark the magic before the spell is performed."

"Right," I nodded. "That makes about as much sense as anything else."

Brandt snorted.

The conversation carried on around us as Eric and Beck debated potential candidates for testing and discussed the merits of being transparent with the town so the local omega population could consider the changes coming their way.

The air felt charged with anticipation. Changes were coming to Shifters Sanctuary, and for shifter-kind in general. Whatever the future had in store, though, I was glad that I had already found my mate. Together, no matter what happened around us, we would be just fine.

With my arm around his waist, I tugged him closer to my side.

"You good?" I murmured while everyone else was distracted.

He nodded, brushing his hand over his belly.

"I am perfect."

I grinned. "Yes, you are."

The End.

Thank you so much for reading *His Unicorn Alpha*. I'm well and truly settling into Shifters Sanctuary now, and I really hope you enjoyed this one.

I'd love it if you could leave a review on your retailer of purchase or wherever you read and write reviews. Reviews not only tell the algorithms that our books deserve attention, but honest feedback also encourages and inspires me to keep writing. Even a star rating helps, and I greatly appreciate you taking time to do so.

Speaking of my writing, if you want a glimpse into Book Four of the Shifters Sanctuary world, titled *His Dragon Duo*, keep turning the pages because the first chapter is waiting for you.

Also, if you'd like to read about Beck & Ollie discovering all the fun they can have with the bond in a short novella (which functions as an extended epilogue for Book 1, *His Alpha Unlocked*), you can subscribe to my newsletter and snag a copy at:

https://annasparrows.com/newsletter-subscription/

If you're already signed up and still want a copy, you can visit:

https://books.bookfunnel.com/annasparrowsbonus

to claim copies of the bonus content you don't yet have.

Please also consider following me on my socials at:

Website: https://annasparrows.com/

Facebook: https://www.facebook.com/AnnaSparrowsAuthor/

Instagram: https://www.instagram.com/annasparrows

...And now, without further ado, the sneak peek of His Dragon Duo awaits!

His Dragon Duo

Chapter One - Sage

"**Y**ou're an omega, Dex." My younger brother, Eric, sounded on the verge of throttling my closest friend. He raked his fingers through his unruly blonde hair as he tried to explain, "You've got the birthmark and all. I highly doubt you have a hidden alpha side."

Instead of explaining his true reasons for wanting to attend an Unlocking party, which I assumed were purely sex-related, Dexter gestured lazily across the table towards my older brother, Brandt. "*His* alpha was a whole different breed and designation, and *he* still magically transitioned into an alpha."

"Micah didn't have a mark, though," Eric argued back, referring to Brandt's alpha. "Neither did Beck, Rex, or Brandi. You do."

I was still trying to wrap my head around the logic behind any of it, if I was being completely honest. The alphas who had thought themselves human made sense to me in a roundabout way. But throwing Micah into the mix had changed everything we (okay, Eric) had hypothesized about.

Micah had been born to shifter parents. He was unmarked—that was, born without a birthmark distinguishing him as an omega or, though they'd been thought extinct until recently, an alpha— just like any other beta, and he had grown up as such. He was a horse shifter and, as far as I knew, had never had reason to question whether he was anything different. But, to cut a long story short, he and Brandt met, mated and bonded, and suddenly Micah was an alpha...and a unicorn.

A freaking *unicorn*.

Until I'd been sent on a fact-finding mission, I hadn't known they were real. (And, yes, the irony of a *dragon* not believing in unicorns wasn't lost on me.)

With Micah's unexpected alpha tossed into the mix, and my older brother pregnant for a second time, this time with boys, there was a sliver of hope for our all-male subspecies after all. But it also raised a whole slew of extra questions and possibilities for shifters in general. Questions which the two successful Unlocking parties we had thrown so far had yet to answer.

"I still think we should attend one of those Unlocking parties," Dexter drawled. "Why let all the betas and humans have all the fun?"

I sighed, regretting coming up with the concept of mass Unlocking events. It had taken six months and a lot of trial and error —none of which I had been privy to, seeing as I missed the science gene in our family— before my brothers and our unicorn shaman, Sergio, nailed down the correct combination of synthetic pheromones and spell crafting to remove the mystical block over a potential alpha's abilities and designation.

After that, Brandt and Eric were run off their feet with half the town clamoring to see if they had an alpha side to unleash. So, I suggested adapting the pheromones and spell to assist larger groups at once.

Eric hated the idea, but with the influx of visitors and an increasingly agitated pack full of shifters at his door day and night, he eventually agreed to try it.

And so the Unlocking parties came to be.

The thing about the whole Unlocking process, though, was that it threw every emerging alpha into a rut-like state as soon as the spell was cast. One of the first new alphas to go through the trial, a hedgehog shifter named Mark, said it was kind of like being high, drunk, and horny all at once...and that he didn't really recall much of his forced rut at all after the fact. It wasn't until the lust had passed and he had slept the experience off that he was able to shift.

Thankfully, his Unlocking had taken place under controlled circumstances, without any omegas nearby. The poor guy had only had his hand to sate his desperate need to fuck and knot something, and he had ridden the desperation out in a locked, dragon-guarded room. Fortunately for him, it passed within a handful of hours; something Eric assumed was due to the synthetic pheromones wearing off. But Unlocking a bunch of alphas en masse meant we couldn't really contain them all.

Hence the parties, which were basically orgies once the spell and pheromones kicked in. And *that* was why I regretted coming up with the idea.

Dex had been desperate to attend one of the events ever since their creation. Luckily (or, from his perspective, unluckily), our Pack Alpha, Beckett, declared that only potential alphas, human men and beta males could attend the parties. His argument was that, until we could trust that the synthetic ruts didn't compromise an alpha's ability to control themselves around potential mates, it would be safer for omegas and women to stay away. I agreed with him. Dex, on the other hand, did not.

My best friend was an acquired taste. I mean, there was a reason we stopped speaking for a hundred years or so. Dex loved to push buttons. He was a pain in the ass. And, having grown up together, he knew exactly how to get a rise out of me. But having him back in my life had made me realize just how much I missed him.

Except for during moments like this one.

I watched Eric groan and pinch the bridge of his nose.

Eric was usually the most patient of we three Weldman brothers, but he was also incredibly passionate about trying to save dragonkind. Being an all-male subspecies with only omegas remaining was incredibly depressing.

Brandt winced and shifted in his seat, rubbing at his comically large belly. He was having twins, and we were all surprised that he had made it almost to full term this time. He had barely made it to thirty-two weeks with his triplets, my nieces. But this time around, only carrying two babies, he had made it further. Of course, it would be just his luck that the one weekend his alpha was out of town would be the time he went into labor. At least he had a large support system here. We all did.

"You good?" I asked Brandt. "We're close to the clinic if you need to go pop a couple more niblings out for me."

He rolled his dark eyes. "I am fine. These boys are just running out of room in there."

I bypassed the opportunity to crack a joke about how large his belly was. I didn't think he would appreciate it.

"All the more reason for them to come out and meet their favorite uncle," I grinned, ignoring Eric's pointed throat clearing.

"Uncle Beck will be their favorite," Beck argued from his place at the head of the table. While our Pack Alpha was a wolf shifter and wasn't related to any of us by blood, he was one of Micah's best friends and the closest thing Brandt's alpha had to a brother.

"Aren't you afraid of infants, Alpha?" Dex taunted him before I could come up with my own rebuke.

The handsome man in charge of leading our pack huffed and crossed his arms over his chest, dipping his stubbled chin in near petulance. "I'm not *afraid* of babies," he took the bait, even as Eric, Brandt and I all shook our heads. "Just because Ollie and I are waiting for Rory and Duke to be..."

"Less evil?" Dex offered, as Beck seemed to struggle for the right words to describe his rambunctious children.

Beck narrowed his eyes. "More independent."

"Good luck with that," Dex stretched his hand out in front of him, idly inspecting his perfectly manicured nails. He was such a brat, but I couldn't help how funny I found him sometimes.

"Anyway," Brandt interrupted, wincing again, "I hate to admit it, but I do think Dexter may be onto something."

In his seat across from me, Dex visibly brightened. "You do?"

"I do. We need to study the effects of the forced ruts more than we have, and we really should be taking more samples for our research to compare genetic makeup now that we have a much larger data pool to work with."

Dexter slumped in his seat and pouted, a lock of his blonde hair falling into his eyes. He made no move to brush it away. My fingers itched. "I wanted to go for the orgies."

"That's not a surprise," Eric rolled his eyes. "But Brandt's right. We really should be trying to understand *why* these people have hidden alpha sides, and whether there is a test we can run to determine who does and doesn't, rather than playing the hit-and-miss game of seeing who is affected by the pheromones and spells during the parties."

"Plus," Beck added, leaning forward over the glossy timber surface of the boardroom table, "with our pack producing so many alphas all of a sudden, we're definitely in the Moonmusic peoples' crosshairs more than ever. It would be nice to have more of a game plan than just unleashing a bunch of alphas for the hell of it."

"It's not really for the hell of it," Eric argued. "We're restoring magical balance and trying to save a few subspecies on the verge of extinction."

"Yeah, well, Morstein isn't going to see it that way," Beck told him. "The existence of one alpha was a threat to his whole cult-y system. Suddenly, there are at least...what? Twelve out there now?"

"Morstein?" Dex butted in before Eric could reply to Beck, sounding uncharacteristically serious all of a sudden. "The weasel who tried to kidnap your children?" There was a growl to his accented voice which was kind of sexy.

No, brain. Stop that.

"The one and the same," Beck nodded. "He's been quiet the past couple of years, but I'm sure that with us suddenly having a magical way to unleash more alphas, and word spreading about it, he's going to feel more threatened than ever by our existence."

Moonmusic was the organization masquerading as a shifter religion, and they were the reason many packs were still treating omegas as little more than property. They had set themselves up with betas in power, seeing as alphas had all but gone extinct before Beckett had accidentally unlocked his own alpha side.

The Moonmusic organization's leader, Joe Morstein, had made his stance on Shifters Sanctuary very clear. We were an aberration: a threat to what he called the 'real' way of shifter life. The fact that he was losing control of the people he had convinced to send him tithes and fund his cushy lifestyle was the actual threat.

Even though I hadn't met him, I hated him on principal. People like him had destroyed things for shifters far more than the humans who'd run us all into hiding a couple of hundred years ago had. Not that shifters were in hiding anymore. But that was beside the point. The point was, Morstein was a manipulative, controlling sleazeball on a power trip.

"Are you sure we can't just shift and eat him?" I asked. "It seems like the easiest way to deal with him, really."

"We're not stooping to his level," Beck chided, but he sounded amused. "And I doubt he'd taste nice, anyway."

"I hate having morals," I complained. "Does he honestly think he's got a chance against us now that we have so many alphas on our side? Even those that are leaving to return to their own packs would be our allies in a fight against Moonmusic and all of the packs they've got under their not-all-opposable thumbs."

"I mean, he hasn't issued any outright threats since we stopped that kidnapping attempt a few years back, but the ongoing silence is concerning, especially now that we've cracked the code on unlocking alphas." He nodded towards Brandt. "Which takes us back to why learning as much as we can is a good idea. Knowledge is power and all that jazz."

"So...does this mean we get to go to an Unlocking party?" Dex asked.

Eric sighed. "Make sure your Pill is up to date. Or don't," he shot my best friend a wry grin. "We could use more little dragons, after all."

The look on my best friend's face was priceless, even if I did have to smother a stab of jealousy at the idea of him hooking up with an alpha.

The fact that I also had to convince myself I was jealous of him and not the fictional alpha in that scenario also made me squirm.

Bad thoughts, Sage, I told myself. *Don't go there.*

If only feelings were that easy to ignore. You'd think that after a hundred years or so I would have gotten over them, but...nope.

"You'll come with me, won't you, Sage?" Dex implored, pulling me out of the start of one of my usual spirals.

I blinked at him, taking in his wide, hopeful blue eyes and the almost aristocratic slope of his nose. Dex was so handsome, and his English accent was my kryptonite. Even though I had never admitted it, I thought that he knew it, too.

"Fine," I agreed, even if it sounded reluctant to my own ears. Then I turned to my brothers. "What information do you need us to collect?"

About the Author

I am a bi Aussie author living in Brisbane, Australia. I've been writing* for as long as I can remember. I started with silly short stories as a kid, moved on to fanfiction in my teens, and then to publishing original fiction in my thirties.

I have been an avid reader of MM romance my whole life. (Ask me about my beginnings with *Buffy* fanfic, haha!) I wrote a sweet and kinky MM romance novel in 2022 and the reader response changed my life. From there, I knew I had found my niche.

And thus Anna Sparrows was born.

*All of my writing is 100% my own. No part of it is generated by Artificial Intelligence (AI) software of any kind. Yes, that means that it's sometimes flawed, but I'm okay with that.

Follow Me

Website: https://annasparrows.com

Facebook:
https://www.facebook.com/AnnaSparrowsAuthor

Instagram:
https://www.instagram.com/annasparrows

Newsletter:
https://annasparrows.com/newsletter-subscription

<h1 style="text-align:center">Also by Anna Sparrows</h1>

I write ridiculously sweet & steamy MM romance with guaranteed HEAs...and sometimes with a side of kink. My backlist can be found at annasparrows.com

Littles & Lace Series

The Littles & Lace series is an MM Age Play series, following a group of like-minded friends in the BDSM community. You'll find mild ABDL, light Pet Play, Femme Play and more here.

Book 1: Asher's Answer

Book 2: Matteo's Mettle

Book 3: Ted's Temerity

Book 4: Spencer's Satisfaction

Book 5: Chance's Choice

Book 6: Josh's Jackpot

Dads & Adages Series

Visit Australia's sunny Gold Coast where an assortment of single dads find love and even learn a few life lessons along the way.

Book 1: Where There's A Will

Book 2: You Don't Know Jack

Book 3: A Match Made In Evan

Book 4: Speak Of The Neville (release TBA)

Related: A Surprise For The Holidays

Written in 3rd person POV, *A Surprise for the Holidays* is a sweet, fluffy MM Christmas novella with a grumpy former soccer player turned coach, a golden retriever younger player, and a precocious little girl. Featuring an Aussie Christmas, grumpy/sunshine vibes, an age gap and sand where you're used to snow, this novella brings additional heat to the festive season in more ways than one!

Shifters Sanctuary Series

In a world where alphas are thought to be extinct, a number of men are about to have their worlds rocked.

Book 1: His Alpha Unlocked

Book 2: His Prodigal Alpha

Book 3: His Unicorn Alpha

Book 4: His Dragon Duo (TBA)

Down Under Daddies Series

Set in rural Western Australia, come meet the and the kinkiest and queerest band of stationhands any outback cattle station has ever seen.

Book 1: A Stable Daddy

Kinks & Conundrums Series

A spin-off from the Littles & Lace series, this series follows Daddies, Doms, Littles, and Pet Players as they discover their kinks and find love.

Book 0.5: Baron's Boo-Boo

Book 1: Anson's Awakening

www.ingramcontent.com/pod-product-compliance
Lightning Source LLC
Chambersburg PA
CBHW030802210726
48290CB00002B/390